Read atleast two More!

The Dark Roads

By Wayne Lemmons

For my lovely wife, Sue.

You've made every good thing possible.

Prologue

In 2015 the winter was unseasonably warm. I remember it well enough to feel a pang of sentiment toward those days. Children were playing in the sunshine, bathing suits donned long after swimwear should have been traded for jeans and sweaters. We were all so happy that Jack Frost had forgotten us that year.

We didn't know any better, but it should have been our first hint that the world was going wrong. Five years later, when the crops were all burnt, and the sun wasn't drawn with a happy face on a child's illustration anymore, we would all have chance for regret.

The funny thing about the change in climate was the way everyone talked about it on the news. Some of the scientists thought that the temperatures were a good sign. They said that the ozone layer was repairing itself and would be as good as new by 2050 or 2060. They said that the warm weather was a temporary glitch that would right itself and that all of the bad things that had happened to the environment since mankind had started damaging the earth would reverse. They said that the greenhouse gases being contained by the ozone layer were the culprit behind our easy suntans in January.

Nobody contradicted any of it because scientists are supposed to be smart. Right.

There were all of these numbers and percentages ticking across the bottom of every news report between 2015 and 2017 showing how great everything was going with the proverbial blanket that protected us all from the sun's radiation. Christ. They even told us that if the layer was actually falling apart that the climate would be getting *colder*. Nobody had the sense enough to call bullshit until 2019 and by then it was way too late. Skin cancer rates were on the rise, had gone up like 400%, and we were all just sitting on our thumbs thinking that it would all turn around. Nature wouldn't dare try to burn us off of this rock. We were the supreme species. Everybody's air conditioning was running at full blast and kept us comfortable as long as we stayed in the house.

In 2020 things started speeding up. Direct sunlight started to get acutely harmful to your health if you were in it for more than an hour. We were becoming vampires, so fearful of the light of day that the streets were always empty until dusk when the cursed sun set on whatever side of the world it was broiling. Before long the power grid was suffering so badly during the afternoon hours that we started having brownouts on a daily basis.

I keep echoing it, but I can't seem to express it well enough to suit myself. We didn't know what was going on. None of us did. All we could do was wait for our governments and scientists to come up with something. We waited, but nothing came other than the usual warnings. Stay cool. Stay inside during the day. We're working on it.

I remember the last time I saw the sun. It was October of 2020, not long before I would meet the young men I'm going to tell you about. I lived north of the Canadian border where it used to seem like winter lasted nine months of the year. I was watching as the evil fireball rose into view. I know it doesn't really rise, but that's what it looked like then, like the sun was climbing to the heavens to preside over all of us, to kill as many of us as it possibly could. It got its share of victims by the end of things.

I only talk about all of this ancient history so that I can tell you about the men who saved my life. They saved so many of us that my own neck doesn't seem so grand in comparison, but trust me when I tell you that my life is the most valuable thing I have. I'm sure that your own means the same to you.

We live because of them, maybe not as their disciples or subjects, but I, at least, will play their apostle.

What they started here, in Alaska, has saved and renewed lives without number. That wasn't their intention from the start. They only wanted to survive, to exist beyond their twenty-second year, if possible. Luckily for me and so many others, they aspired to that goal.

There are startlingly few people left on the third planet from an insufferably deadly sun, but more of us are being made by the day. We have a shot at survival, even if it's a long one.

So, I'm going to tell you about them. I knew them as well as anyone outside of their own friendship could, so I have a little bit of insight. As with most stories, this one is a journey that begins with walking.

American Highways

Chapter 1

Sheridan, Wyoming
January 12, 2021
2:17 AM   99*F

Elvis was constantly wiping at his face with a grubby blue bandana, trying to keep up with the steady stream of sweat dripping from his hairline. Buddy, though usually a quiet and patient guy, had started giving him shit about it just after they'd commenced walking for the night and wasn't letting up. Richie had been trying to ignore the bickering between his two compatriots, but his own patience was wearing thin.

They were all shirtless and carrying their packs with dish towels folded beneath the straps to avoid chafing. Shirts would be a better buffer against the pack straps, but it was too fucking hot to even consider more than the barest of clothing.

Elvis had once started the night walking in the nude, but soon became embarrassed. Benny had still been around then and couldn't stop giggling at the way Elvis' equipment was swinging with his legs. Richie had tried not to laugh, but every time the guy took a step his equipment slapped against his thighs. It *was* pretty damned funny. Shorts were pulled on within the first hour.

Benny was long dead, along with most of the humor they could draw from their situation. Walking from full dark to just before dawn every night for the past six months was actually incredibly exhausting. It was also draining on the spirit to keep moving without any kind of change in scenery. There was road and road signage. There were houses. There was night.

They were always tired, cranky, and scared to death. None of those conditions were good for morale.

"Dude!" Buddy exclaimed, "Will you quit with that fucking rag?!? It's wetter than that pile of shit on your head. Can't even be doing anything for you anymore."

"Can't help it, Buddy. I hate the sweat on my face. Always have," Elvis said, looking down at the soft asphalt of the road.

Buddy pulled his coke bottle glasses off and grabbed his own bandana from a cargo pocket. He wiped sweat from the lenses roughly and started to put the cloth away again. He looked at it, his hand stopping close to his hip, and seemed to consider something.

"Hundred fucking degrees in the middle of the night. Fuck! I'm sorry man. Here."

Richie looked up from the road to see the next part of this exchange. Buddy gave Elvis the dry bandana he'd been cleaning his glasses with. Elvis took it as if it was the holy grail and promptly soaked it with his own sweat.

The look of supreme satisfaction on his face made Richie think of the way you looked when a cool breeze hit you on a normal hot day. If there *were* any cool breezes or normal hot days, they wouldn't be in this mess in the first place.

The thermometer he kept in his ruck sack hadn't shown less than 98 degrees above ground in the last three months, no matter where they walked. He didn't want to know what it showed when the sun was out.

"Fucking sun," Buddy muttered, through with aggravating Elvis for the time being.

"Couple more hours, guys," Richie said, "And we'll find some cool and have a little water."

Neither of his longtime friends had any comment on that. They'd stopped looking at anything other than the road. They were hurting. *He* was hurting.

7

The trees along the two-lane road they were pacing were all barren of leaves, their bark darkened and made brittle by the sun's rays, as was every plant they'd seen since October when going out during the day had become truly dangerous.

By November daylight had actually become life threatening. What had once caused a darkening of pigment on the skin over a period of hours now caused a blistering and painful burn in seconds. Minutes of exposure to the sun was fatal.

It was January now and though winter, whatever that meant to them now, was supposed to be in full swing, it was just getting hotter at night and scarier during the day. There wouldn't be any snow to worry about.

They'd started in Florida, one of the worst states to be in when winter time decides that leaving town seems like a good idea, and had steadily traveled north since June.

Richie almost laughed when he thought about being hot. Florida had seen record highs before any of the northern states had figured out that the shit was hitting the fan. Miami had been melting, actually fucking melting, when they'd taken to the road.

They'd stopped at a beach near Tampa to take a dip and cool off a little, thinking that the water there must be cooler than the piss water on the Atlantic coast. Elvis had suffered second degree burns on the ball of his left foot within seconds of stepping into the Gulf.

What had looked like waves crashing against the shore was actually the ripples of boiling water. Swimming was out of the question forever.

That had been their last daylight adventure, one begun only moments before dusk. After that, they waited for things to cool off after sunset. It usually took a few hours, but the heat dropped with the sun. That meant waiting from the very start of dawn until ten or eleven at night, holed up in whatever squat they were able to find.

They tried to sleep most of the time away, but it was never comfortable. No matter how far they could get underground, the temperature always stayed higher than eighty-five. Sleep is hard in that kind of heat.

They kept walking. Before long they were silent, conversation lagging and leaving each of the three men in his own mind.

***

It was close to five a.m. when they decided on a place to crash for the day.

They'd come upon an old farmhouse with a tornado cellar a mile or so behind them and chose to go back rather than hope for something better to show up.

Buddy and Elvis were clearing the rooms of the two-story structure, making sure no one was holed up inside, while Richie set to work picking the master lock on the outdoor entrance. If the two inside found a door to the cellar they wanted to be able to re-lock the one leading from the outside.

That was the main reason for picking the lock rather than busting it apart with a hammer. None of them liked the idea of someone barging in on them before they were ready to leave.

"No door inside," Buddy spoke up from behind Richie.

"Shhhh! I almost got it," Richie replied.

The tumblers on this one were sticky and he was close to resorting to just raking the pick across and hoping it would pop. He wasn't the best B&R guy in the world, but he was getting better. The lock was old and rusted, making things that much harder. For the hundredth time he reminded himself to look for some type of lubricating oil.

9

Richie put a bit more tension on the key slot, slipped the pick back a quarter of an inch and the lock popped open. He was slightly surprised, but very pleased.

"We're in," he said, pulling the lock out of the clasp and tugging hard on the warped wooden doors.

Elvis walked up, holstering his revolver, and helped to pull the cellar doors open. It only took a moment, but they were both exhausted by the end of it. Buddy had been covering them, holding his pistol at the ready, and waited until the shriek of the hinges hit his ears to holster it. They all walked the stairs quietly, each listening for any kind of movement, hoping to hear a rat.

Buddy and Richie got busy laying out camp while Elvis rummaged in his pack for a slingshot and a bag of ball bearings. This was the usual routine. Nobody spoke as they went about their chores, making sure not to spook anything that might be in the basement with them.

Buddy looked up from the sleeping bag he was rolling out when he heard the twang of the slingshot band. Elvis had found something and was getting ready to shoot. Still, they were quiet.

THWAK!

"Got you, sucker," Elvis whispered, tossing the dead body of a thin rat back over his shoulder.

THWAK! THWAK!

Twice more Elvis whispered. Twice more a rat was tossed close to the center of the room. He kept hunting, kept looking until he'd killed six of the bastardly thin things. Richie pulled the small sharp pocket knife from his pack and set to work dressing the rodents. Two apiece. They'd eat well today.

When the skinning was done Buddy took the small bodies to the top of the cellar stairway and dug a small hole. He laid their dinner into the hole and covered it, knowing that the day's heat would cook them without burning.

10

If he left the animals above ground, they'd be burnt to a char by the sunlight. They'd done that on the first day of December and had been sorely displeased by the lack of edible meat.

Buddy had come up with the idea of burying their kills and it had been a happy success. He did wonder, however, if that would change in the future. If he dug too shallow a hole, the rats were rubbery and hard to eat. Deeper holes countered the issue, but he could only dig so deep. It was getting hotter out.

Their water had already been pulled from the packs and set in the farthest and darkest corner of the room. They couldn't drink it until they allowed its heat to dissipate a bit. They always tried to find a lake or stream at the end of the night, after it had time to cool, but that wasn't always possible.

Finding clean water was becoming a problem, but there were still lakes that they could draw it from. There was no need to purify it, as it usually spent the day under boil. The taste wasn't great and the refreshment of a cool drink was a thing of the past, but at least they could stay hydrated. That was a major need.

"How hot you think it's gonna get, Richie?" Elvis asked, speaking above a whisper for the first time since they'd entered the cellar.

"Don't know, man. We aren't very deep in here, so it might get sweaty."

"Wish we coulda' found a mine. Don't you wish we coulda' found a mine, Buddy?"

Buddy, who had just closed the cellar doors, said nothing as he walked down the steps toward them. He simply nodded his agreement and began stripping his pants and shoes off.

They'd gotten past modesty under the light of a single lantern and were naked as soon as they were readied to sleep. Clothing was not conducive to these climates just lately.

11

"Tennessee was good for the mines, but that's the last we've found of them," Richie said.

"Gotta be more of them, right?" Elvis asked, hoping to be reassured, "Will you look at the map, Richie?"

It wasn't a bad idea. Richie opened his pack to search for the road atlas he'd picked up before they had left Miami. The plan was to head toward Alaska and hope for cooler nights. He'd done the math, Elvis watching with wide and hopeful eyes just as he was doing now, and figured it would take two hundred days. It was looking more like three-fifty at this point, due to the fact that they were losing strength earlier and earlier in the night, but it was still doable. Even if it took them four hundred, it was something to try for.

"We should be in Montana in a few nights," Richie told the others, "At least I think so. I didn't notice any signs tonight, but I'm pretty sure we're still on the right road. There are mines in Montana. Deep ones."

Elvis smiled in the lantern light, obviously remembering how cool it had felt so deep under the Tennessee dirt. They couldn't see any sunlight there at all and it had been quiet. The smell of damp that you'd expect in a mine wasn't there, the moisture in the dirt and clay having evaporated in the past months.

Every body of water they passed was getting shallower, disappearing into the atmosphere, so why wouldn't the dampness of the mines do the same? They hadn't really thought about it, were too comfortable in the depths of the earth to complain about anything, but Richie was worried. If the heat was growing exponentially, would the underground sanctuaries be any cooler than the cellar they were staying in? Could the constructs dry out to the point of collapse? If so, would they be safe going underground?

"Alaska," Buddy said with a sigh.

"Alaska," Elvis said with a smile.

"Yeah. Alaska," Richie said with fear in his heart.

***

"90 degrees," Richie answered Buddy.

He couldn't see his friends in the darkness of the cellar, but could still make out the numbers on his thermometer. His night vision was getting better out of necessity, as was everyone's.

He laid his head back on the make shift pillow of his ruck. Elvis said nothing, only tried to suffer in silence as the day wore on.

Richie went over the facts silently, again. He wondered if anyone was left in Alaska, anyway. It wasn't important, not really, because they needed somewhere to go. They needed a purpose in order to survive the constant misery of the days and nights, so finding more people was at the bottom of his priority list.

Buddy was snoring. At least someone was getting some rest. Elvis might not sleep for the rest of the night. Richie knew that sleep would be impossible with Elvis tossing and turning.

He felt bad for the guy, as he always did when someone was restless. It meant that they were hurting in some fundamental way that his reassurances couldn't touch. It meant that his friend was in pain.

Twenty-two years old. They were all the same age, had grown up together. Benny, of course, had been one of them, but wasn't around to keep them company anymore.

Their unfortunate names had brought them together in the first place, toward the end of elementary school when children found the ability to be truly cruel. Circumstance had made them stand up for each other and fight with the bullies as a team.

Each of them was named after one of those old rock-legends, or so it seemed. Other than Elvis, the boys' names were coincidental. He was named after the long dead "King of Rock n' Roll", but Richie was named for a great grandfather, Buddy was nicknamed because of those thick fucking glasses he wore, and Benny was just a version of Ben.

Elvis was born Down syndrome and his mom was idiotic enough to stamp him with the name and the hair that would make him a target for ridicule. Richie never cared for the woman, nor had Buddy.

They'd come together at Buddy's apartment just as the heat started really building up and decided to take off. None of their parents had survived, most lost to the fatal choice of going outside too often, and the only other family any of them had ever known was each other.

Richie decided on Alaska and the others followed without much question. It was go or stay and staying was off the market in Florida. There were hotter places, but not by much.

Richie suggested that they stay to the highways for the easy navigation and drew a route that would take them across the Midwest. When Benny asked why they didn't stick to the coast, the others just looked at him as if trying to analyze his density until Richie finally spoke up, his voice firm and his tone mimicking those of many of their old teachers.

"Salt water can't be drunk, Benny. There are more lakes and rivers moving through the Midwest so water will be easier to come by."

"Don't forget the complete lack of fucking basements on the east coast. The ground is too brittle in most spots. You can't sleep underground if there isn't an underground," Buddy added.

Elvis watched the exchange, his head moving back and forth as if he was a spectator at a tennis match. *His* decision had already been made. Where Buddy and Richie went, Elvis went.

14

Benny sputtered a bit, wishing he had a way to argue the point, but finally conceded. There was no good reason to stay on the coast. It wasn't even the shorter of the two routes.

"So we'll go northwest," Richie said, "It'll take the better part of the year to walk it, but we don't have much choice in the matter. Cars won't run worth a damn in this heat. Probably couldn't get past all of the break downs even if they *could* run."

They all nodded at this. The ability to travel had become difficult during the decline, motors overheating only minutes after being turned over and tires exploding at random. Opening up a hood to add coolant had become a frightening task. Batteries had a tendency to explode lately. Bicycles couldn't even be ridden due to the tires falling apart. Elvis and Buddy had even seen the foam filled wheels of a forklift falling apart. Walking seemed to be the only way to move.

Richie was roused from his memories as Elvis stood, his visage short and stocky, and walked to the stairway to sit on the bottom step. The slump in his shoulders, the way he leaned forward, the way his forearms propped against his upper thighs were all signals shown for Richie to read.

His friend hadn't been getting much sleep over the last week. Richie was keeping a close eye on him, remembering the signs Benny had shown before going over the edge. He didn't want to bury Elvis until he was old and gray if such a thing was possible.

Richie rolled over to face him, deciding on whether it was worth it to get up and sit with him. Would they gain anything from conversation? They hadn't been talking a great deal recently, so it might not hurt. He *was* tired and needed some rest, but knew that it would elude him if Elvis continued sitting watch over them. He sat up, the bones in his lower back crackling loudly against the silence. Buddy kept snoring.

15

"What's going on little brother?" Richie asked him as he approached.

"You haven't called me that in a while," Elvis said thickly.

"Move over."

He did, allowing Richie to sit, their legs almost touching in the narrow area. A fleeting thought reminded Richie to be careful sitting on old wood steps with a naked ass. Splinters in the behind would be just what he deserved for doing it.

He noticed that Elvis was losing weight, just like the rest of them, but it looked worse on him. His muscle tone was weak because of the Down's.

"I'm thinking about Benny," Elvis told him, knowing that he would ask.

"He's gone," Richie said, the image of Benny pointing a pistol at him playing on the movie screen in his mind.

"I know that. I know he left on purpose. Doesn't mean I don't miss em'."

Richie nodded.

"Do you ever think about it? Givin' up, I mean."

"Yeah," Richie admitted, "Sometimes. I'd never do it, though. Chicken shit way to go out, Elvis. You aren't thinking that way, are you?"

"Nah. Just talkin'. You know I'm not chicken shit."

"Besides, if I did something like that you'd be stuck with Buddy every night. You two would get lost as shit and end up in Mexico if I wasn't around."

"Me and ole' coke-bottles would get to Alaska in a week without you to slow us down."

They laughed, chuckled really, together in the dark. Richie loved the innocent way that Elvis laughed. Even when he was trying to be quiet it was close to a guffaw. His whispers were bellows in a crowded room, full of life even if the man himself didn't seem so.

***

16

"You know, I never thought I'd eat a rat," Buddy said, his tone thoughtful, but light.

"Me neither," said Elvis.

"I used to eat them all the time," Richie added, waiting for the other two to catch it.

"That's because you were always a pussy... Cat," Elvis testified.

That surprised all of them into a laugh for a moment. It was proceeded by jibes at each other that they'd gotten away from giving. It was nice to talk the way that they once had, before any of this started. Even if it was a conversation over a dinner of rat carcass, it was still a conversation.

"Do you think anyone around here lived through it?"

Buddy's tone sobered with the question and they became quiet. Richie started to speak and it was obvious that Elvis had an opinion, but they didn't want to say the actual words. It would be too much like dancing in a graveyard. They just kept eating, hoping that Buddy would either forget that he asked or decide he didn't want the answer. Buddy gnawed on tiny leg bones and considered the thing.

"I think there must be people up north. That's the only way to go to get away from the heat. My grandma lived in that condo on North Beach. You guys remember?"

Richie and Elvis nodded.

"She always left in April or May and went up to Michigan for the summer. She said that the humidity wasn't as bad there and it wasn't near as hot. Fucking Michigan, right?" Buddy paused for effect, "But that's the way all of the old folks did things. Snowbirds. They came south for the winter and north for the summer."

17

"Your grandma didn't go to Michigan," Richie said, "She stayed with Elvis' grandpa in Tampa and fucked her wrinkly old ass off all winter long."

Elvis guffawed some more as Buddy shook his head. Richie stood and made a bump and grind motion with his hips to accent the comment. His thin hips made the motion look almost unsettling.

"Your grandpa couldn't get it up any more than I could when your mom tried to jump my bones."

"Richie's mom's pretty, Buddy. I got it up for her every time," Elvis said dryly, eliciting stunned silence and laughter soon after.

"Dude. You just got burnt by the King of Rock N' Roll."

"Fuck," Richie said in return.

They concluded their meal and packed up their basement camp, making sure to leave nothing other than rat bones in their wake. Buddy checked their water and doled out enough to keep them alive but not a drop more. They drank, though it was still too warm to be good. All of them wished for a cold glass of water in a silent prayer to a God that must have abandoned them. After that, it was time to start the night.

"Who checks?" Buddy asked, knowing that he'd been the man to do so on the previous night.

Elvis started to rise, but Richie grabbed his shoulder and made him sit back down. Richie stood, pulling his coach gun out of the pack, checked the breach to see that it was loaded with shells, and walked toward the staircase.

He held the barrels to the doorway above, aiming low in case of any intrusion. They'd learned to do this at the beginning of each night early on. Sometimes people showed up. Usually they weren't nice. When food becomes scarce, there are those who don't want to bother with finding rats to eat.

Richie used his shoulder to shove one of the doors open so that he could keep the gun in hand and was blasted by hot air.

18

It was like a furnace in the basement, but was closer to hell outside. He was efficient without ever being taught and was able to clear the area quickly. He opened the other door with another hard shove and signaled for his friends to join him on the outside. They did, holding their own weapons at the ready.

"Safety's on, asshole," Richie griped at Buddy.

Buddy looked for a moment at the pistol before realizing what Richie was saying. The look on his face was amusing.

"You're a dick. It doesn't have a safety."

Richie grinned in the moonlight. To the others his face looked like a death mask.

Chapter 2

<u>**Wyola, Montana**</u>
<u>**January 24, 2021**</u>
<u>**12:02 AM 101*F**</u>

Montana wasn't as empty of life as Wyoming had been. They'd spent the last week walking its roads in near silence. There were signs everywhere that people were traveling the same highway, but they were either too far ahead to catch up to, or they didn't want to be seen.

Buddy was so tense that he slept with his pistol in hand. Richie and Elvis were afraid to wake him for fear that he would shoot first and ask questions later. It was distressing for all of them.

Elvis had gone mostly quiet, barely talking to either of his comrades, and it was a bad sign to Richie- who'd watched Benny go from talkative to quiet, and finally, to dead.

They'd tried a mine a few nights before and found it too dangerous to inhabit. Richie's thoughts about dry soil had proven accurate. They'd found three of the four shafts that branched off from the ballroom of the mine caved in.

They decided to find another basement instead. It didn't matter much. The mine's depth wasn't what they'd thought it would be and the temperature wasn't very different from the surface. It was disappointing, but not surprising. Time was running out for everything.

Richie wasn't troubled by the idea of other people being in the area. On the contrary, his spirits were lifted. If there were other survivors taking the same route, that meant that there was something to the idea of Alaska. Others might already be there. It might be safe and comfortable. There might be food that hadn't spoiled, water that was cool to drink and swim in, and life.

LIFE had become a word on a huge flashing sign in Richie's mind. Life meant being somewhere that wasn't so consistently dangerous, a place where he and his friends might be able to survive.

"Hear that?" Buddy asked in a hushed tone.

"Yeah," Elvis uttered, pulling the pistol from his hip.

Richie hadn't heard anything, being deep in thought, and said so in his own whisper. All of them had weapons at the ready, looking around for the source of some sound that Richie hadn't registered. All he heard now was the blood rushing through his ears. They were silent. No one moved for fear of making noise of their own that might be detected.

"We're safe. We have no weapons. Please don't shoot," a man's voice declared from somewhere close by.

Richie searched for the source of the intonation, unable to make anyone out in the night. A small superstitious part of him wondered if they were listening to ghosts. He shook the thought away and continued to scan the area.

"Let us see you. We won't shoot, but we aren't putting em' down," Buddy replied, still aiming at everything in front of him.

Three forms, specters in the shadows, seemed to materialize ten feet in front of them. Two teenage girls flanked a tall older man in a misshapen Stetson. Their hands were raised in surrender, but the man seemed, to Richie anyway, ready for anything.

No one spoke for a moment, both groups adjusting to the idea of other people being within view. As tense as they were, the smallest of movements at that instant would have caused a fire fight.

21

"I'm Steve Dundel and these are my girls. This is Annie," he said pointing to the girl on his left and then to his right without dropping his hands, "And this is Theresa."

"I'm Buddy. These two are Richie and Elvis."

One of the girls giggled, nervously, making Elvis uncomfortable. Buddy was taking the lead, quite easily, and Richie was impressed. The thought that Buddy might shoot them as soon as he could see them had crossed his mind. He was handling things calmly and logically. It was something Richie hadn't expected and he was thankful.

"We aren't going to hurt anyone," Buddy said, finally, and holstered his gun.

Richie followed suit and looked over at Elvis to see if he had. Elvis' pistol wasn't holstered, but he wasn't aiming it at the three newcomers anymore. Richie started to tell his friend to put the gun away, but something in the man's eyes told him that he might not listen.

Elvis doesn't like something about this, Richie thought and filed the notion away for later consideration.

***

Dundel had prepared well for the apocalypse.

The home he'd built in 2016 was actually an underground bunker, the entrance standing above ground, discreetly, among the surrounding hills. The place was powered by solar panels and hooked into an underground well.

The solar hadn't stood up to the intensity of the new dreadful sun, but the water still ran. It was warm and distilled by the heat of day, but it was better than what sloshed around in their bottles and was free of sediment. There were four rooms in the dwelling and an actual bathroom that the three men used with unexpected pleasure. Anything civilized in this new world was a luxury to be appreciated.

Richie, Buddy, and Elvis marveled at these temporary lodgings. None of them knew that there could be such comforts as this after society had collapsed. For the first time in months, none of them felt the pressure of the sun beating on the roof of their habitat.

They were all sitting around a scored kitchen table with Formica peeling away at the edges. The girls had brought in folding chairs from one of the other rooms so they could all sit. Things were still divided, the three men sitting close together on one side of the table while the girls sat with Dundel on the other. All of them had cups of warm water in hand, sipping as they spoke.

"My girls were keeping track of everything," Steve Dundel began without a trace of the accent all of them expected, "They were watching the news and listening to the radio. I didn't bother much with the media. I could see what was going on just by looking outside, so I stayed here and waited for my people to show up. After a while, they did."

"It was a good thing you just happened to have this type of place to stay in," Richie said, raising his eyebrows in question.

"It was," Dundel agreed, "Having this place built was one of the best decisions I ever made."

"But why did you build an underground house?" Buddy broke in, "I've never even heard of anyone doing this kind of thing."

"Oh, there are a lot of these places. I don't think there are many of them in Montana, but there are quite a few people living like this in the Midwest and up in Canada. It got fairly popular in the late 90's and improved with the technology. Solar used to be the hardest part of it, but enough people worked on it to get power running without the big companies. It's not worth shit now, but it was efficient before the sun started burning everything up."

23

"You didn't answer me," Buddy said, challenging Dundel, "Why did you build an underground house?"

Dundel smiled slightly, just a twitch at the corner of his mouth, and met Buddy's stare for a few seconds. He seemed to be weighing something in his mind, deciding whether to tell them more. The look in his eyes was one of debate and Richie watched as his inner turmoil seemed to fall to the side.

"I built it because the ash trees were healthy all of a sudden."

Buddy said nothing, only waited as if he understood something about the statement. The others sitting around the table looked at one another without a clue. *What in the hell do ash trees have to do with anything?* was the obvious question in everyone's mind. Richie looked to Buddy, who nodded to Dundel for the rest.

"Any of you ever heard of the Emerald Ash Borer?" Dundel asked the group, knowing that none did.

"Never," Richie said for all of them.

"Back in '02 the ash trees in Michigan started falling to shit. They figured out that there was a dirty little bug called an Emerald Ash Borer causing the mess, but they couldn't figure out how to contain it. By 2015 the Borers had spread all over the country, causing all sorts of havoc on the forests, which caused all sorts of havoc with lumber yards and the pockets of all sorts of carpenters. You know what baseball bats are made of? Ash. Hammer handles? Ash. How about guitars? Ash again.

"So the EPA and all of the conservation groups were trying like hell to get rid of the Borers and no one was having any luck at all. The government even tried to quarantine any affected unfinished wood. You could see the problems with those trees if you went to the woods at all. We had major problems around here and, for me at least, it was obvious. One day, though, I noticed that the trees were coming back."

24

"The sun was killing the Borers," Buddy said softly.

Dundel pointed a finger at him, cocking his thumb, and nodded. He looked around to see if everyone was following, but it didn't really matter if we were.

"Pests don't just go away when they have a nearly unlimited food supply. Something has to happen to force the point."

Richie nodded slowly. It made sense.

"So I started working on this place. I didn't really know what was going to happen, but I wanted to be prepared for anything," Dundel grinned, "I even had some of the framing built with ash."

"I'd say you managed your goal," Buddy acknowledged, holding his cup in the air as a salute. Dundel raised his own in response.

"When it got to the point of not being able to go out during the day, at all, Annie and Theresa got their butts over here. Their step-dad, Ronnie, had walked outside right at dusk and was sunburned so badly that he could barely move. Their mom told them to head over after dark," Dundel explained.

"Mom said that she would stay with Ronnie until he got better and then they'd come. That was in October and they haven't been here," Annie said tonelessly while her sister nodded her verification.

No one spoke for a moment. Buddy had been the first to stumble upon someone who hadn't been able to get underground before sunrise.

He'd gone off into the woods to get rid of dinner scraps and found a full grown man who'd tried to hide in the shade of the trees. His skin was charred as if someone had soaked his body in gasoline and lit a match. He'd brought the others to see it, knowing that they should get the shock of it out of the way. They'd be looking at more bodies along the road.

"So we stay in here during the day and do our chores at night to make sure the water keeps running and the septic tank can hold everything we need it to. It's a lot of work, but the girls pull their weight. If it wasn't for these two, I'd be

25

up a creek," Dundel said with a smile for each of them, though the looks they returned to him didn't seem very warm to Richie.

"You've got a radio. I saw it on the way in," Richie stated.

"I do."

"Have you been able to talk to anyone? Is there anywhere that isn't fried?" Richie asked hopefully.

"Mostly it's just static, since most of the antennae were above ground, but I've gotten a few people on the HAM.

"They're all saying that we have to go north, but I don't know if that's a good idea or not. Unless somebody up there has some kind of power source they'll be cooked there, too, sooner or later."

Dundel shook his head at the thought as if he'd been privy to something that nobody else had a clue toward. He closed his eyes for a moment before he started teaching his guests about what was really going on.

"Before all of this started, what did you boys do for a living?" Dundel asked them.

"I was in data entry, Buddy worked on cars, and Elvis helped Buddy out in the garage," Richie volunteered.

"Good jobs. I was a mechanical engineer. Worked for one of the smaller oil companies and made a good living. Got to know a lot of people in the EPA because I was always working with environmental regulations. The job was boring for the most part, but it paid really well. A while back, I retired. I wanted nothing more than to drink good bourbon and read a lot of books until my ticket got punched. Kept in touch with a few people from the old job, but for the most part I kept to myself."

"So I get a call, before things started to get bad, from an old buddy of mine, an EPA guy who hadn't had the good grace to retire and he asks me what I'm doing now. Did I ever build my man cave on steroids? 'Of course I did' I tell him. 'That's a damn good thing,' he says. Then he starts telling me about this nationwide conference call he'd been on that morning," Dundel said with a growing frown.

He ran a hand through salt colored hair and sighed.

"Here's what you've got," Dundel started again, "The sun's surface temperature runs at 5500 degrees Celsius and its rays are pure UV radiation. For as long as we've been on the earth the Ozone layer has absorbed at least 97% of that UV radiation acting like a shield for the surface of the earth.

"We didn't even know there *was* an Ozone layer until the late fifties, so up until then and quite a while after, we as a species set about destroying it. Nobody really paid much attention to it until the winters started getting warmer and shorter.

"There was always somebody trying to stop pollution, to save the ozone layer, but it was like some kind of fad. It was "in" one year and "out" the next. They even made some kind of holiday out of preserving the layer in 2009, but it was probably too late to fix things by the 70's.

"In 2003 the UN started lying to people. They used the media and some scientists to tell everyone that the holes were closing and the shield was getting better. In 2015 NASA told everyone that the holes in the Ozone were closing.

"That was a huge line of bullshit. Things don't repair themselves without action, just like pests don't go away on their own. All we did was stop using some of the chemicals that speed up the damage to the stratosphere. Nobody *did* anything as far as the public knows.

"When everyone started feeling the real heat of the thing, it was way too late to take any kind of action. I know that the UN and all the major government players had some bunkers built over the last twenty years. With a little research we could probably even find one of them if there was a working computer around.

27

"I'm sure that our president is sitting in a climate controlled room, either helping them try to figure out what to do or hoping for winter to come back, but that isn't helping anybody on the outside, on the surface."

"So the call was about the ozone?" Buddy asked.

"It was. It was about the known depletion and what the higher ups called "Cause for Concern". The big wigs said to be ready for climate changes, but not to worry about it too much. There were safeguards in place for everyone. It probably wouldn't be all that drastic, most likely. My friend said that they even made a joke about needing raises to pay for all the extra AC they were using. What they were really doing was protecting themselves, creating scapegoats for when fingers would be pointed. The EPA is a pretty powerful agency, but they weren't always a required entity. They were worried about their jobs, which is funny as hell considering how much money a man needs to get by when there isn't a store open for business or a house you have to pay taxes on anymore.

"What they told their people was that the ozone layer had been weakened to about 89% absorption. That means that in the last two years we were being hit with 11% of the sun's UV rays. Now I wonder if it wasn't closer to 80% absorption.

"Basically, we're being burned to death by too much direct sunlight and unless you have a tube of SPF-5,000,000 in your hip pocket, it's smart to stay inside during the day. And it's getting worse."

"I knew I should've gone into politics," Buddy said, cutting the tension a bit.

"Me too, son. Me too," Dundel said, "I don't know what happened to the friend that called me, but I hope he had his own plan. He was a good man."

The girls to his left and right hadn't said much, but both of them had been listening as if they'd never heard his explanation before, though Richie was sure they had. They nodded in the right places and looked somber when it was required.

For some reason, though, Richie didn't like the way it all came across. He might have been drawing off of the look on Elvis' face when they'd all met because Elvis had been good at knowing who to like and who to avoid all of his life. It was like an internal radar told him who would be mean to him.

Elvis was looking at the girls with an "avoid them" look that Richie recognized immediately. He also noticed that Steve Dundel didn't touch them in the way that most fathers do when close to their daughters. In fact, he hadn't touched them at all.

Maybe he was just reading into the dynamic too deeply. Wasn't it possible to be away from people for long enough that you didn't really connect with them in that way, anymore? Sure it was.

"I hate to ask you, sir, but do you have anything to eat?" Buddy asked, still playing the spokesperson of the group and silently telling Richie and Elvis that they shouldn't continue the conversation.

Dundel smiled at Buddy's question and stood without a word. He walked to a door and opened it, revealing a pantry stocked with dehydrated meals. He grabbed six of the packets and sat them on the table in front of the three travelers. He motioned toward the sink.

"The only good thing about the water being hot is that you don't have to worry about boiling it first. It's not the best chow you'll ever eat, but there's plenty to go around. Eat up."

***

The walls of the shelter were thick concrete, providing insulation against the heat emanating from the surface. It wasn't cool by any means, but Richie's thermometer showed the ambient temperature at just over eighty degrees. If they were able to sleep, it might actually be restful.

They'd eaten their fill of the dehydrated meals, not really caring what the food tasted like. In these times quantity was a big leader over quality. Elvis had stuffed himself, eating the two dinners he'd been given and finishing anything his friends had left over. He was full, but didn't seem as happy as he usually became when he'd been able to eat enough.

"I think they might be mean," Elvis had said seconds after they'd been left in the main room to set their sleeping bags.

"Why? Did they say something you didn't like?" Richie asked more out of curiosity than anything. There *was* something off about the daughters. Dundel seemed on the up and up, but Annie and Theresa projected a bad vibe toward them.

"Don't know. It ain't the man. It's them girls that give me the willies," said Elvis the mind reader.

"I think we ought to keep a watch. You know? Sleep in shifts," Buddy suggested.

Richie nodded his agreement, but decided against saying anything further about the family that had taken them in. He wondered if they had become less secure with being around people because they'd been alone for so long. Living souls were few and far between on the road these nights and it had been months since anyone had made their presence known to them.

Civilization had crumbled to a point where a person didn't want to meet another person for fear of being robbed of their few possessions or killed for food. Cannibals weren't common, at least not so far on their travels, but there were groups of them running the roads in search of meat.

There were many books written and movies made about the end of the world and a few of them seemed more like premonitions than stories. Short of the actual cause of the world's ruination, a lot of them had proven accurate guides to what was happening. Buddy was the reader out of their little group and had opened thirty books, at least, that covered the fall of structured government, the loss of life, and the cannibalism that resulted from food shortages.

If they hadn't seen the people who'd decided on that course of survival, none of them would have thought it possible. De-evolution on a grand scale was in progress.

"You guys sleep," Richie offered, "It'll be a while before I can close my eyes, anyway."

"Sure?" Elvis asked, already laying back, but serious about the question.

Richie nodded his encouragement and laid the coach gun to his right and under the sleeping bag he was sitting on. He didn't think it wise to leave the weapon in plain sight just in case one of the Dundels came to check on them, but he did want it close and ready. Elvis and Buddy readied their weapons in the same fashion. Nothing wrong with being prepared.

Buddy laid back, his fingers linked behind his head for support, and closed his eyes. Elvis followed suit, imitating Buddy in the way that he'd always been in the habit of.

Richie had to smile at the similar postures. He extinguished their lantern, leaving their world pitch black for the few moments it took his eyes to make the adjustment. Soon he could see their forms again. It was comforting. They'd been together for a long time.

Moments like these, when he was by himself in thought, always seemed to stretch for Richie. Buddy was always calling him "The Thinker" after that old statue. Richie didn't mind the comparison because it was apt enough to be stated. He *was* a thinker and was able to sort his thoughts into nice even piles when left to his own mind. It was like having a desk in his brain, manila folders sat here and there waiting for the proper arrangement to occur.

31

On that night, his thoughts turned toward a conversation he'd heard a few years before.

He'd been at work, getting a cup of coffee with a couple of the other employees who were busy discussing the state of the planet Mars. They were going back and forth about some theories as slightly intelligent people had a habit of doing and Richie listened in before going to his desk. The guys were entertaining.

"You know that Mars used to be like earth, right?" one of the men said while stirring powdered creamer into his cup.

"I've heard that," the other said.

"Well, just think about it. You have to imagine that the whole world was covered in water, like ours, and the atmosphere was good enough to support life and plants."

"Right."

"I've seen some things online that show Mars billions of years ago and it looked pretty close to the way Earth looks now."

"Yeah," the other man began, "But how could we know that? What's to say that the place hasn't always been what it is today?"

"Nothing at all, but what's to say the opposite. Just imagine what would happen to our world if something crazy went on. Maybe we're like a second version of the original Martians and we're headed down the same path."

"All things *is* possible," the man said jokingly, "Like you getting something done today other than bending my ear."

"Bite me."

Richie almost laughed, sitting in the darkness of an underground house with his hand on a shotgun. The conversation hadn't been long or detailed, but it crept back to him. Was it possible that the happenings on Earth were just a mirror of what had happened on a dead planet billions of years ago? Sure. Why not?

The world was in some definite trouble at the moment. People were wandering toward the same list occupied by the dinosaurs and the dodo bird. They were doing it in the most frightening style that they could manage, too. Sure. Why not?

The next hour was filled with thoughts of that comparison. It became like a dream as Richie dozed from time to time. He could hear the soft snoring of his friends as they slept.

***

Buddy sat up suddenly, a few hours later, with his gun in hand. He searched for the source of whatever had caused him to wake until he was sure there wasn't a threat. He *did* see Richie and could tell by his posture that he was close to falling to sleep.

He thought about trying to catch another hour, but his concern for Richie overwhelmed his own need. He looked over at Elvis to make sure he was still sleeping soundly and was rewarded with the sight he'd hoped for.

"Bad dream?" Richie asked in a low voice.

"Nothing new."

"Yeah."

They sat there for a few moments more, enjoying the almost mild temperature of the place, before either of them spoke again. Buddy was the first to break their silence, but he regretted doing so. Silence keeps a dangerous situation at the back of the mind. Words bring it to the front.

"You want to sleep a little?" Buddy asked, "I'll take the rest of the watch and we'll let the King sleep."

"Yeah. I'm bushed."

"Lay down then."

"Want the coach? Easier to shoot when you don't have to aim and it'll scare the hell out of anyone who tries to come in."

"I'm good."

"Suit yourself."

Richie laid back, his eyes finally closing, but knew that sleep would elude him for a few minutes more. He'd been thinking about their situation for the last couple of hours and badly wanted to compare notes with Buddy. He was hesitant, but things had to be said.

"I think we need to leave tonight."

"Yeah," Buddy confirmed with a disappointed sigh, "So do I."

"Elvis knows something. He just can't say it. Doesn't know how."

"He said he thought they were mean. That's good enough for me when it comes to Elvis. He may be a little soft, but he isn't dumb."

"I agree," Richie said, "But what's the deal? They've got food, shelter, water, and relative safety. I don't think they could want anything from us."

"They don't want nothin'," Elvis spoke, scaring the hell out of them, "Sometimes people are just mean."

"Be nice if you'd tell us you're awake instead of making me piss my pants, dick," Buddy snapped.

"You're a sissy, Buddy," Elvis said without much thought, "They won't be mean to you guys. I don't think they like *me* being here."

"And you're such a sweetheart. How dare they?" Buddy retorted.

"I am," Elvis agreed.

"He is," Richie said from his own edge of sleep.

Richie was soon in the hands of slumber, satisfied that the others agreed with him. He'd been wondering if he might be paranoid, but his friends reassured him by either validating his paranoia or joining it with their own.

It wouldn't be easy to leave a place where they didn't have to eat rodents on a daily basis, but it was better than what could happen if they stayed. He was drifting away when Elvis asked Buddy one last question.

"Do you think we'll make it to Alaska?"

***

The three guests were quiet. Dundel knew that what he was hearing wasn't their doing. He knew the sounds of his home well and the movements happening now were obvious to him.

The sound of a kitchen drawer sliding open and cutlery being rummaged through was one he didn't want to hear in the current situation. The man sat up in bed, knowing he was going to find something he didn't want to see.

Dundel stood, alone in his bedroom, and looked around. Nothing out of place. His shotgun still hung on the wall.

He thought about finding his shoes and decided against it. Whatever was going on in the house was something that called for silence and bare feet were better for that. His door was slightly ajar, letting a very dim light in, as if someone had been looking in on him. He used the partially open door to exit the room and closed it behind him, taking care to let the latch close gently.

The doorway to his daughters' room stood free of obstruction, so he looked there first. Dundel wasn't very surprised to see that his girls were no longer in bed.

It was the boy, Elvis, that they were probably after and he couldn't allow them to do anything to him. There were so few people left in the world now

35

that anyone with any sense had to try to preserve what life could continue to exist.

Dundel closed the door and turned away. He padded toward the kitchen area, passing the room he'd lent to his guests. They were all sleeping, though one of them was obviously supposed to be holding some kind of watch over the others.

They'll have to get better about that, Dundel thought as he reached the portal to the kitchenette.

They were whispering, his two girls, each of them holding a kitchen knife. One held a chef's knife, its edge honed by Dundel's hand just the day before, while the other held a serrated bread knife. That one would prove to be very wicked if used on flesh.

The girls hadn't noticed him yet, too caught up in their plans and fearful memories, allowing him to watch them for a moment.

Annie was sixteen and homely. She was just tall enough not to be considered short and was pudgy for most of her life. She'd lost weight in the last few months, but her body wasn't made to be a thin one and she just didn't look right without the extra pounds. Her rust colored hair could've been beautiful if her mother had ever taught her how to keep it, but her mom hadn't proven to be the most nurturing woman.

Theresa was thinner, at fourteen, had always been, but her looks weren't much different from Annie's. They both might have grown into themselves if their lives hadn't been filled with so much suffering.

Dundel wasn't a piteous man, but for his own daughters he held pity and regret. He'd known that they'd been through *something* at their mother's house, but they'd never let him on to what. The appearance of the boy Elvis and their obvious dislike of him was cluing him in.

"We don't have anything to eat that requires cutting," Dundel said finally, startling the two in his kitchen.

"Daddy," Annie began breathlessly, "He's bad."

"Who is?"

"That retard boy," Theresa answered, "He's like David."

Dundel could say nothing. He stood in the doorway, blocking the path to the boy his daughters had such terrible plans for. He was shocked and saddened. He hadn't known that there was anything going on with his ex-wife's step-son and his daughters, but he should've.

Steve Dundel was a thinking man, one who took the time to analyze everything, but he hadn't thought of this. He'd known that there were problems with the boy, David, but not to what extent.

It was a mistake that he would regret.

"He's not bad," Dundel choked out, "He's just a boy."

"He's a boy like *David*," Annie said, walking toward him, "And we got to get rid of him."

Theresa followed her sister's lead, staying in pace with Annie as they moved toward their father. Dundel refused to move. They stopped within a foot of him, holding their knives in a threatening stance.

"Move, daddy," said Annie, "We have to do this."

"I won't," Dundel returned sternly.

Their eyes met, father and daughter, and he felt that in a battle of wills he was more than capable of asserting his. This wasn't such a battle, not a mental one, and he could do nothing to stop the surprise of the chef's knife cutting across his chest.

Dundel grabbed for Annie's wrist just as the blade came away from his skin, the gash sending shooting pains throughout his upper body, and caught it. At the same time, he reached for his other daughter. He caught Theresa seconds

37

before she would've stabbed him in the throat with her bread knife. He twisted both wrists with strong hands and both blades dropped.

Lord, he thought, What could've been done to you to cause this?

Dundel let go of Theresa for the short time it took to hit Annie hard enough to knock her out, before rounding on Theresa to do the same. When they were both on the ground he took the time to touch the wound on his chest. It was deep and nasty, but it wouldn't kill him if he got something on it. He wouldn't treat the wound, though. He walked to the pantry, reached down to the floor, and came up with a handful of bungee cords.

Tears spilled along Dundel's cheeks as he tied his girls, hoping that they wouldn't wake before he was done with what he needed to do.

In the next room, his guests slept.

***

Richie woke to the sound of footfalls. Buddy was pacing around the room for some reason, his revolver in hand, and shaking his head back and forth quickly. Richie thought he might be doing this to stay awake, but dismissed the thought quickly. Something was wrong.

"You okay, man?" Richie asked quietly, hoping he wouldn't startle his friend.

"We gotta get out of here, Richie."

"Something wrong? Did something happen?"

"I don't know man, but the fucking front door just opened *way* too early. It's still fucking *light* outside," Buddy answered in a strained voice.

"Who the fuck opened the door? Elvis, wake up man. Did you see anybody walking around, Buddy?"

"Fuck! I think I must have nodded off. I don't fucking know. I didn't see anything, but that doesn't mean I didn't miss something."

Elvis stirred for a moment and muttered something unintelligible before sitting up and looking around.

"Richie? It's not night yet, is it?" Elvis asked.

"Don't think so. Just get your shit ready. Something's going on," Buddy demanded.

Elvis hurried at the tone, packing their gear as quickly as he could in the gloom. He'd already gotten his pack ready and was working on Buddy's when they heard the main door swing open and then closed.

Richie was up and on the balls of his feet, pulling clothing on and trying to hold his shotgun ready at the same time. The barrel of the thing wavered in his grasp, but never really aimed away from the main stairwell.

"You want the light?" He whispered to Buddy.

"No. Put that thing down and get dressed before you blow your fucking foot off."

Their whispering was harsh, but so quiet that no one could have heard them. Their hearing had adapted to the quiet whispers out of necessity. There were no footsteps on the stairway, no telltale creaking under the weight of a person, but they were waiting for someone to enter.

Buddy was aiming at the doorway that led to those steps with his finger on the trigger rather than the guard. He wasn't going to waste time. Richie, now clothed, followed his lead, aiming the barrels of his coach gun toward the lower half of the portal. Elvis was close to finished with the packing and would soon join them.

"What time is it?" Richie asked without looking away from his predicted target.

"Little after seven, I think. You're the one with the watch. Somebody popped the door three hours early.

"I heard someone walking. I was freaking out and thinking about waking you guys up, but what in the fuck can we do? We can't leave yet. The goddamn sun's still out. We couldn't even go if they'd waited until after sunset because the ground's too fuck hot to walk on. What the-"

"Dude. Calm down," Richie cut him off, "We're with you now. We'll figure it out."

"It's one of them girls, Richie," Elvis chimed in, "One of them girls went outside, I'll bet."

"No fucking way," Buddy said, "That would be-"

"Suicide," Richie breathed.

They all looked at each other in the darkness. There wasn't very much to say about what was going on until they decided on what to do. If one, or both, of the girls had walked outside then there wasn't anything to be done about it.

Anyone crazy enough to go out into the sun would surely be dead within moments, or at least very close. There was nothing to ponder or debate. It was what it was.

"Check on them?" Buddy asked.

Elvis nodded. Richie shrugged. That was enough of a vote to pass the motion.

***

Knocking on the two doors that could house Dundel and his daughters proved fruitless. No one seemed to be home, which put more of a strain on Elvis than any of them.

He started rattling out questions as to where they could be, but not listening for an answer. His whispering was failing in places as he tried to catch his breath in order to ask more questions.

Buddy was ignoring it and moving quickly through the quarters to make sure the others hadn't gone into some room they hadn't noticed. Richie was trying like hell to calm his friend down and failing miserably. Anxiety was contagious and Elvis was spitting it out with every exhalation.

"Give me some light, Richie," Buddy said, walking back to the first door they'd tried.

The place was suddenly flooded with illumination, making them squint against the glare at first. Nothing seemed out of place. The area was as tidy as when they'd first been invited to enter. The doors to the rooms where their hosts should have been sleeping were closed. Buddy twisted a handle and the latch opened freely. Richie held the lantern up to check the area and found it vacant.

"The other one," Buddy said, making his way to their last option.

The door swung open just as freely as the first and the empty room was the thing to finally silence Elvis' machine gun questioning.

"Well that's not what I was expecting at all," Buddy said.

"Nope," Elvis agreed, looking around the place as if it should have been bigger.

Richie glanced at the table at which they'd been sitting earlier in the night and noticed a piece of paper laying in the center. He picked it up without much hope and began reading, silently. The other two looked at him as he read, being patient with his reticence. He looked at the page for a long time before folding the note and putting it in his pocket.

"Do we have any room in anybody's pack?" Richie asked them.

"I got a little," Elvis said, "Why?"

"We're taking as much of the food as we can carry, filling our water bottles, and getting the hell out of here as soon as it's cool enough. Eat as much as you

41

can first, because we won't be able to take most of it. Drink the water too. They won't be needing it anymore."

Buddy and Elvis asked no questions, knowing by the look on Richie's face that he couldn't answer them yet. They would just do as he'd instructed and wait for him to explain.

They got to work, packing away everything that they could carry. Richie said nothing as he poured water into six meal packs and set them on the table to hydrate. He splashed water into glasses and set them out to cool before filling each of their bottles.

The work was helping him to get past the things he'd read. Part of him was angry and afraid. The other part was thankful to Steve Dundel, who had done something for them that he'd never be able to undo.

***

The night was still, without wind, and that was good. They were out a bit too early, but the situation had made their need to leave more essential than their comfort.

Buddy walked beside Richie, waiting for an explanation while Elvis trudged ahead, wiping his face and cursing the heat. Richie was quiet. He didn't want to let anything out, yet, and his friend knew to wait.

When they'd exited the underground home of Steve Dundel, Richie had made sure to get out first and lead the others away from the bodies that were surely laying at the entrance. He wasn't worried about Buddy seeing what had happened, but Elvis might have been more upset by the scene.

The door hadn't been pulled closed properly, which was why Buddy had heard it opening and closing on its mechanism. The bolt had been thrown, somehow, so that when the hydraulic arm that controlled the entrance tried to pull it shut, it would have to start the open and close process again after a set time. It had been a nerve racking sequence as they waited to leave.

Their bellies were full again, which was something to be happy about, or at least content. They'd gathered enough food for a week, or maybe two if they were prudent.

The dried stuff wasn't much better than the sun fried rodents as far as taste went, but flavor wasn't something of necessity. The parcels were, however, packed with nutrients that they wouldn't get from the small meals they'd gotten used to.

Richie thought they might even be able to stretch the stuff for a month if they could keep hunting the basements at night to supplement their appetites. As usual, it was a coin toss.

"Elvis," Buddy beckoned, "Trade me rags, man. That one's drenched."

"Thanks, Buddy," Elvis said, switching with him, "It's hotter tonight, huh?"

"Only a little," Buddy answered, giving Richie a look, "It'll cool off in a few hours."

Elvis nodded, thankfully, and wiped at his brow some more. Richie and Buddy had gotten into the habit of trading out Elvis' bandana with their own in shifts. They'd gotten pretty good on the timing and were able to keep the things drying in a somewhat regular cycle during the past weeks.

They were able to ignore the steady sheen of running sweat on their faces, were in fact thankful for the liquid as it proved that they were still hydrated enough to keep going. Elvis couldn't copy that ignorance. The sweat was a constant nuisance for him.

Heat stroke was a worry that none of them really discussed. If the sweat stopped running they were screwed, because drinking water throughout the heat of the night was almost impossible.

They'd tried to keep drinking steadily during their first few months of travel, but had become nauseated by the fullness and sloshing in their bellies. Buddy believed that the water was actually heating up even more inside their stomachs. Elvis just didn't like drinking water that had warmed almost to the point of boiling. Richie chose not to think about it, knowing that he wouldn't find a real answer through discussion. They simply filled their stomachs at the beginning of the night and waited until they stopped walking to have a drink unless it was absolutely necessary.

"You going to tell me?" Buddy asked without looking Richie's way.

"Not yet," Richie replied, his eyes never leaving Elvis' back, "After he goes to sleep."

"We can't keep anything from him, man. You know that."

"*This* we can keep from him. Trust me, Buddy. He doesn't need to know about any of that shit."

"What'll we tell him when he brings it up?" Richie asked, "You going to lie to him? I say *you* because you're not telling *me* shit."

"The truth. We don't know why they were gone. The letter explained a few things, but not everything. Just go with me on this one."

Buddy finally turned to look at him, but quickly looked away. There wasn't anything to be done for the time being, but to keep walking.

***

"It's fucked up, Buddy, but Dundel saved Elvis' life," Richie explained, long after Elvis had rolled over and fallen to sleep.

"What does that mean, Richie? I've been cool so far, but you're gonna have to spill."

They were sitting, nude and sweating profusely, at the top of a stairway that led down to the cellar they were holed up in for the night. The door was uncomfortably near and they could feel the heat baking off of it.

Neither man wanted to be this close to the surface, but it was the only way to talk so that Elvis wouldn't hear them if he woke up.

The sun was out, but luckily there were no cracks in the barrier above them. Even a stray beam of sunlight could cause their skin to broil. The night seemed miles away.

"I'm going to. Just let me get to it my way," Richie said, "It's a tribute to how screwed up the world was, even before this shit happened."

"Okay."

"You remember how Dundel said that the girls' mom and step-dad stayed behind?"

"Yeah," Buddy responded, wiping sweat away from his brow with a forearm, "But they didn't show back up. What's that have to do with anything?"

"What they didn't tell us was pretty fucking important. What they didn't tell us is why Dundel had to drag his daughters into the light."

"Fuck you," Buddy said a bit loudly.

"Yeah," Richie agreed, "Fuck me. Fuck all of us."

They were quiet in the darkness for a few minutes. Richie unfolded the piece of paper he'd pulled from his pants pocket before they'd crept to the top of the stairs and looked at it for a moment. There was no way to read the words in the darkness, but he could almost see them, anyway. Dundel's handwriting was neat and legible. It was actually in cursive, which had become a sort of lost art in recent years. Richie knew that some people couldn't even read the style of writing anymore. It had become a different language, like hieroglyphs.

"Light the torch," Richie told his friend.

45

Once there was meager illumination from Buddy's penlight, Richie handed over the paper.

Boys,

You're going to want to get down the road after you've read this. I'm sorry that things have to be this way. You don't know how sorry. My girls have gone bad inside and I'm sure at least one of you noticed.

The boy in your group, Elvis, bears a striking resemblance to Annie and Theresa's half-brother David. He's also got Down's, but I'm pretty sure that's where the similarity ends.

That boy wasn't right from day one. He did things that didn't make any sense to anyone. Let's just say that my ex couldn't keep a pet cat or dog with him around. They came up missing for a while and then they'd find the poor animal in pieces somewhere on their property. The boy did it.

Everyone knew, but nobody did anything about it.

Once he got older, he got after those girls in ways I don't even know about. They were young. Hell, they are young. Nobody really knew what was going on and I wasn't around at the time because of work. They learned to hate him. I don't think I need to spell it out for you. You're smart boys.

Until you three showed up, I thought that their half-brother died of going outside too early, but I think maybe things were different than how my girls explained them. They were planning the same thing for your friend and I caught them at it. They fought me on it, gave me a taste of what they were going to give him, I think.

They were poisoned by what they went through. For that reason, I forgive them and hope that you will, too.

I've got both of them tied up, right now. It won't hold until nightfall, but I think I'll be able to get through this letter before they can get loose. I can't risk letting them hurt anyone that doesn't deserve it. There are too few of us left to allow that.

The other problem is this. Without my little girls, I can't keep living. So that tells you what I need to do and why I'm doing it.

Make sure that you get deep underground within the next few months, boys. This is all going to get worse if I'm right. Alaska could be safe, but I don't know.

Take the food and water. Stay in the house if you want to. We're going outside, so we won't need them anymore.

Don't let this sacrifice be in vain.

Steve Dundel

Secrets are hard to keep, but from time to time they have to be kept. Richie and Buddy decided to keep this one to themselves, saving Elvis from something he might or might not be able to understand. Neither of them stated their intention, sitting together in the heat of the stairwell, but both of them knew what needed to be done.

They stood, one at a time and went down the stairs, made alone by the darkness, but held together by pain. They slept through dreams that would never hold in their minds and were grateful to wake up without memories of them.

Chapter 3

<u>**Billings, Montana**</u>
<u>**January 28, 2021**</u>
<u>**1:21 AM 97*F**</u>

The going had been easy during the last six nights. They were far from the underground home of Steve Dundel and hadn't been very successful on the front of putting the things that happened out of their minds.

Elvis was in his usual jovial mood, but Buddy and Richie were pensive at best. Elvis hadn't asked about the letter anymore, had just accepted the fact of leaving in a way that made Richie wonder if he had some idea of what he'd escaped. The very notion that someone would consider killing their friend was beyond Richie's ability to reason. It was a ridiculous idea.

Buddy was walking ahead of Richie, Elvis behind him, and they both appeared to be lost in thought. They were silent. No hectoring or bitching was able to get past the thickness of the air.

Richie had been watching the yellow lines in the center of the road and listening to his friends' footsteps for a few hours without interruption. Their pace was good. They were making some headway on their journey. By Richie's calculations, they would be out of Montana and across the border into Canada in less than two weeks.

"Holy shit," Buddy said from up in front.

"What?" Elvis asked, but was soon standing next to Buddy in the middle of the road.

Buddy began to laugh, as did Elvis, which made Richie look up at them for the first time in hours. When he did, he had to join them in laughter. They had stumbled into some good luck, after all.

"Do you think it's empty, Buddy?" Elvis inquired once he'd stopped laughing.

"Don't know, kid. Only one way to find out."

"Might be. We're in the middle of nowhere," Richie added.

They started walking again, this time side by side, as they always did when approaching something risky. It was instinct, more than anything, to make a larger image of their group than would be interpreted if they walked single file.

Each of them pulled a weapon, but didn't hold them at the ready quite yet. They were too far away from their destination to justify pointing the guns at anything but the ground.

"First one we've seen in Montana. Thought these places were like McDonald's. One on every block," Buddy said.

"Don't care. I'm getting some new boots and about fifty bandanas if they got em'," Elvis pronounced giddily.

"I'll get fifty more if it'll stop your whining," Buddy countered.

"To hell with all of that," Richie said, smiling nearly from ear to ear, "If I have to I'm going to force a shit just so I can use toilet paper to wipe my ass."

This cracked all of them up. They didn't stop laughing until they reached the parking lot of the Walmart Supercenter and headed for the back entrance. Their guns were now raised and ready.

***

The thing that all of those books about the apocalypse never consider is how unpredictable weather can really get and how much that can affect everything.

Things like canned goods and carbonated beverages become useless in extreme temperatures. If it gets too cold, everything freezes. If it gets too hot, soda cans and canned food can actually explode, wreaking havoc on everything that surrounds them.

Luckily for Richie, Buddy, and Elvis, most department stores don't store the food next to the clothing, and water is usually sold in plastic containers. The plastic bottles *can* melt, but the thicker ones usually warp rather than dissolve.

Richie took a few minutes to pick the lock on the back door while his friends kept a look out for anyone that might approach. When the door swung open they all nearly cheered aloud. It was nice, at least to Richie, to be in high spirits over something. It wasn't really happiness, but it was as close as they were getting to such an emotion just then. As they entered each of them had a similar thought.

The place was quiet and obviously deserted, but they still walked the entire store to clear the area. No threats emerged from the aisles. There were no squatters near the end caps. Nothing moved or made a sound other than a few rats that were living in the shelves. Elvis noted their locations for further investigation. They would need some fresh meat and they'd have to eat something other than their current stock of dehydrated meals if they wanted to make them last.

The rats had been a happy little coincidence from the onset of their journey across the United States. It seemed that they were the only sizable animals with the sense to both get under cover and stay there. The animals seemed to be plentiful in most of the squats they'd used and all of them hoped that they would keep up their appearances. Meat was hard to come by.

"I'll bet they have a slingshot in here somewhere," Richie said, "You could probably use a new one by now, Elvis."

"Yeah. I could," Elvis replied happily. He hadn't even thought about the possibility and was eager to take a look around for such a prize.

"Ammo, too," Buddy remarked.

"They probably have marbles, but I don't know about bearings. Don't wanna use marbles 'cause they break, Buddy. I got enough bearings for now if they don't have 'em."

"Duh Buddy," Richie taunted.

"Yeah. Duh Buddy."

"Get bent," Buddy said as they completed their circuit of the place, "Let's go shopping."

They pulled two shopping carts from a line of them at the front of the store, which looked as if it hadn't been touched by looters or even the odd shopper in a hurry. They walked through the grocery aisles while clearing the place and had seen the mess made by exploding cans, but didn't linger. There was nothing for them there. All of the food had long passed the point of spoiling and barely held the smell that would have assaulted their senses months before.

There was an abundance of water to be had so they each grabbed a warped gallon jug from the shelves, tossed another into one of the carts, and began to drink the warm liquid as they shopped.

Buddy led them, still holding his revolver in one hand, while Richie and Elvis pushed the carts. Better safe than sorry was their motto whenever they entered a structure like this one. In consideration of that, one of them would cover the other two at all times.

They picked things off of shelves as they passed making Richie nostalgic for the days when the three of them would do the same thing on a weekly basis.

51

They'd been soft then and were happy in a way that they'd likely never be able to duplicate. He pushed the thought away while taking a long swig from his water jug.

They came to the toiletries aisle and Buddy stopped, abruptly. The other two men tensed, waiting for him to say he'd heard or seen something, but they relaxed when he turned to them with a huge smile on his face. Buddy took a bar of soap from a stack of ten and ripped it open.

"Elvis, kid, how much water do we have with us?"

Elvis grinned, already twisting the cap off of one of the jugs.

Richie laughed as Buddy laid his pack on the ground, stuck the now unwrapped bar of misshapen soap between his teeth, and stripped. Elvis squeezed the plastic jug, spraying his friend with water, and Buddy began to wash for the first time in more than a month. Richie held his coach gun at the ready, laughing at the two of them as he scanned the area for danger.

The smell of the soap, one he'd never thought he'd miss so much, was absent. It had been stolen by the same heat that seemed to pilfer everything from the world. It barely mattered to him. Barely.

"I'm next!" Elvis shouted, which would usually have drawn ridicule from his companions. This time no one reprimanded him.

For the moment, at least, they were safe enough.

***

Three hours remained before sunrise. They'd each bathed in the middle of the toiletry aisle before making their way to the stock room at the back of the store to see if it had a basement. As luck would have it, the store actually had one. Usually they didn't.

Richie and buddy took turns at point, clearing the parts of the store they hadn't been through, and found nothing to be alarmed about. Once the basement was deemed safe they went back to the main aisles and outfitted themselves with new clothing. They tossed their old garments into the child's seat of the carts for later disposal.

None of them liked the idea of leaving evidence of their invasion. They'd even taken the time to clean up the mess from their showers. It was another of the habits they'd picked up in this new world that hadn't proven a bad one, as of yet.

They replaced gear that had gone too many miles with new stuff from the camping and sports sections, where they stumbled onto another great treasure. On an end cap, in the section marked for fishing and camping, they found another stock of dehydrated meals.

Arm loads of the packets were thrown into the cart. They would eat well without having to hunt if they chose. It was a luxury of epic proportions and each of them privately thanked whatever force might be helping to keep them alive.

Elvis, the great hunter of creatures great and small, waited patiently for the other two men to walk into the aisle full of glass cases that he'd been the most excited to see. There were rifles and shotguns stored along with boxes of ammunition, but that wasn't what he was interested in.

While Richie worked on the lock that held the glass cases closed, Elvis searched the shelves for a slingshot that would replace his weathered weapon. When he saw it, one of those models with the wrist support, he pulled it from the shelf happily and placed the old one in the cart.

By the time they'd decided on going back to the basement there was an hour left before the sun would peak over the horizon. They would sleep easily, on this day, safe from the sun and most other threats.

Each of them worked during the next hour. They barricaded all of the entrances to the underground stock room with pallets full of items that would never be restocked. They walked the wide open area to ensure that there wouldn't be any surprises. They covered vents if they were big enough to allow someone to breach them. None would've supported the size of anyone over one hundred pounds, but caution won out and they covered them.

When the three men rolled out new sleeping bags in the corner farthest from the main door all of them were tired and ready to sleep. The temperature was rising steadily, but would max out, soon. It wouldn't be like sleeping in the comforts of Steve Dundel's home, but it would be much more comfortable than most of their recent lodgings.

"It was a good night," Elvis said before drifting off to sleep.

***

"One more day," Richie said.

"Yep," Buddy replied.

Elvis was walking the perimeter of the basement with his slingshot. He was creating a small pile of meat for the next evening.

They'd been in the basement for two days, resting and recuperating in the way they always did when they found a safe spot to sleep. They never stayed for more than two days before this, but the distance between stops had been longer this time, more grueling. All three of them were in need of some time indoors.

The walk would continue soon enough.

Richie was working out the route that they would take once they crossed into Alberta. The Canadian road system was unfamiliar and it was taking some real concentration on his part to figure the plan.

Their atlas was open on the floor in front of him and he was jotting notes on a small pad he'd had since the three of them had started this journey. A yellow highlighter lay in the crook of the atlas' binding, ready for use when he needed it.

Buddy's nose was in the pages of a hard cover novel and he was intent on finishing the thing before they ventured back into the world. Richie remembered the book shelves that outnumbered everything else in Buddy's small apartment. The shelves seemed to be a starting point for a trove of books that were always laying everywhere.

Most men's apartments needed a good cleaning about once per week to gather the fast food containers and clothing laid around the place. With Buddy, you had only to pick paperbacks up off of the floor to make it look clean.

"You wonder why your eyes keep getting worse," Richie had remarked to him on some long ago day, "You read so much that they're giving up in protest."

"Is that why your right hand has gotten so much weaker than your left?" Buddy asked without missing a beat.

"Yes. That's how I know," he replied, "But you're likely the expert."

Richie wasn't going to say anything about Buddy's small pleasure now. He wouldn't even pick at him to keep himself from going crazy right now. Buddy deserved his book as much as Elvis deserved his slingshot.

Richie wondered what it was that he deserved and realized that he was enjoying his own prize. His friends were safe. For Richie, that might actually be enough. It wouldn't be a lasting thing, as the road beckoned to them even now, but he had it for the moment.

THWACK!

Buddy looked up from his prose to grin at Elvis. It was something that he didn't have reason to do for the most part, but the grin felt good. Elvis grinned back, loading a marble into the cup of the sling to replace the spent one.

As he'd told them, marbles shatter, but that didn't matter here. He could hunt and not have to risk losing any of the steel balls he used elsewhere. There were four bags of ammunition next to his sleeping bag.

"We needed this, you know?" Richie asked.

"You think?" Buddy remarked.

They slept well for the third day in a row. They woke with dusk, ate, packed, and left the place behind. Buddy turned the last page in his book an hour before they left.

Chapter 4

<u>**Livingston, Montana**</u>

<u>**February 7, 2021**</u>

<u>**3:00 AM 98*F**</u>

They weren't making bad time, putting miles and experience behind them. The nights were seemingly longer as they continued their journey to the north.

They started to notice signs of other travelers again. They would see the left over scraps or bones of an evening meal on the shoulder of the road, or a discarded piece of clothing. Elvis bent down in the middle of the road to pick up one lone shoestring and began wrapping it around the insides of his fingers only to unwrap it a moment later. He grew bored with the game after a bit and slipped the string into a pocket. Richie watched this with well rested eyes.

He'd been worried about Elvis for a while there, but their little break from the walk had done him good. It seemed that he was truly enjoying the exercise now, as opposed to shuffling dreadfully along with no real end in sight.

Richie didn't know whether he was out of the proverbial woods yet, but he was definitely on the right track. Buddy thought the same thing and had mentioned it to Richie. They smiled at each other for a moment. Both men were happy to see that their friend would likely be alright.

Buddy had always been an odd duck, but his friendship with Elvis regulated his weirdness a little. Elvis and Richie had been close too, but Buddy was around him so much more that he'd become a real brother to The King.

He was constantly letting him help when there was a simple repair to be done on a car at the garage, or taking him to the library when he needed a new book.

The time they'd spent surviving had just made them even stronger as a group, which was more of a need than a want. They were all that they had left. All of them would have been alone if not for one another.

"I feel like finding another Walmart, with a basement, and squatting there for the rest of my life," Buddy remarked.

"Spoken like true white trash, my friend."

"Have I told you to fuck off lately, Richie?" Buddy asked sweetly.

"They probably have them in Alaska," Richie added amiably, "Probably a bunch of them."

"Hard telling until we get there."

"You remember when we would've just pulled out a phone and looked it up?"

Buddy smiled at this. It was true that there had been such a time. Everyone had knowledge of everything in their back pockets. You had only to swipe your fingertip along the surface of a touchscreen to answer any question you might have had.

That was one of many things that all of them, the entire human race it seemed, had taken for granted. He nodded his head toward Elvis.

"He's the lucky one out of the three of us. Never even *had* a phone. Didn't want one," Buddy said, "The only times I ever saw him touch one of the damn things is that time I downloaded Pacman. He killed the battery every time he got hold of it."

"Blame him?" Richie asked with a chuckle, "I'd kill me some Pacman right about now."

"Not if Elvis knew you had it. I'm pretty sure he'd grab it and run like hell."

"You guys talkin' about me?" Elvis asked them.

"Oh yeah. We were just saying that you might be the last man on earth who can jerk off with either hand," Buddy said.

58

"You think so?" Elvis asked, the look on his face shocked and serious.

A response was impossible, as was continuing to walk. Both Buddy and Richie were doubled over with laughter. Each tried to say something in return, but couldn't get anything out that would be understood.

Elvis decided to give them the finger and say nothing more. Before long he was laughing right along with them. It was a good moment.

***

Once they'd gotten past their laughing fit they'd been able to find their pace again with Richie taking the lead.

The road had become hilly, small inclines and declines mixing with short flat areas and blind curves. Normally curves were approached with caution and blind ones were avoided completely if it was possible. There wasn't much of a choice on their current route, so they'd started taking the blind turns, too.

The moon was full and the stars bright, so they didn't have flashlights on to show their position. Nothing made a sound as they came up on a turn that Richie didn't care for.

There were cars blocking the roadway, broken and dirty thanks to their environment, and a shopping center blocked the next stretch of asphalt from view.

Strip malls, like this one, were always frightening. There were plenty of places for someone to hide in the abandoned storefronts to go along with the fact that they were just spooky, like small ghost towns with broken windows and angry spirits.

They hunkered behind an old Buick with Montana plates and busted tail lights. Richie scratched at the stubble on his freshly shaven face, grateful for the grooming they'd all been able to do recently, and looked at the curve.

Buddy's eyes were on the shopping center, magnified by thick lenses that were looking a bit worse for wear.

Richie wondered if he had an extra pair of the things or if he'd just be blind if they were destroyed. He thought about asking, but re-focused his attention instead. There were more important things to worry about.

Elvis had decided that a closer look was in order, shed his pack, and untied a pair of binoculars from the side of it. He'd picked the new pair up during their rest and had been eager to use them for something other than looking down long stretches of road at nothing.

The moment the lenses were to his eye lids, he sucked in a breath. Elvis handed the field glasses to Buddy and gave Richie a harried look.

"Somethin' moved." Elvis said as Buddy searched the area ahead of them, turning his head this way and that.

"Buddy?"

"I don't see shit, Richie," Buddy answered, "Where Elvis?"

Elvis duck walked until he was behind Richie and put his hands on the other man's shoulders, aiming him to the area he'd been looking at. A few seconds later Buddy handed the binoculars to Richie.

"Don't know, man. I don't see anything," Buddy told Elvis.

"Sure you saw something?" Richie asked as he scanned the area.

"Somethin' moved," Elvis reassured them.

"A person, you think?" Buddy asked.

"Don't know. Somethin' moved."

Elvis' face had gone pale, making his hazel eyes stand out intensely. Buddy was grinding his teeth and considering the situation. Richie kept looking, but saw nothing.

Finally, he took the things away from his eyes and looked down at this watch. They were two and a half hours away from sunrise, which made time and how they used it incredibly important. They would have to be quick about making a decision, or risk being caught outside.

The group liked to be secure and camping at least an hour before the day actually started. Delays were like flying bullets to them. Both could get a man killed.

"Here's what we have. If we keep walking, get past the curve with no trouble, we'll probably come up on a neighborhood in half an hour, but we'd have to get moving. Otherwise it's an hour back track to that place we passed earlier. That cuts it a little closer than I like, but it's doable," Richie explained, looking hard at both of his companions, "I'm for the easy walk if we can get by it. Buddy?"

"Shit," Buddy said, looked down at the asphalt for a moment in consideration, before looking back up, "The curve."

"Elvis?"

Elvis stared at the cars blocking the road ahead of them. This wasn't anywhere near the first time they'd come up on a road packed with cars, but it *was* rare. When people were afraid of going outside, they didn't really try to drive anywhere. He shook his head as if he was going to choose the house they passed, but looked at Buddy and Richie without saying anything for a full minute.

"Don't like it, but don't wanna get a sunburn," Elvis told them, "How do we get by, Richie?"

Richie looked at his watch again, followed the thin hand as it ticked seconds off of their lives, and began to talk.

***

It was surprising, to Richie at least, that they hadn't run into more trouble on their journey than they had. Sure there had been problems finding food, water, and shelter, but there hadn't been many people around them, so there hadn't been altercations for the most part. In fact, when they *did* happen the confrontations hadn't really gotten violent. Excluding what had almost happened at the Dundel home there hadn't really been much of a human threat at all.

Richie had been waiting for the other shoe to drop, for their luck to run out for so long, that when it did he wasn't surprised in the least. Being prepared for such an event was another thing entirely.

The plan was simple. Richie would take point, darting between cars as he went, up to the open area just before the turn. Elvis and Buddy would spread out staying to either side of him without bunching up and giving someone an easy target on the three of them. They would continue this pattern, slowly, until they'd completely cleared the turn

. Weapons would be drawn and ready to fire, but they would leave their packs hidden under the vehicle they'd started out behind. Once all was deemed safe one of them, most likely Elvis, would go back for their supplies. If everything went smoothly, they wouldn't lose more than fifteen minutes of darkness.

It started out in just that manner, Richie jogging in a crouch along the center line of the road, taking cover from time to time at the front or rear of a broken down vehicle. Elvis and Buddy were doing the same along the shoulders and staying hidden well enough.

Richie was becoming more and more at ease. He was starting to believe that Elvis had been mistaken about spotting movement, as he rounded the first part of the turn. His coach gun was cocked and ready, but he didn't think he'd be firing it at anything.

When the first burst of gunfire filled the air, cutting the wind around Richie's crouched form, he just stopped. He stood for at least three seconds, not comprehending what had happened. The only thing that saved him from being mowed down on the spot was their attacker's inability to aim. If he'd been a little better with his rifle Richie would've ended his journey abruptly.

Instead of dying, he dove back and to his right to the cover provided by an old Toyota Corolla. He could only hope that his friends had been so lucky, or hadn't been fired upon as he had.

The sound of semi-automatic gunfire stole the silence of the night. The only other thing that could be heard was the impact of the bullets on vehicle bodies and the breaking glass of windows.

For the moment, Richie could only make a smaller target of himself. He crouched low, covering his head with his forearms and praying not to be caught by one of the fired rounds. He'd closed his eyes at first, but soon opened them to look for signs that his friends were okay.

He thought to shout for them, but knew that they wouldn't be able to hear him over the barrage that was being laid down before them.

All at once everything was quiet. Whoever had been shooting at them had either stopped to inspect the damage they'd dealt, or was reloading. Richie's mind was whirling with the possible actions to be taken along with the need to know if his group was safe. He chose to believe that Buddy and Elvis were fine, but couldn't be sure since they'd decided to stay quiet along with him.

He heard something hit the ground, a hollow metallic sound, from far in front of his hiding spot. He braced himself without thinking as bullets started flying again.

Fucking waste of ammo, a part of his mind scolded the person or people firing on them.

He didn't think they were doing anything other than destroying busted down vehicles and hoping for a lucky hit on them. Richie was proven wrong when the asphalt next to where he was standing seemed to come alive.

He wondered how in the hell they were doing that from their position and promptly stopped worrying about it. Richie ran from his spot behind the Toyota, past the empty area between cars, and to the front grill of a BMW. He looked back as the ground exploded in the exact spot where he'd been squatting.

The firing stopped again, but he was sure he didn't have long to act this time. Richie stood up, his head popping up over the top of the hood to look for his friends. Looking to the right paid off with the image of Buddy hauling ass toward him. Looking left didn't help him to see Elvis at all.

Buddy stopped, abruptly, looking with wide eyes to where the attack had come from and fell backward on purpose to avoid a few badly placed shots. Richie and Buddy could at least see each other now. Elvis, though, was Richie's new concern. Where in the hell was he?

They waited through another burst of enemy fire, watching the ground for signs that their aggressor was firing low again. No asphalt was eaten on this round before the weapon ran out. Buddy ran toward Richie, his boots sliding along the pavement when he came to a crouch at the hood of the BMW.

"The fuck, man?" Buddy whispered, "Can you see em' anywhere?"

"Can't look for long enough to spot the pricks. They must have an armory up there to be shooting like this."

"Yeah," Buddy said, "What ever happened to conservation?"

"You see Elvis anywhere?"

"Was going to ask you the same thing."

64

They looked at each other for a long minute, neither of them wanting to think that Elvis had been caught off guard. They said nothing of the sort, choosing instead to figure out a next move.

"Try to flank them or run like hell?" Buddy asked.

"If we run it'll take too long."

"Yeah, but if we flank we might get dead quicker."

As if Buddy had told their assailant the same thing, more bullets came at them. It seemed that whoever was up ahead had an infinite supply and was intent on target practice.

"I think it's only one guy," Buddy said.

"Why?"

"Because if there's more than one of them we're fucked. Flank him."

Richie nodded. As soon as the shooting stopped again both he and Buddy stood and bolted for the outer lanes of the road. They stayed low enough so as not to be easy targets, but were both moving too fast to be completely safe.

When the gun started up again, they didn't dive for cover. Richie heard it, but didn't hear impacts near where he was, so decided that Buddy had been right. There must've been only one person shooting, or only one gun working. He risked standing up to his full height to see where the source of all the noise was standing.

He *did* catch sight of the person with the rifle, noted his general area, and ran for it. The rifle went silent just as Richie was coming within range of the man and he took advantage of the situation.

Richie pointed the miniature shotgun at the guy and almost yelled for him to stop what he was doing and put the weapon down. He immediately thought better of it and fired both barrels.

Flames licked out of the front of his weapon, lighting up the night for a moment, and the man who'd been trying to replace his ammunition clip and throw the rifle bolt, fell hard to the ground.

Buddy ran up to the other side of him, aimed, and put two more shots into the guy for good measure. Their eyes met for a second, both knowing that their actions had been the only chance at survival, and they nodded to each other. Job well done.

More gunfire erupted behind them and they turned, both hoping that there wasn't someone else with a long range rifle targeting them. Three more shots sounded, but no impact noises were evident near them.

"Elvis," Buddy said, turning to run.

Richie followed, cracking open the breech of his weapon and reloading as he went.

***

Elvis had been thinking clearer than either Buddy or Richie. All they'd been able to focus on was getting past the turn and had panicked for the first few moments of the attack. Elvis had no trouble understanding what was going on, though he couldn't have been sure that he was right without checking.

His intuition, though simple, had always been trustworthy. When Richie and Buddy started running toward the man in front of him Elvis had reversed toward their supplies. When he got back to their starting point it was just in time to see their packs being stolen.

A young girl, probably in her early teens, and a boy of about the same age as Elvis were doing their best to pull the supply packs from the underside of the car where they'd been left. The only thing that had slowed them down enough for Elvis to catch up was the band on his slingshot.

He'd stowed the thing in a side pocket on his own pack and somehow the rubber sling had bound up on the bottom of the car. He almost laughed at his good fortune.

"Wait!" he yelled, "Leave that alone!"

They couldn't have heard him over the gunfire, but he yelled twice more as he aimed his revolver. On the third yell he must've been louder, because they both turned their heads toward him.

Behind him, the roar of the coach gun canceled out all of the other noise. He knew that Richie had probably gotten to the person who'd been shooting their way. He wouldn't have fired if he could miss. Elvis knew that.

He held his aim on the two thieves, walking toward them, and remembered what all of the TV show cops usually said. He didn't want to shoot these two. They didn't look like bad guys to him, so he wanted to let them go if he could.

He wasn't above killing them, not even Elvis could pretend to be so innocent in these times, but that didn't mean that he would like it.

"Hands up," he told them, thankful that the noise had stopped and that he didn't have to yell, "And step away from the backpacks. Don't make me shoot you."

They did as he'd said without hesitation. These strangers had noticed the silence and had an idea that they wouldn't be getting any help from the man at the curve. It wasn't their plan to hurt anyone. All that they could do was hope no one would harm them.

These were the thoughts that Elvis imagined that they were having. He couldn't have known what they were thinking at all. When a stream of sweat filled his left eye and he raised his left hand to wipe it away, all hell broke loose.

The girl was the first to jump at him and the first to be shot. Elvis hit her twice in the chest before she could get to him, but didn't wait to see her fall before targeting the boy who'd been with her.

Elvis took aim as the boy tried to hide behind the open car door of the Buick and fired three times at the skin of it. The boy fell without ceremony. There weren't any last words from either of them. They were just dead now.

"Why'd you make me?" Elvis asked the dead boy, before turning back to the girl who was very close to dead, "Why'd you make me shoot? All you had to do was listen!"

Elvis abruptly emptied his gun into the girl, ending her life before she could answer him. He threw the revolver to the ground, tears dribbling down his cheeks, and walked over to the boy he'd killed.

"Stupid fucker!" he shouted, kicking the body hard in the ribs over and over, "Stupid fuckin' asshole!"

When Richie and Buddy arrived, he was still kicking the dead thing, screaming at it as if the boy was still able to learn something. Great streams of saliva and snot were running down Elvis' face as he raged at this person who'd made him do something he didn't want to do.

His friends turned away, both to leave him to the task of getting his anger out and to cover their backs in case the noise alerted anyone else to their presence. Richie looked at his watch and then up at Buddy.

"He's going to need to hurry this up," Richie whispered, "Two hours."

"Let him go. We'll make it," Buddy said, his eyes wet and shining in the dark, "You can't always hold it in, so let him go."

***

They spent the day in a den of ghosts.

68

The house they came to after leaving the newly dead group to rot on the road behind them had obviously been the place where those people had been living. There wasn't any food, which was probably why Richie and his friends were accosted, but there was water and the blankets they'd been using for beds. Buddy and Richie drank the water, but Elvis refused.

They kicked the dead's sleeping garments into a corner and spread out their own. They slept in shifts, as they'd been doing more often than not before their little vacation in the Walmart basement, and both of Elvis' friends knew that he wasn't sleeping well. He asked to take the second watch for them, admitting that he wouldn't be able to sleep at all.

"I don't like bein' stared at," Elvis told them.

"We aren't staring at you, kid," Buddy assured him, "It's too dark to see you, anyway."

"Not you guys," Elvis said and would say no more.

Richie was pretty sure that he knew what his friend meant and accepted it. He and Buddy laid down and dozed, but didn't truly sleep. The temperature wasn't any worse than it had been in any other basement, but it was stifling in a very different rite.

Later, when Buddy and Richie talked about the place, they both agreed that it felt haunted. They'd all killed at some point, but none of them had really accepted it as a normal turn of behavior.

When night fell and they'd given the outside world enough time to cool off, they left, clearing the entrance in the same way they'd grown accustomed to.

The only difference was Elvis' weapon. Buddy had picked up his revolver from the road, but Elvis told him to keep it. He wanted nothing to do with it. Instead, he'd retrieved the rifle, one Richie thought might be an M14, along with ammo for it from beside the dead rifleman. He aimed it along the length of the road, nodded, and slipped the shoulder strap onto his arm. He would use this from now on.

"It's better anyway," Elvis said, "Don't gotta be so close."

His friends nodded their agreement.

Chapter 5

Basin, MT

February 19, 2021

4:32 AM 95*F

Richie's stomach was tight with worry. They'd been walking for most of the night without seeing any sign of former civilization other than service stations speckling the roadside. No houses or factories meant no basements and no way to get underground.

There was no going backward, as the last place they'd seen was near the place they'd started their night. Elvis was silent. Buddy was searching the road as if his head was on a swivel. None of them had any solid ideas to pose in the event that they might not find shelter. At this point they were looking at a very possible end to their trip and it wasn't likely to be a pleasant one.

"Gas station up ahead," Buddy declared angrily, "We haven't seen a basement on one of these things since fucking Missouri."

"We'll check it," Richie said, "How far do you think it is?"

"A mile. Maybe two."

"Shit," Richie cursed, looking at his watch for the umpteenth time in the last hour, "Let's make it closer."

They picked up their pace, nearly jogging toward the lone building in the distance. They were all breathing hard, but Elvis was the loudest. He hadn't complained, hadn't started praying to the God of men who don't have shelter, hadn't said a damned thing over the last few hours.

Richie was becoming frustrated with his silence. He'd been quieter since their altercation in Livingston, and Richie understood that without a doubt, but he

71

was close to screaming at the guy for some reason. Maybe it was just the stress. *Maybe? Of course it's the fucking stress! You're dragging ass and tired of helping* them *drag ass, too!* his mind screamed.

Richie slowed a step or two, shaking his head to quiet the anger in his thoughts. It wasn't like him to be enraged with anyone in the type of shape they were in, especially when it came to Elvis.

Who could be frustrated with a person for *not* complaining? He knew that he had to get a grip on his emotions. He picked the steps back up and ignored the oddity for the moment.

"It's got a restaurant attached," Buddy said breathlessly.

"Maybe a storeroom under?" Richie hoped.

"Fuck! Maybe."

Buddy's pace didn't flag, but Richie could see how tired he was. *Pick it up! For God's sake, man up and run!* he shouted silently at his friend.

He closed his eyes to fight the thoughts back again. Now it was Buddy who had drawn his quiet rage. What in the world could be pushing him to such emotional outbursts? He tried to breathe deeply, but it was nearly impossible when he couldn't even get air into his lungs.

Hurry!

The station was drawing nearer and they would be there in the next few minutes. Richie looked to the face of his watch again, hoping that he wouldn't trip and fall due to the lack of attention on the road and saw that ten minutes had passed. They were close, sure, but this was where they would *have* to stay for the night. They couldn't possibly have time enough to get anywhere else.

***

Basin, MT

February 19, 2021
4:56 AM 99*F

The fueling station, a truck stop with a fast food restaurant attached, was deserted. They knew that almost without clearing the place.

All of the windows had been shattered and there were food stuffs everywhere spoiling on the shelves. The carcass of a dog greeted them within a few feet of the front entrance. The place wasn't huge, but it wasn't one of the tiny gas and go places that they'd been seeing throughout the night. Elvis and Richie walked the aisles of the place, quickly, to make sure they were alone.

"Running out of time," Richie whispered as he searched for a door that would lead to their salvation.

"Shit!" Buddy shouted, "No basement."

"Okay," Richie said, trying to keep some kind of self-control, "What else?"

"What else? What the fuck do you mean? We're dead! Didn't you hear me? No fucking basement!"

"I know what isn't here, Buddy," Richie admitted, surprised by his calm tone of voice despite the roiling acid in his stomach, "We need to know what else is here. Is there a store room?"

"Fuck," Buddy said in answer before nodding and turning to the opposite end of the convenience area, "I'll look."

"Elvis?" Richie beckoned.

"Yeah?"

"Check behind the counter at the fast food place. See if there's anywhere back there to go. We need a room with no windows."

Elvis nodded and sprinted away. Richie looked around the area, carefully, thinking and not wanting to miss anything.

73

What did he know about these places? Gas stations? Not a thing, really. Restaurants? He nodded to himself. He'd dated a girl in high school that part-timed at some fucking place that spit out burgers for money. What had she always talked about?

"Think, damn you," he whispered, "Think."

***

Basin, MT
February 19, 2021
5:04 AM 108*F

A freezer! Richie's mind exclaimed as he felt the temperature rising.

"Elvis!" he yelled, "Look for a freezer!"

Richie ran toward the counter where god knew how many meals had been handed off, grabbing Buddy's attention along the way. His friend followed him to the back of the kitchen area where Elvis stood staring at a large stainless steel door.

He looked as if his entire world had crumbled and Richie was very close to turning him around for a slap. The heat was coming. They all knew it, so why wasn't Elvis doing anything?

"Open it!" Richie told him loudly, "That's where we need to be."

"It's locked, Richie," Elvis said as he turned, tears starting to stream down his cheeks.

Richie grabbed the door latch, pulled, felt no give in the door, and pulled harder. Nothing. His mind raced, wondering what could possibly keep the door closed. He yanked again on the handle with the same result. Buddy took his own turn before stepping back.

74

The three of them stood for a moment, gawking at the only chance they had, Elvis crying without making much noise. Richie's mind raced along the tracks of his memory, pondering any conversation he'd had with that long ago girl that might just save their lives from the past. What in the fuck had she ever said about freezer doors in a restaurant?

"Oh fuck me," Richie said with a grin as he reached forward to a spot opposite the door handle and pulled a latch outward. The door swung open quietly.

The stench of the walk-in freezer was strong and immediate. All of them stepped back, wishing that the smell hadn't been sealed in for however long it had waited for them.

***

Basin, MT
February 19, 2021
5:13 AM 124*F

"Jesus," Richie spoke, the crook of his arm covering his mouth and nose, "We gotta get in."

"I think I'll just die," Buddy said.

"I'm with Buddy," Elvis proclaimed before turning away from them. The wet spatter sound of vomiting filled the room.

"Suck it up," Richie said, "We can get most of it out, but we don't have a lot of time here."

"Can we even survive in there? Is it going to get too hot?"

"I don't know, man," Richie admitted, "But we need to give it a shot. It's our last chance."

Elvis nodded. He'd turned back to them and was staring into the room with a disgusted look on his face. Richie took Elvis' sweaty bandana and wrapped it around his friend's face. Elvis breathed deeply and nodded to Richie thankfully. It wasn't great, but it was better.

Richie repeated the action with his own bandana, not able to suck in nearly as much breath. For once he wished that he sweated as much as the King. Buddy took a shirt from his pack, wrapped it around his face and looked to his friends. He gestured to them and then to the room in which they'd have to stay for the night.

They didn't have time to empty anything out. The temperature was rising much faster than any of them had expected. They would have to exist with the smell of badly rotten food for the day.

"Shit," Richie said as he walked into the stench of rot and decay. His friends followed.

***

Compared to the temperature of the outside world, the walk-in was cool at just over one-hundred-twelve degrees, but the day was uncomfortable to say the least. They didn't sleep for more than a few minutes at a time and even during those few precious minutes, no one slept deeply.

The heat was bad, but the smell was much worse than anything they'd had to deal with before. Outside, where the sun was able to strike and bleach the aroma of death away, nothing was that offensive. In this well-insulated room, however, the qualities of decay had been held in wait.

Buddy and Richie tried as many ways to distract themselves as was possible. Elvis seemed not only to deal with it, but was a rock compared to the other

76

two. He got more rest than his companions and was obviously better suited for the experience.

When Buddy asked how this could be, Elvis simply shrugged and told him that he should've thrown up before they walked in. Richie could say nothing in return while Buddy shook his head in amazement.

"It's frigging hot!" Buddy shouted at one point.

"Not as hot as it is out there," Richie contended, "We got lucky this time."

"You ain't lyin'," Elvis added.

Both Buddy and Richie looked his way with more head shaking for Elvis. They were always surprised when he spoke in certain ways. This was one of them.

The day lasted an eternity. They'd come close to not finding shelter before, but had always lucked out at what they believed was the last minute. This was a lesson that it could be cut much closer, time slivering away as if sliced with a hot wire, but they might not be so lucky the next time.

The problem with learning that type of lesson was that they might not have a choice in how they learned, much as they hadn't had an option this time. They could try staying in one spot for extended periods of time, but that could prove even more hazardous.

North was the only way to go. Stopping would mean a death doled out by the lack of forward motion and none of them was willing to accept that fate.

A lesson that they *could* take and make use of was that there was an alternative to the basements and store rooms of the world. Though that option might not be very attractive.

When darkness came, they walked on, grateful for their lives and the chance to keep moving.

Chapter 6

Sweetgrass, MT

March 10, 2021

10:51 PM 96*F

Richie was the first to see the Canadian border. The customs center was almost camouflaged by the grime that had gathered upon it. He saw that it must've been a madhouse near the end. Cars were lined up for half a mile on the U.S. side, empty of passengers. Large trucks were pulled across the lanes to try preventing the mass migration.

There were bodies all over the place, but it was impossible to tell how long they'd been there, or how they'd actually died. The flesh had been distorted by many days of direct sunlight.

He still smiled before turning back to his friends who'd been walking twenty or so feet behind him. They were looking in the same direction, but hadn't yet made out what the building meant. He would tell them in a moment, but right now he was too busy marveling at what they'd done. He was nearly elated by the notion that they'd made it this far and had only lost one of their original group.

His mood was hampered only by the thought of the one they'd lost.

***

Benny. Benny hadn't ever been the best of them. He was weak in a fundamental way and had proven it not long after they'd begun the trip to Alaska. Even before things went bad with the world, Benny was always afraid

78

of something, whether it be a bully giving him a hard time, or a teacher that made him take a test over when he didn't think he should have to.

He wasn't necessarily intelligent and had no athletic gifts. They'd always taken pity on him. Even when he'd go too far with teasing Elvis, the others were quick to forgive him because he didn't really understand what he was doing.

Buddy had been the one to finally lose his patience with Benny while they were still south of the Alabama line.

Benny had been quiet, isolating himself from the rest of the group for some time. During the first weeks of their trip he'd been a constant complainer, rubbing against the nerves of everyone, but that fell away once he'd stopped conversing. On his last night of life Benny seemed to burst out of his shell. He became manic and was screaming at the top of his lungs.

"I sure am glad I get to walk up this fucking road until dawn! It sure is great!" Benny yelled at the top of his lungs.

"Enough Benny," Richie had said to him, quietly.

"No way! I'm so goddamned excited about this that I just have to shout it out!"

Buddy was staring at him, now, but Elvis kept walking with his head down. He didn't like yelling, even when it was safe, and Benny was a champion screamer. The shouting put them all even more on edge than they'd already been.

"I'm just gonna walk all night long! Maybe I should sing about it!" he continued.

The singing, Richie thought as he neared the last car that would be waiting in line forever to get into Canada, was what set Buddy off. The shouting would've bothered him enough to say something, but the singing was what made him act.

79

Buddy quickened his pace so that he could round on Benny and be in front of him. He stopped, halting Benny in his tracks, and so did Richie and Elvis. They could see that it was going to go bad, but they couldn't have predicted how so. Neither of them, however, wanted to stop Buddy. Enough was enough.

"If you say one more fucking word, Benny," Buddy told him, their faces now only a few inches apart.

"What are you gonna do, Buddy?" Benny asked in that same faux happy tone, "You gonna hit me? I sure would like that! Go right ah-"

Benny was on the ground before he could finish his rant. Buddy stood over him, shaking and enraged. He was done listening to it and had made that clear with a fist to the jaw. Benny was quiet, finally, so surprised that he couldn't even think about getting up off of the ground.

"I warned you, Benny. That kind of shit could get us all killed. If you get up, do it slow and easy. I'm not going to let you hit me back."

Richie noticed that Buddy hadn't even removed his glasses, as he'd done on the few other occasions where some altercation might come to blows. He was confident that Benny wouldn't even try to strike him in retaliation.

"Now get your shit and let's go."

Benny did get up, but left his pack on the ground. He looked Buddy in the eye without saying a word before turning to the others. He seemed to be studying them, trying to find something in their faces.

Richie stared back at him and was unsettled by the look in his eye. It was that moment when Richie realized that Benny had cracked. Buddy's punch had been the last straw. Benny had been steadily worsening since they had left Miami, but Richie hadn't thought much about it. They were all under an incredible strain, but were handling it. From the look of things, Richie knew now, Benny had stopped handling.

"You can all fuck off," Benny told them quietly before turning to walk in the direction they'd already been going.

They all started the walk, again, Buddy picking up Benny's pack and shouldering it by one strap. He didn't look like the extra weight was affecting him, but after a while Elvis took a turn with it and Buddy didn't try to stop him. Richie took the pack from Elvis after a few miles and they began taking turns with the thing until they were ready to stop for the night.

Benny didn't speak, nor did anyone try to break words with him. The time for cooling down mentally had come.

Later, when they came to a place with cellar doors on the side, Benny didn't walk toward it. He just kept moving down the road. When Richie ran to him, trying to pull him back to the house, and finally screamed at him that it would be dawn and he was going to get himself killed, Benny simply pulled his pistol and aimed it at Richie's face.

"Fuck off," Benny whispered, "I'm not going anywhere with you pricks."

"Come on, man. Don't be stupid," Richie told him, trying to ignore the black hole of the pistol.

"Stupid?" Benny started, "I've followed you and Buddy around for fucking *years*. I've put up with all of your bullshit. I even helped protect your pet moron over there."

Elvis looked up sharply, a shadow of anger strolling across his features. Buddy didn't move toward Benny, but he didn't try to help Richie pull him in either. There would be no love lost between those two.

"You want to die Benny? Is that it?"

Benny pointed the pistol away from Richie, fired it, and returned his aim as the barrel puffed out a stream of acrid smoke. His eyes never left Richie.

"I said to fuck off," Benny said in a voice that was almost unrecognizable.

Richie could only raise his hands and back away. If Benny was going to shoot him for trying to save his life, then he could go on his way. Elvis said nothing during the exchange, nor had Buddy. They watched as their old friend walked away without so much as a look back over his shoulder.

They stepped past his blistered body the next night, a mutilated figure huddled in the road as if he'd lain in wait for death. Each of them mourned Benny in some way, but they did it alone.

***

Richie and his friends stepped into Canada over two hundred days after they'd left Miami, Florida. They'd traveled more than 2600 miles on foot and had a long journey ahead of them before their faction would reach Alaska. They were happy, but it was a subdued joy.

"Fucking Canada," Buddy said.

"Hopefully they're still the polite type," Richie added.

Elvis laughed heartily.

Canadian Roadways

Chapter 1

<u>**Coutts, AB**</u>

<u>**March 11, 2021**</u>

<u>**2:31 AM 94*F**</u>

Richie was working through his maps by lantern glow, outlining the same roads over and over with the yellow highlighter. Consequently, the lines on the map had gone from black to a muddy yellow.

His eyes were dry from staring at the paper without blinking for too long. His enthusiasm for Canada's s shortest route to Alaska had been fading over the last few minutes. The roads looked straight, not too many blind curves for them to navigate, so that was good.

The thing that kept cycling through his mind was the discernable lack of civilized areas once it ran through the Yukon. He'd begun debating as to whether they'd be able to find accommodations. Once upon a time the ground was more frozen than not through most of northern Canada so they might not have been really fond of digging out cellars.

Buddy, who'd found a paperback when they'd ransacked a drugstore earlier in the day, was sharing his light. He was laying on his stomach like a young kid, enraptured in the story of the thing. Richie didn't really know why he didn't carry a book in his pack all of the time. The weight wouldn't slow him down. It was just something that Buddy didn't like to do.

Richie had seen the look on Buddy's face when he'd spotted an abused book on the coffee table of his cousin's apartment. He'd looked as if someone had jabbed him with a needle. Maybe he just couldn't bear to damage a book in the way he would if he packed it away. Maybe.

84

Elvis was playing with his slingshot, having killed every rat in their current basement lodgings within an hour.

It was funny that the rats had survived. The only other animals he'd seen were lizards. Hell, even the insects had been mostly killed off. Rats were survivors as long as they weren't being targeted by Elvis' sling. It was just another of those things about the world that made little sense to Richie.

He didn't know if the others had questioned their good fortune at still being able to get hold of some kind of meat, but he'd made the choice not to ask too many questions long ago. By the grace of God, the survival of rats and men would always be.

He shook his head from side to side, as if to clear it of these thoughts, and looked at the map again. He would have to voice his concerns to the others soon.

"Water?" Buddy asked, offering his mostly full bottle without looking up from his book.

Richie took it, swigged the warm stuff, and handed it back to him. It wasn't too bad, a bit gritty, but otherwise okay. Piss warm. Probably warmer.

"Elvis wants music," Buddy told Richie, his voice barely audible, "You know. Like a guitar or something."

"Can he play?" Richie asked.

"Says he can. I've never heard him play before, but he was saying that he wanted to get a guitar if we see one again."

"Elvis playing guitar? I gotta see the king play."

They were grinning at each other over the lantern like a couple of kids. They turned to Elvis, but he didn't immediately look up at them.

"Little brother," Richie called to him, "You wanna get a guitar and be a rock n' roll star?"

Elvis' face pinched as if he was waiting for someone to strike him, but the look cleared away almost instantly. He smiled at them, knowing that Richie wouldn't make fun.

"Nope," Elvis replied through a dopey grin, "I wanna be the King."

They all laughed with him, not at him, and that was alright with Elvis.

***

Milk River, AB
March 12, 2021
1:02 AM 95*F

They were walking along the northbound lanes of Highway 4 in the only direction that mattered. The three men were side by side and looked more like 35 than 22 by this time.

They were road weary and haggard, but still walking, still breathing. The one in the middle had sprouted a thin beard, the auburn facial hair making his pale skin look even more white.

All three had long and tangled hair, but the man walking on the right side looked as if he'd been growing his deep brown curls long before the others had begun. His glasses shone in the moonlight, hiding his eyes from outside speculation.

The third had the beautiful, smooth, face shared by most of those born with Down Syndrome, but his eyes were sharp and alert under a mane of, considerably, darker hair than the others.

When the man in the middle spoke the other two didn't turn to him, but were listening intently nonetheless.

"Well you better share, then," Buddy said as he held a fresh bandana behind Richie's back for Elvis to take.

"Yeah," Elvis agreed, trading out his drenched rag for Buddy's fresh offering.

"How many of those things do you two have?" Richie had to ask.

"Dude, I have like ten folded up in my pockets. By the time the wet one, over there, gets through with all of them the first one's dry again."

Richie regarded Buddy with amusement. He'd not snapped at Elvis about the bandanas in a long time, and Richie was pleased to see that they had gotten a system down in order to avoid any more anger over such small fare. He hated to aggravate their good thoughts with his trepidations, but there wasn't an alternative.

"We've got choices to make as usual," Richie offered, "There are two routes that'll get us to where we want to be and both of them suck. One a little more than the other."

"Doesn't sound like we're going to have to think real hard on this one," Buddy said.

"Why's it suck more, Richie?" Elvis asked, "No stores?"

"Kind of. The first option is switching roads a lot and being able to get supplies up until we hit a spot in British Columbia. After that it gets dicey. The road's also curvy as shit."

"And the second option?" Buddy asked.

"We go up 4 until we hit 2. We get on 16 and walk forever. We hit 37 from there and we're home free. It's a pretty straight route with few curves that runs through the middle of nowhere. It would also save us about a month of walking."

"Sounds like the better way to go."

"Yeah," Elvis said, "We don't need no more curves if we don't gotta."

"But we don't know if there'll be houses with those nice basements to squat in," Buddy said as if he were pulling the words from Richie's mouth.

"Or places to get supplies."

"We should find a gas station," Elvis suggested.

"A gas station? For what?" Buddy asked.

"They got those books, sometimes, where it tells you where you can stop when you're goin' somewhere. My mom used to get em' when we'd drive up north."

Richie nearly slapped himself on the forehead. He hadn't thought of that at all.

"You got it Elvis!" Richie laughed, "There's bound to be some info on the road to fucking Alaska. Why didn't I think of it?"

"Cause you're a little slow, sometimes," Elvis told him.

***

Truck stops had been fairly easy to find along the major highways of the U.S. and, luckily, Canadians had followed the same philosophy when building their routes of transportation. They found a sizeable one a couple of miles down the road, the parking lot filled with tractor trailers and RV's.

As they walked through the graveyard of recreational vehicles, Richie couldn't help but think about how much easier things would have been if they had left Florida just two months earlier. The cars had still been running, though not well, and the trip wouldn't have taken more than a few weeks at a snail's pace.

The automatic doors at the front of the building were wedged open, saving them the headache of picking the lock. Elvis strolled in as if he were stopping in to grab some candy and a soda for the road. He probably could've had the

88

candy, but it was likely that the taste of it would've already been stolen by the heat.

With the doors open as they were, there wasn't anything that the elements hadn't gotten to. They kept their eyes open and weapons at the ready. Buddy and Richie cleared the place while Elvis searched for a book that would tell them something more about their new environment.

"We're good here," Buddy said, "Want to check for a basement?"

"Will do," Richie said looking at his watch, "It's only two, you know."

"Yeah, but it can't hurt to know something more before we keep going."

Richie nodded his agreement and veered toward the back of the store. He strode away from them and began his search. He could hear Elvis muttering to himself as he passed.

The beam of the penlight Buddy had turned over to him was weak, but there wasn't a need for anything brighter in the dark corners of the truck stop. Their night vision had become quite strong since they'd become primarily nocturnal beings.

Richie could see everything he needed to see under the soft light and was in the midst of checking behind the closed doors of the place when he spotted something on the floor in front of one of them. He stopped moving, listening for the smallest of dins.

Richie tapped the light against the barrels of his shotgun lightly, hoping to get Buddy and Elvis to notice that he wanted them there without speaking. They did, both of them quickly and silently walking over to where he was standing.

Buddy's eyes were wide in question while Elvis saw the problem right off. He looked at the floor and then back up at Richie in alarm. Richie nodded toward the door, asking for their opinions with the gesture.

89

Elvis nodded. Buddy hesitated, but nodded also. They could've left and found what they needed somewhere else, but they were here already and didn't know how long that would take.

Buddy stared at the trail of blood they'd found on the floor leading into a door marked "Storage" that was very likely a basement. Richie reached for the latch, his hand pausing over it for a moment as he listened for the sounds of another person and heard nothing. Elvis stood back from the doorway, aiming his rifle at the lower half of the thing. Richie turned the latch quickly and opened the door.

Darkness. Until Buddy took the penlight back and aimed it down the stairway, there was only darkness. Once it was brightened, however, many things came into view.

There were boxes on shelves that would have been used and restocked hundreds of times. There were crates of aluminum cans and plastic water bottles. There were two sleeping bags laid messily on the floor, blood spattered along the length of one of them. There were two middle aged people huddled in a corner, one a man and the other a woman.

One of them was unconscious from the look of his posture while the other was facing them with a stern expression on her face. She seemed to be protecting her man from something. At the moment, Richie guessed, *they* were that "something".

"Leave us alone," she said, firmly, her voice raspy but strong.

"We ain't gonna hurt you," Elvis told her.

"Do you have a gun?" Buddy asked her, "If you do, don't shoot us. We're coming down."

Richie hadn't lowered his weapon, but his friends were putting theirs away. He wasn't afraid of the two they'd found, but he wasn't going to trust them until he knew more. He wouldn't let his guard down just yet.

90

"We don't have a gun, anymore," the woman said, "We dropped both of them."

She was visibly shaking, though she still looked as if she was going to defend against them, no matter what. The man behind her hadn't been awakened by their talk. He was definitely out.

Richie thought he might be the one bleeding. Something occurred to him, suddenly, and he had to ask the question that seemed to eclipse every other thought in his head. These people looked like they were being hunted.

"Is anyone after you?"

Elvis and Buddy turned toward Richie with confused looks, but recognized his reasoning without much delay. People didn't hide without motivation. They also didn't bleed without a cause.

"We ran. They were chasing us," she replied, tears coming suddenly, "You aren't with them?"

"Fuck. Elvis, go clean up the blood on the floor. Make sure you get it all. Make it look like nobody was ever in the store and get your ass back down here," Richie ordered, "Buddy find a first aid kit if you can. Clear the medicine aisle if you have to. Don't use the light much and hurry it up."

Buddy cursed as he ran up the steps with Elvis on his heels. They went as swiftly as they could, hoping to find the things they needed to accomplish their orders. Richie turned toward the couple.

"Is he shot? Stabbed?" Richie asked, putting his pack down and opening the top of it. He didn't set his gun down, couldn't let it out of his grasp, but he didn't point it at anyone either.

"Shot. It's his shoulder," the woman said, still tensed for a fight, "They shot him and he bled all the way back here. He passed out a few minutes ago."

"Once my friends get back we'll need you to let us see him. He could be bleeding out."

91

"Are you a doctor?"

"Lady, do I look like a fucking doctor to you?" Richie snapped, and was immediately ashamed, "We've all had to learn some things recently. I've found a talent for not getting myself killed and bandaging people who are bleeding to death."

"What if you make it worse?"

Richie, who was close to shouting at the woman, said nothing for a moment. He took a deep breath, let it out, and then took another.

He was getting too worked up. He needed to calm down. He didn't like being in the darkness of the basement storage room without his friends. He could barely hear them moving up there, which was a good thing. They were surely doing what they needed to do. He knew that they were covering each other and covering him. It would be fine. He just had to deal with the woman.

"What's your name?" Richie asked her.

"Amanda."

"Well, Amanda, whatever we do is going to be better than doing nothing. Once my friends get down here we're gonna try to save your man," Richie explained, "Now tell me what happened."

"You didn't tell me your name," she sniffed.

"I'm Richie. My friends are Elvis and Buddy."

"Really?" Amanda asked, noticing the odd nature of their names.

"Yeah," Richie said, involuntarily smiling a little, "But we're not in a band."

***

"Could you have taken longer?" Richie asked without turning toward his friends as they returned.

92

"Fuck off," Buddy said mildly as he began laying bandages and medicines out on the floor, "There was blood *everywhere*. I can't believe we didn't notice all of it."

"It's all clean, Richie. And I found the book we wanted," Elvis told him, holding a small pamphlet for his inspection as he knelt down.

"Thanks, little brother. Does that door lock?"

"It's locked. We almost closed the front doors, but the King here made a good point. If anybody was looking and saw something different, they'd want to check it out."

"Nice."

"Yeah. What's up with our friends?"

Amanda had stepped out of the way of the man, who she said was Alek, as she'd been telling Richie about their problems on that night. Richie had already cut his shirt away and had been looking at his bullet wound by lantern light.

Richie introduced them all without ceremony as he began unrolling a large roll of gauze from the first aid kit and drenched the material with a bottle of peroxide. He held the dark brown container up and aimed the mouth of it toward the gaping hole in Alek's left shoulder.

"He might wake up in a second," Richie guessed, "I need you guys to hold his arms. Amanda, stay where he can see you as soon as his eyes open. I don't want him to freak out on us."

"Gunshot?" Buddy asked.

Amanda nodded as she crouched down and put her face less than a foot from the wounded man's visage. Buddy and Elvis each took one of his arms, being gentle on the wounded side.

"Did it go through?"

"There's a hole in both sides, so I think so. Get ready. This is going to frigging hurt and he might try to jump."

Everyone did as Richie said. When the peroxide hit the entrance of the injury, just north of his shoulder blade, the man moaned without waking. By the time the liquid had flooded the area, turned to a light pink color, and spilled from the other side, he was awake and nearly screaming.

His arms strained to pull away at first, but Amanda's constant flow of reassurance calmed him. He barely knew what was going on, was in an incredible amount of pain, was bleeding profusely, but still trusted her and was able to absorb all of it. That proved, to Richie anyway, that they were more than just acquaintances.

Richie wiped away the fluids with a roll of paper towels and had Elvis hold the wounded arm up so that he could bandage it. First he pressed a wad of the soaked gauze into the wound, actually penetrating the entrance and exit wounds, before taping a square of the stuff over either side to secure the wads. Then he began to wrap the rest of it around and around the area, finally taping it all at the collar bone.

Alek had been conscious up to the point when Richie had pressed the material into the entry wound. He'd passed out with this new agony, revealing that it was even worse than the pain that had roused him.

Elvis and Buddy propped the injured man against the wall again, instead of laying him down, at Richie's urging. They needed to try and keep the bleeding to a minimum, which meant keeping the shoulder higher than the heart. At least Richie thought that would be the case.

"Is he gonna be okay?" Elvis asked.

"I don't know, man. I don't know," Richie answered.

After all, he wasn't a doctor, as he'd already admitted.

***

94

Richie told Amanda to begin at the beginning. When she started telling them about the night so far, Buddy stopped her.

"Uh-uh. He said 'The Beginning'," Buddy clarified.

Elvis was paying attention to the conversation, but his eyes kept straying toward the broken man whose bandage was already turning pink at the thickest spots. Elvis had been the one holding the wounded arm throughout the bandaging and his hands were tinged with the same rust color as most of Alek's upper body. He was slowly cleaning the blood off with his sweat drenched bandana as Amanda talked.

"We lived in Wyoming," she began, "Not too far from Montana. No kids. Not many friends because we lived out in the country. If I wasn't so stubborn we'd have come north long before we did. Alek kept saying that we should, but I didn't want to leave our home."

Her voice had taken on a jerky monotone that Richie understood, but didn't really like. Regrets could be so painful that you had to separate the emotion from them or you'd drive yourself crazy. He could relate, but that didn't mean he had to enjoy it.

"We've been walking for months. We were living in our basement before that, but the food and water were running out. I finally gave in and we left. Alek said that we had to get as far north as we could. He said we'd go to Santa's damned workshop if we could have found it. I don't know if he was right or not.

"This place was full of supplies, so we stayed for the last couple of days to rest. We were just going to check out the area for another place and come back tonight, but we ran into some of those... people."

"What people?" Richie asked, although he had a fairly good idea as to what the answer was going to be.

95

"We think they're cannibals," she said, tears welling in her eyes, "I think they wanted to eat us."

Elvis looked up sharply, but looked back at Alek after a few seconds. He knew about the cannibals. They all did.

"They didn't say anything when they were walking toward us," Amanda continued, "That's what tipped Alek off, I think. He grabbed my shoulder and turned me back this way and told me to run. As soon as we started running they started shooting at us and chasing. I didn't even know Alek was shot until we were almost back here."

"How many?" Buddy asked, "And how did you outrun them."

"Eight or ten, I think. We didn't outrun them. We got around a curve and got behind some cars. Alek saw a trunk that was open and we got in. We waited in there for a while, until I didn't hear anyone anymore. We came back here and he managed to get down the stairs before he passed out," she said, looking at her husband, "He was so strong."

"He'd better be strong," Richie said, "He lost a lot of blood from the sound of it."

"How far away from here were you when you hid?" Buddy asked her, "Do you know how long it took to get here?"

"An hour? Maybe a little less."

"That's not good," Buddy said, his eyes meeting Richie's, "That means they aren't too far away."

Richie checked the time before saying anything. He motioned toward the packs and Elvis went to work unpacking.

"Won't make any difference," Richie told his friend, "Sunrise should be happening now. Unless they have the world's biggest sunbrella, they aren't coming today."

"Does it stay cool down here?" Elvis asked the woman.

"As cool as it is right now," she answered.

"How hot is it, Richie?"

When Richie checked his thermometer, he was astonished. He hadn't really noticed the ambient temperature of the basement due to all of the excitement. When he looked up at his friends, there were tears in his eyes. The thermo hadn't read less than eighty-degrees underground in a very long time.

"It's seventy-eight," he said, quietly.

"Fuck you," Buddy said, reaching for the thermometer and reading it himself.

"Yeah," Richie said, grinning, "Fuck me."

"It's cooler," Elvis whispered as a smile sprouted on his lips.

"Thank God," Richie said, covering his face with the palms of his blood stained hands.

***

They ate leftovers from the night before, opening the re-sealable dehydration bags with matching grimaces, and offered some to Amanda. She took the food and ate without speaking.

She thanked them in a way that no words could equal by offering some of the food that she and Alek had been living on. All three men were near tears as they tasted the tablespoon of powdered peanut butter, trying to remember when they'd last enjoyed such sweetness.

"Jesus!" Buddy exclaimed, "That's so good. Where did you find it?"

"We had a box of packets at home. Alek packed it as a treat."

"I hope he wakes up soon. I wanna thank him," Elvis said, licking his spoon so clean that it shone in the dimly lit basement.

Richie volunteered to take the first watch. No one argued it and everyone else in the basement was asleep in moments. Richie watched over them, his weapon pointed at nothing and aimed at everything. He thought about the most wonderful number in the world. Seventy-eight.

He'd held to the idea that going north as far as they could would save them from the ever-increasing heat, but it was a hard notion to keep hold of when there wasn't hard evidence to support it. This, however, this chink in the armor that the world seemed to be trapped inside of, was so uplifting that he thought he might weep.

Wouldn't it be a sight for his friends when they woke. Richie would be lying on the ground, clutching the thermometer that had given him such terrible news in the last few months, and crying like a baby. He would have to control himself instead.

The real questions would come soon, though. Was it just the insulation of the basement that had caused this? Was the atmosphere actually cooler once they went outside? Was it a one-time thing, or would it be lasting? Was the world really less miserable at the end of these miles of travel?

He didn't know the answers, hadn't actually looked at the thermometer that night above ground, but they would all soon find out.

When Elvis woke to relieve him of his shift, they barely spoke. Elvis was still half asleep and Richie was too lost in his own thoughts to let anything intrude.

When Richie laid down to sleep he did it with a tired mind. It wasn't long before he crossed the line between the real world and the one where dreams take you away. His dreams were filled with falling snow.

***

Alek took his last breath some time during Richie's slumber. There was no last word or moment for the man. He simply ceased to exist. There were tears for him from Amanda, and a sadness felt by everyone in the room, but there wasn't anything to be done for the man.

They laid him down on the blanket upon which he'd slept so many days away, and carried him to the surface once the land fell under the shadow of night. Buddy and Richie put his body in a place where there would be no shade to stop the angry sun and walked off a little way to let Amanda have a last minute with her husband. They would keep heading north and she would go with them.

They walked. They walked. They walked.

The scenery didn't change a great deal as they made their way down the straight stretch of road that would lead them to Alaska. Small buildings cropped up here and there, but there was nothing they needed inside of the structures just yet.

Their little group was the only living thing for miles, as far as they could see. No man-eating men roamed this area. More of them were sure to arrive, but for the moment they were safe.

Miles would fall behind them on this night with minimal conversation. Death was unremitting and they'd all learned how to handle it in their own ways, but Alek's passing was still a blow to their resolve.

Richie, Buddy, and Elvis were strangers to the dead man, but had given their effort toward saving his life and had failed. That failure would hang over them as they traveled.

What if it had been one of *them* who'd been wounded? Would they be able to do anything more for one of their own than they'd been able to do for Alek? Would they try harder and find some other way if it was Buddy on Death's doorstep? Or Richie? Or Elvis?

We couldn't have done anything more than what we did, Richie thought, He'd lost too much blood already.

99

Who knows where the bullet really was? thought Buddy, He was probably dead before he knew it.

This sucks, Elvis said to himself, This really sucks.

They walked.

Chapter 2

Calgary, AB
April 2, 2021
2:38 AM 93*F

Elvis could barely contain himself. They hadn't seen a department store since crossing into Canada, but there was one floating in the distance now. All of them were ready for a break, especially Amanda, who'd done more of her share of their nightly tasks. If they could rest for even two nights Richie was sure that things would get better for her.

She hadn't had time to grieve for her husband, not really, as they were keeping a ceaseless and rapid pace on their nightly travel. The big blue sign next to the huge white structure was an oasis, like a mirage, further up the road.

They approached the place with caution, as they always did, checking the area around the building for any signs of squatters and looking at the state of the entrances. This store wasn't untouched, by any means, but the windows were mostly secure and all of the doors remained locked.

If the inside proved to be a safe haven, they would have to find some way of patching the single front window that had been shattered. Someone, who was less subtle about entry than they were, had made his own way in.

Amanda stayed with Richie, covering his back as he worked on the bolt lock of a back door into the building. Buddy and Elvis were set to enter through the broken window. They wanted to secure the place from both sides. It would be much more efficient than entering as a complete group. The convenience of having four people rather than three was not lost on the three men and they were grateful for Amanda's presence.

Richie had improved upon his lock picking, but was having a hard time with the door. It was taking much longer than he liked and the delay was tapping on his nerves.

When the latch finally turned it was with an ease that he wouldn't have normally expected and he dropped his tension wrench to the ground. The tinkling sound of aluminum against asphalt pervaded the silence. The door swung open as he was fumbling for it and the barrel of a gun pressed against the top of his head.

Richie froze, refusing to look up, his eyelids slamming closed over his vision. He sincerely hoped that the person holding a gun to his head was one of his other two friends and that they were pulling some kind of a prank.

When he gathered the courage to open his eyes, seconds later, he saw an unfamiliar pair of hiking boots before him. No luck on the practical joke theory.

"Ma'am, if you would, just go ahead and drop your weapon that would be great," a man said from above him.

The clatter of the revolver hitting the pavement stung Richie's ears. His eyes went to the coach gun that lay to his right. The thing was just out of sight of the doorway, but he didn't dare reach for it.

He didn't want to look up and see the man's face for fear that it would cause him to squeeze the trigger. He waited, his breath going shallow, until the man that could kill him so easily spoke.

"I'm backing up just a little bit, but don't think I'm not still pointing at you," the voice said, "Now stand up and keep your hands where I can see them."

Richie did as he was told. When he finally got to see his aggressor, his appearance was surprising. The man was only five-eight and probably weighed one hundred forty-five pounds at best. He was clean shaven, and somehow his blonde hair was short and neat. His voice was much more rough than his appearance. He smiled at Richie, as if he weren't holding him in the sights of a weapon, but rather inviting him inside for a drink.

"Names?" he asked.

"Richie," he said.

"And you?"

"Amanda."

He looked at Amanda for a long moment, giving Richie time to contemplate the situation. Elvis and Buddy might already be inside and looking around. If so, he would need to figure out some way to warn them. If this man was the only one occupying the store, his friends would have a chance to either help Amanda and him, or get out of there.

That would be *their* choice, but if he knew Buddy, there would be a fight. If more people were inside, then there wasn't much he could do to even the odds now that he'd lost his weapon.

There was one more possibility that he dared not entertain. Maybe this man was actually friendly, but being as careful as Richie, himself, would have been. Maybe they would all end up as cohorts against the dangers of this new life they were leading.

When the man looked back to Richie, the jovial smile had vanished, revealing a severe look of dislike.

"You can call me Bail. Now get the fuck in here and join your buddies."

Richie's mind reeled at the statement. Elvis and Buddy had been captured.

***

"Right through that door," Bail told them from behind.

He'd backed into the building, keeping his weapon trained between the two of them, making sure that Richie knew that either one of them would be shot over any sudden movement. Since then, he'd been directing them through the store. He was following them with his pistol in one hand and the revolver he'd made Amanda drop in the other.

Amanda hadn't said a word, but Richie could tell by the look on her face that she was fighting to stay calm. He could empathize with her on that.

Richie pushed through a swinging door, thought about turning on their captor, and decided against it. One of the others might be hurt or killed if anyone heard the sounds of a struggle. He wasn't willing to risk their lives, just yet. Instead, he and Amanda passed through the entry without incident. Bail followed.

"Leave him alone," Elvis' voice echoed in the storeroom as Richie approached.

"Shut up, you fucking retard, or you'll get some, too!" yelled an unfamiliar voice.

Richie stiffened as he heard the sound of a fist hitting skin. When Bail told them to turn the last corner they could see the source of the noise.

Two men were holding Elvis by the arms, while two more were in the process of beating Buddy to a pulp. One was gripping his arms at the elbows from behind as the other took shots at Richie's friend. Richie almost ran to him, remembered the barrel of the gun that was surely pointed at this back, and chose to wait for a better opportunity.

"What the hell are you doing?" Bail asked the other men, "I said to hold onto em', not beat one to death."

"He took a swing at Jessie," the fellow who'd just punched Buddy in the stomach explained.

"Oh," Bail said, "That's fine. Quit it, though. He looks like he's had enough."

The two men dragged Buddy over to where Elvis was being held and dropped him. Elvis was let loose and fell immediately to Buddy, checking to see if he was still breathing, trying to make sure his friend would be okay.

Elvis looked up at the men as they backed away. Richie had seen anger on his friend's face many times, but never a pure and vengeful hatred as he saw now. Those men would be smart to keep an eye on Elvis. If they didn't, regrets wouldn't have time to be had.

"Go over by them," Bail told Richie and Amanda, "And don't get funny. There are a lot of guns at your backs."

Amanda joined Elvis, kneeling down to look at Buddy. Richie positioned himself between Bail's group and his own, protectively. He didn't think he'd be able to do much to save his friends, just then, but he wouldn't cower to these men. He heard Buddy cough and was glad. That meant they hadn't hit him hard enough to kill him.

"Also," Bail said, redirecting his attention to the men on his side, "Please don't use the word 'retard'. It's not civilized and I won't hear someone spoken to like that."

The men nodded, obviously taking Bail's command seriously. Richie was sure, now, that Bail was the most dangerous man in the place. He would have to be if the others took his commands so submissively.

"Okay. Let's get to business here. What did you four think you were doing? Trying to break in on us? Wasn't smart maneuvering," Bail advised, "Coming in for supplies? Am I right?"

"That's all we were doing," Richie told him.

"Well why were you sneaking around like thieves, then?" Bail asked.

"We weren't."

"Picking a lock seems like something a thief would do. Don't you think so?"

"We do that so that we don't damage the mechanism. It's so we can use the locks if we decide to stay the night."

Bail nodded, a look of admiration slipping across his features. He looked around at his group and gestured toward Richie in a way of congratulation.

"Not bad. Makes sense."

Richie waited, not breaking eye contact with Bail.

"One problem."

"Yeah?" Richie asked.

"You picked the wrong place to check out."

"It's the only place for miles. We didn't think anyone would be here. Just let us go. We won't come back."

"I'd really like to do that, Richie. I really would," Bail said regretfully, "I'd like nothing more than to stock you four up with whatever you need and send you on your way."

"Then do it," Richie urged, "Please."

Bail seemed to consider the thought. It actually looked like he was thinking about it long and hard, but Richie knew that something else was running through his mind. A man doesn't gain power over so many others by being merciful.

"I'll tell you what, Richie," Bail offered, "Three of you can leave. We need to keep one to pay our taxes with."

Richie's heart began to race. He knew what would come next. He also knew that he wouldn't be leaving anyone behind when he left this place.

"We'll do just what I said. We'll stock your packs and set you loose. We'll have to keep your guns, you understand, but you'll get to walk out of here. No harm. No foul."

Bail paused, looking at the three people on the ground. Richie could hear Buddy trying to get to his feet, the scratch of his boots on concrete as he slipped once or twice before planting his feet.

"You just have to pick which one of these three you're going to leave behind."

"Why would I do that?"

"Richie! I'm sure you went to school somewhere and learned the rules of commerce!" Bail announced, "Just because it's gotten a little warm out during the day doesn't mean we all don't have to answer to someone. We've all got to pay our dues to keep the machine running.

"The thing is, we need to give a body up to the local feeders in order to continue our days in this safe place. Usually we go looking for somebody, but here you are. You've saved us some effort, which is why I'm letting you keep most of your group."

Bail walked toward him. He took slow, sure footed, steps until they were only a foot or two apart. He winked at Richie and leaned in close.

"Me personally, I hope you leave the girl. I wouldn't mind a shot at that one before we give her up to the stew pot. I'm sure you fellas have had your share already," Bail said with a lecherous wink, as if they were two friends about to have a beer together, "But I'm not going to make any choices for you."

"Let them go," Richie said, "Keep me."

Bail laughed, waved his index finger back and forth, and shook his head. His demeanor was almost jovial, friendly as any neighborhood watch member, but false. Richie could see the steel in the man without looking too hard.

"Sorry, Richie. That wasn't one of the choices. Now I'm going to take away points."

He looked at the group of them for a moment before pointing to Elvis. Two of Bail's men immediately grabbed Elvis by the arms and drug him a few feet away. Guns that had been pointed casually at the ground were now pointed at

Elvis. His oily black hair hung down in his face, but the anger was still there in his eyes. He shook his head at Richie, telling him instantly that it didn't matter. He would survive these people if he was left.

"You have until I count to three. After that, you'll only have two to choose from. I hate to do it, Richie. Hell, the feeders won't even take him if he's dead. Spoils the meat, I guess. But don't test me, son. Now let's get this done."

"Feeders?" Richie heard himself ask from a thousand miles away.

"Oh, you know. Some of our fair race has developed a taste for... Well, have you ever heard the term 'Long Pig'?"

"Cannibals," Richie said, his eyes switching to the men in the room, counting the odds quickly, finding them impossible without weapons, and then back to Bail.

"You got it," Bail said grinning, "We don't share their appetites around here, I'm glad to say, but we still have to pay the piper. Can't have them picking off one of my boys whenever they get hungry."

Buddy and Amanda were standing together, now. They weren't saying anything. They just watched, each of them realizing what was about to happen. Richie glanced at them as Bail began his count.

"One," Bail said, "Hope you have someone in mind."

Richie's watch ticked away at the seconds. Sweat was springing out on the nape of his neck. He was thinking hard and fast.

"Two. Hard position you're in. I'm sorry it has to be this way. Really, I am," Bail said without meaning a word of it.

Would they really let them go? If he had to leave someone behind could he live with himself? He knew who he'd have to choose.

"Three," Bail said, "Choose."

A plan formed in Richie's mind. It was rough and incomplete, but he didn't have time to consider the details. It would be more likely to work if he kept his strategy vague.

"Amanda," he said, turning to her, seeing the shock at his betrayal in her eyes, "I'm so sorry."

"Well, damn it all. You took my advice after all. Smart boy," Bail pronounced, motioning toward the woman with an open and empty hand.

Amanda was restrained by the same two men that had been after Buddy. Elvis was let go and went to Buddy, helping him to stand. Richie continued to hold the same posture.

He looked down into Bail's eyes. He heard Amanda screaming at him, telling him that she hoped he'd rot in hell, as the men pulled her away.

"You boys go on, then. I'm a man of my word."

The other men escorted Richie, Buddy, and Elvis out through the swinging door, one of them backing through first so there wouldn't be any unseen actions. Richie was out first, listening to Amanda's screams until they were at the front of the store where her voice would no longer reach.

***

They were shoved into the night, the back door of the place slamming shut behind them before anyone spoke.

"What's the plan, Richie?" Buddy asked, turning on him, "What are we doing?"

"Why'd you leave Amanda, Richie? She's our friend," said Elvis putting Buddy's glasses into his hand. Richie hadn't seen him pick the things up, but he was glad Buddy would be able to see. He would be needed.

"Didn't have a choice. Come on."

109

Richie bent down, reaching out for the double barreled coach gun, before walking along the back wall and away from the door. Buddy hadn't noticed the absence of the coach until that moment and followed his friend with Elvis in tow.

Richie rounded the corner of the building, walking as quickly as prudence would allow. He was almost sure of their next move, but didn't want to say anything until he knew what the front of the building looked like. At this point, he was the only one with a weapon and that made things much more problematic.

As they neared the front of the place, Richie planted his back against the wall as he walked, making a small target of himself if anyone came around the corner. His coach was held at the ready. His friends emulated his posture and followed.

At the edge of the building, Richie took a deep, calming breath before peeking around the corner. No one was there. He crouched down and motioned for Buddy and Elvis to do the same. They did.

Richie saw that Buddy's frames were out of true on his nose and immediately dismissed the thought. That wasn't what he needed on his mind just now.

"Okay. Shit," he began in a trembling voice, "How did you guys get caught?"

"We got in through the window and were walking the aisle back to where we thought you'd be. Then they were all around us."

"Okay, but where did they come *from*?" Richie asked.

"I'm not sure," Buddy answered, spitting a gob of blood onto the ground in front of him.

"The water." Elvis said.

Both of them looked to Elvis expectantly.

"They were carryin' water when they caught us," Elvis said, "So the water aisle's where they came from."

110

"Good," Richie nodded, "That's where some of them will be, then. They probably hadn't gotten the job done before they found you. The others will be back in the storeroom."

"With Amanda," Buddy added.

"Yeah."

"So what do we do with this?" Buddy asked, flicking the barrel of Richie's gun with his middle finger.

"We get you guys some weapons."

Richie stood, again, and walked over to the broken storefront window. He knelt down to look inside, hesitated for a few seconds, and finally entered. Buddy and Elvis watched him. They looked back at each other, to make sure of their agreement, before following him through the break.

***

Bail smiled, as he usually did, and strolled toward the woman. His steps were slow and sure. His hands were stretched out beside him as if he were offering an embrace. Amanda's eyes stayed on him. He was the only one she *really* needed to watch.

The other men were smiling widely. They hadn't had a woman in quite a while and it would be a nice change of pace. Some of them would've never thought about taking a woman by force in the old world, but this wasn't the old world.

They might have been accountants, or construction workers in a civilized time. Now they were a different kind of people, a rougher sort. Each of them looked to Bail for their next move.

The man who had become their leader wasn't the biggest or strongest of them. He probably wasn't the smartest. What he *was* could be considered the most important type of person to have in any group.

Bail was an animal that would bare teeth and use claws to survive. He would maim or kill at the drop of a hat if it meant living for one more day. His strength was a cold fist against the harsh heat of the day. His thoughts were that of a cornered beast who'd gotten out of the corner but hadn't forgotten it.

They all feared him.

"It's okay, honey," Bail reassured Amanda, "We aren't going to do anything you don't like."

"Yeah? What do you think I'll like?" Amanda spat back.

"My boys and I have some needs, sure, that we'd love to have you take care of. If you do, well, I might just think about finding someone else to trade to the feeders. Wouldn't that make you happy?"

"I'll tell you what," Amanda offered with a suddenly sweet tone, "You bring anything near me, any little thing at all, and you won't be able to use it on anyone again."

Bail's laughter bounced off of the walls, the sound deep and honest, as he took another step toward the woman. His eyes changed from a cold imitation of amusement to a real one.

He looked around, again, at his flunkies, and continued his laughing fit even as he called out a name that she could barely recognize as a word.

"The rest of you need to go on back to your chores," Bail commanded, "You'll get your turn after we get her ready."

The men that Bail hadn't called upon exited the room with little argument but many grumbles. They hated the idea of being left out.

"Now, sweetheart," Bail said, "Why don't we just talk this over?"

Amanda started to ball her fists, thought better of it, and shaped her fingers into claws. If they came for her they wouldn't walk away unscathed.

One of the men stopped, just inside of the exit, and turned back toward them. Amanda noticed this, but Bail seemed in ignorance of it.

"What do we do about the ones we let go?" he asked.

"They have no weapons and they're running out of time before dawn. That means they'll look for shelter and weapons before they think about coming back here," Bail answered without turning, "They'll be dead by tomorrow night if they come back, but I highly doubt we'll be seeing *them* again."

He smiled at Amanda wickedly and puckered his lips in a terrifying mimic of a kiss.

***

Five men, Richie thought as he walked through the department store.

His footsteps were almost silent against the background noise of a woman screaming to be left alone. Each vocalization made Richie's stomach turn. He hadn't had much of a choice in the matter, had to choose Amanda as the one to be left behind.

Not only was he thinking about who he would need in order to get someone back from these people, but who he could bear to lose if the rescue failed? He could live with someone's death on his conscience if it was someone he barely knew, at least he thought he could, but he couldn't lose Buddy or Elvis. They were his brothers in this world and he couldn't be without them, wouldn't be able to go on.

Richie was nearing the aisles where bottles of water would be stacked up to the ceiling when he heard male laughter. It was quiet and close by. He knew the others were behind him and would follow his lead, so he ducked into an aisle just before the one where the sound had originated.

He got low, pacing slowly toward the sound of two men talking. They were so sure that the men they'd shoved outside didn't have weapons, that their guard was down.

Richie braced himself before turning the corner to see the backs of the two men as they pulled large totes of water from the shelves. Richie saw that their guns, both pistols, were tucked into the back of their waistbands. That helped to make his next decision.

Rather than firing his coach and alerting everyone to his presence, Richie uncocked the hammers, flipped the gun in the air, caught it by the barrels and used it as a club on the back of both heads in quick succession. He'd managed to do this so fast that the two men hit the ground at nearly the same time.

He pulled the pistols off of them and tapped the barrels together lightly. Buddy and Elvis came running as quietly as they could and took possession of the things. Richie took one more swing at the heads of the men he'd knocked out, making sure that they wouldn't be getting up again. A puddle of blood began to grow beneath them.

Three left.

The three friends walked away from their first two victims without a word.

They followed the rear wall of the place, checking the spaces between aisles before crossing them.

Amanda was still screaming. As much as Richie hated to hear them, her screams were a good sign. The sounds meant that she was alive. They searched for the next target.

Buddy stopped just as he was about to cross the lane that Richie had just passed. He tapped his pistol barrel against the temple of his glasses once, making Richie turn back toward him.

Buddy motioned toward the area between the two end caps by which they were standing. Richie had a look, noting that someone had just turned down the dark aisle and was staring at the shelves, looking back and forth as he walked toward them. His shoes squeaked on the tiles.

The man was five feet away from them when Buddy pointed to himself and then their target. Richie nodded.

A few seconds passed as the guy turned his body toward Richie's side and Buddy pounced on him, wrapping the forearm and biceps of his left arm around the guy's throat and bludgeoning his temple over and over with the butt of his pistol. It wasn't long before the man was on the floor and Buddy had returned to them with an extra pistol.

Richie nodded again, thinking that Amanda would be needing it. Another man's blood covered Buddy's forearm, but he hardly noticed.

Three down, Richie thought, Two to go.

They huddled for a moment so that they could take stock of the situation. It had only been ten minutes from the time they'd been pushed out of the place. They were moving along well and getting really lucky, but the next step would be the hardest.

Richie signaled to his friends as well as he could manage that there were only two left and that they were in the storeroom. They seemed to get the gist of his hand motions and game him twin "Okay" signs. He led them to the storeroom.

Richie, Buddy, and Elvis were all very surprised at how easily they entered the storage area. No one had been watching the door. Neither of the two remaining men were even looking at the entrance. They were too busy trying to get a hold on Amanda, who was fighting and screaming as loudly as she possibly could.

She'd finally backed herself into the corner and Bails was edging closer to her as the other man blocked her from their direction. Amanda's shirt was ripped and her right knee was pouring blood, but otherwise she looked unharmed.

They crept up on the two would-be rapists, gaining ground quickly with Amanda's screaming to cover the noise they made, and were within a few feet of them when gunfire chewed into the body of the man that wasn't Bail. Buddy looked on as Elvis emptied his pistol into the guy.

Richie had other matters to attend to, namely Bail. He was on the clean cut man the instant that Elvis had pulled the trigger the first time. He'd hit him in the face with his fists ten or twelve times before the gun clicked and the last casing hit the floor. When everything was quiet, including Amanda, Richie stood looking down at the beaten man. Amanda took the time to walk over and spit on him.

That's five, Richie thought, That's all of them.

"He called me a retard, Buddy," Elvis was saying about the dead man on the floor, "Don't like it when people say that."

"He won't be saying it anymore," Buddy said, looking down at the wrecked body with wide eyes.

"And he almost broke your glasses. Don't like him."

"What do we do with this asshole?" Amanda asked Richie.

"We make a decision," Richie shrugged before looking at Amanda, "I'm sorry we had to leave you. I hoped you knew what I was doing."

"Not at first, but I figured it out. Thanks," she said without looking up from Bail's beaten form.

Richie nodded. Elvis kicked the man he'd killed in the head once, for good measure, before he and Buddy joined them.

116

"Pick him up," Richie told the other two men. He wished, in a way, that they would refuse. He wished that they would take the lead of the thing away from him. They didn't.

Elvis grabbed an arm and began hauling the man up. After a moment, Buddy helped, looking at Richie in an intense way.

He didn't care for it, but what could he do about it. He looked at both of his friends for a moment before speaking. *It's like the fucking Lord of the Flies, isn't it? We're changing to fit the circumstances,* Richie thought to himself.

"We can tie him up and leave him here, but we can't leave until tomorrow. The sun will be up soon. If he gets loose, he'll come after us if we're still here. We can set him outside and lock the doors that lead downstairs, but you never know.

"You guys remember what happens in all the movies and books when you leave loose ends. You know what happens when you talk to the bad guy for too long instead of just fucking putting a hole in his head."

The others were all watching him with growing anxiety, knowing what would come next.

"I say we kill him before he wakes up," Richie finished, swallowing the taste of the words, wishing he could spit them out.

Elvis thought for a moment. He nodded.

They looked to Buddy, who looked back for a full minute before agreeing. He cleared his throat.

Amanda took the gun from Richie's hand, her once delicate fingers making the weapon look much larger than it really was. She aimed it at the center of Bail's face, and pulled the trigger twice, considered for a moment, then squeezed off one more shot, just to make sure.

There was no ceremony. There were no real regrets. Elvis had a few small drops of blood on his face. He wiped them away with his shirt sleeve.

117

Chapter 3

They went about their chores as if nothing had happened. Buddy and Richie found and dragged all of the bodies they'd left in their wake to the front of the store, close to the windows where the sun could reach them. Sunrise was only an hour away when they finished.

Elvis and Amanda were each working on a different aspect of food and water. Elvis was making the day's meal and gathering water as Amanda filled a large microwaveable bowl with dry beans and water, sealed the lid with duct tape, and piled bags of mulch over top of it just outside of the back entrance. By nightfall they would have well boiled beans. They would likely be mush, but everyone would eat them with pleasure.

"Wish we could make a fire, some time," Elvis was fond of saying at least once a week.

"You know we can't, kid," Buddy always replied, "Fire inside when you can't get out is dangerous."

"Yeah," Elvis would say, simply, "But it'd be nice."

Richie and Buddy were quiet as they carried the dead, working without saying anything about the task, but it was obvious that Buddy needed to talk about what had happened in the store room.

He'd made the choice right with the rest of them, but Richie could read the guilt written all over his face. Neither of them was ready to broach the subject until after they'd left Bail's ruined body at the front of the place. They both

119

looked down at the man for a long moment, both being well past disgust at the sight of gore. It was common to them, now, and didn't have much effect.

"Are we the same as him?" Buddy asked as they walked away from the pile of dead bodies.

"We're surviving," Richie said in answer.

"So were they."

"They were catching people and giving them over to a bunch of cannibals to save their own skin. That's not the same as what we do."

"How many people have you killed since this started?" Buddy asked, "Because I'm losing count."

"As many as I've had to. Just like you. Just like Elvis," Richie said.

Buddy nodded, his logical mind taking what Richie said as a kind of gospel.

"I just don't want to be the bad guys, man," Buddy declared, "I don't want any of us to be like *them*."

"We aren't and we won't, Buddy. We do what we have to. Nothing more. Nothing less."

"Yeah," Buddy agreed, but still looked out of sorts.

Richie knew that Buddy would come to terms with all of it. *He* was in the process of doing the same. Everything he'd said to Buddy was coming from the internal dialogue he'd been having more often than not lately.

It was as if they'd just stated all of his deepest thoughts in words. Buddy's anxiety was warranted. Richie wasn't worried about *him*. Elvis was the one he was starting to worry about.

They'd have to talk to him, soon, to gauge his state of mind. His anger was coming to the surface more quickly and manifesting in a more lethal way with every confrontation they'd had with anyone. It was something to think about.

When they reached the store room, Elvis was waiting for them with a huge smile, making Buddy reconsider his thoughts about the man for a moment. He was shuffling from side to side, excited about something.

"I gotta show you guys this. You'll like this a lot!" he told them.

They followed Elvis into the store room, starting to wear their own smiles after this terrifying night. Elvis had a contagious grin.

***

"I found it," Elvis told them, "I was just lookin' around for stuff when I found it."

"Found what, kid?" Buddy asked, trying not to giggle right along with him as they walked the length of the store room.

"You'll see," Elvis said as they neared the back wall.

Richie heard the swinging door squeak open and looked back to see Amanda enter the storage area, tugging at the bottom of her new shirt with one hand while draping the old garment across one shoulder. She looked at them quizzically. He shrugged his shoulders and waved her toward them.

"Yeah," Elvis said, "You too Amanda."

They waited for her to join them, impatiently. All of them were suddenly giddy. Richie wondered if it was the stress of the situation they'd just dealt with that was making them a bit manic. He thought better of inward examination for the moment. He was too excited.

"I *found* it," Elvis said again, before pulling one of the large shelves out toward them with entirely too little effort.

They watched as an eight-foot section of the shelf came loose from the wall, slid out past the shelving that had seemed connected to it, and rolled to the side to overlap the next section. They saw a passage in the floor, leading down under where they stood.

"Holy shit," Buddy said breathlessly.

"I second that," Richie agreed.

They all looked at the portal and then up at Elvis, who was glowing with pride. He, after all, had been the one to find it. Richie and Buddy laughed out loud. Amanda simply smiled and shook her head.

"It's safe. I already put all our stuff down there. You gotta see the rest," Elvis told them as he slipped down onto the ladder, the rungs supporting him without a sound.

The group followed their friend down this new rabbit hole in the world. All of them were surprised by the discovery and weary of its existence at the same time. Had the men who'd been staying here as of late been using the area into which they were descending? Had they even known about it? Why was it there?

Richie was the last to touch his feet on the floor below. He was standing in total darkness until Elvis switched on their lantern. He spun around in the twenty by twenty-foot room, smiling again, as Elvis began to point things out, excitedly.

There were stacks of batteries everywhere. There were food pouches that were surely MRE's. There were fold out cots, of which their friend had already set up four. And the most important thing of all was the most evident.

Richie scrambled to his pack and quickly found the thermometer. The mercury line was steady at the seventy-degree hash mark. It was like winter for them.

"What the hell is it?" Buddy asked no one in particular.

"You guys don't know?" Amanda asked, her smile as wide as theirs, "It's a panic room."

"A panic room is hidden under a storage room at a random department store in Canada," Buddy said, trying the thought on for size, "Fucking convenient."

"Not really. I forget that you guys came from the southern states. Up here, we have a speaking relationship with the Canadians," Amanda said, "You remember back in '17 when the terrorist attacks *really* got out of hand?"

Buddy and Richie nodded. There had been a short time when the U.S. had seemed at the mercy of fanatical terrorist factions.

Bombings and shooting on home soil had become an almost daily occurrence by 2017. People they knew had gone as far as moving to different countries, neutral ones, to insure their safety.

Things were brought under control in 2018, when all of the American borders had been closed off completely, going against the very ideals the country had been founded upon. It was late in 2019 before anyone was allowed to leave or enter the country, but by that time the entire world had bigger problems on their hands than fighting over religion.

"Well, if you had paid attention to Canada's statements on the news starting in '16, you'd have been able to predict everything that happened after that. The Canadian government didn't agree with the way the U.S. was handling the terrorists, so they started taking things into their own hands before it got worse.

"Canada closed off travel a year before the states did. They made panic shelters a mandatory addition to every building constructed from the summer of 2016 on, along with any building that would house a large crowd of people, such as a department store. They were all to be underground. They were all supposed to have a hidden entrance so that no one without direct knowledge of the buildings would be able to find or enter them."

Amanda sat down on a cot, stretching her slim legs in front of her. She ran both hands through her filthy mop of blonde hair and pulled it back into a

123

ponytail. Her eyes were closed and her smile stayed strong. They watched, wondering if she might have more to say. She didn't.

***

"How long do we have before sunrise, Richie," Buddy asked, already walking toward the ladder.

"Forty minutes, at best. We need to wrap things up and close ourselves in."

"Yeah, but I need something. I should be back in plenty of time. Wanna come?"

The others watched as Buddy and Richie climbed the ladder. They were making Elvis nervous. He liked things more when they were all together, but Amanda was there to keep him company. They'd already started checking through the battery stocks and were replacing the ones powering their flashlights and lantern.

"I can get most of it," Buddy told Richie, "But I need you to find something for me."

"Okay," Richie agreed, "Give me a hint."

"I need one of those inverters. You know, the ones that hook to a battery and you can run like a lamp or something off of it?"

"Gotcha. That it?"

"Yeah. I can handle the rest," Buddy said with his recently revived grin.

Richie took up a quick jog, trying to remember where the vehicle repair section was. He thought it likely that he'd be able to find the inverter in that area.

As he ran along the center aisle of the store, looking for signs that would signify which section he wanted, something caught his eye and he had to stop, abruptly. He looked at the thing for a long moment, not really knowing if it

124

was worth taking, and finally grabbed the thick sketch pad from its shelf along with a pack of pens that was nearby. He stowed the new property and went after what he'd been told to grab.

Within ten minutes Richie and Buddy were standing outside of the entrance to the panic room, arranging the objects they'd gathered in order to carry them down the ladder without too much trouble. One of the items, a boxed up acoustic guitar, was way too large to carry. Richie finally looked down into the hole and yelled for Elvis.

"Catch this!" Buddy shouted before dropping the guitar. They didn't hear a crash, but instead were treated to the sounds of a very pleased Elvis.

Just before sunrise, they started down the ladder. Richie looked for, and found a switch that would allow him to pull the shelf back over top of the entrance so that they would remain hidden. As they descended, the glow of their lantern replaced the darkness of the shaft.

***

Cardboard scraps were everywhere. The room looked as if a psychotic child had unwrapped and destroyed five Christmas presents.

If Elvis' mother were alive to see the enthusiasm with which Elvis had unwrapped the cheap acoustic, she surely would've keeled over in fright. If she were alive to see the smile on his face as his fingers slipped up and down the frets, squealing on strings from time to time, she may have been happy enough to get back up.

"He's actually really good," said Richie as he watched Buddy pull apart the plastic casing around a pair of hair clippers.

"No shit. I never would've thought it."

Amanda was curled up on the cot she'd sat upon and claimed earlier, watching their friend as he played. His eyes were closed and his mouth moved around silent lyrics. She looked dazed and tired, as anyone who'd gone through her earlier ordeal would be. Richie hoped she wouldn't hold a grudge against him for leaving her for the short time, but he would shoulder the blame if she did.

"You want to be first?" Buddy asked, holding up the clippers.

"Don't threaten me with a good time. This hair is fucking killing me."

They set about dragging a twelve-volt battery to the back of the room where a few shower stalls had been built in, and hooked the positive and negative leads of the inverter to the posts. Richie set a folding chair up and took his seat as Buddy plugged in the clippers.

The buzz of an old barber shop filled the room and Buddy set to work shaving his friend's head to stubble. Within minutes, Richie was a new man rather than an old hippie and was giving Buddy the same treatment.

Elvis played a soundtrack of half remembered songs, humming the lyrics and sometimes, when he forgot himself, singing out loud. Richie and Buddy cringed slightly at the quality of his singing voice, but said nothing.

"You're beautiful," Richie told Buddy as the last clump of his dirty brown hair hit the floor.

"Wish I could say the same for you, my odd looking friend," Buddy jibed, putting his glasses on, "Elvis! Put that thing down for a minute and get a haircut!"

Elvis carefully propped the guitar against his cot and stood, stretching his back. He walked over to them and did something that neither man expected. He hugged them, one at a time, before sitting in the chair and patiently waiting.

Buddy grinned, taking the clippers and going to work on Elvis' head. Elvis was still humming one of the less recognizable tunes he'd been playing.

"Just take a little off the top and sides," he demanded, out of nowhere, "Leave the back natural. Don't want you to mess up my "do"."

"I'll do my best to keep you looking chic, kid," Buddy replied with a laugh.

Amanda had walked over to the hair cutting area and shed her shirt, revealing a too thin figure and a dirty bra. They'd seen her naked. She'd seen them naked. There wasn't a sexual thing about any of it.

"I'm next," she stated, "My hair has to go. Style is my least concern."

"Will do, young lady," Buddy said as he shaved a handful from Elvis' mane, "Just take a seat and wait in line."

"After that, I'll take a pair of scissors to your beards if you've got any. I didn't see any mirrors down here."

"I've got scissors, shaving cream, razors, and even soap."

"Good," Amanda said, "We may use all of it."

"You're done," Buddy patted Elvis on the shoulder a few ticks later, "Water's already by the shower. Do it up."

Once Amanda was in their self-titled barber's chair, Buddy hesitated. It was sad to see such lovely hair, even if it *was* dirty, be ruined. He thought for a minute before starting and asked Amanda for a favor.

"Anything, as long as you cut this shit off of my head," she told him.

"When we get to Alaska," he said, "If it's cool there, grow it back out."

She smiled and reached back for his hand. Buddy gave it to her as Richie watched. She squeezed it once.

"You too," she said to Richie as her hand reached toward him, "And I'll have to say this to Elvis after he gets out of the bath."

Richie gave her his hand, noticing that all three of them needed to work extra hard at washing the blood away from their skin and from under their nails. She squeezed his hand just as she had Buddy's.

"I know that you had to leave me. I know that you were coming back for me, whether I knew it then or not. I know that if you hadn't been able to," she paused, "If you hadn't been able to get back to me, it wasn't because you didn't want to. You tried to trade yourself for all of us, Richie. Don't think we didn't notice that."

Richie looked at the floor as she spoke. Her hands were strong and held onto both men, tightly. She wasn't letting go of them until she'd had her say.

"Thank you. Those men were going to use me. They were going to... Rape me. They were going to trade me to worse men for the ability to continue doing bad things to other people. You all saved me from that when you could've walked away, just like when you tried to save Alek. You're all good men. Thank you," she finished, her voice growing thick, and kissed each of their hands with dry lips.

There was an awkward moment where no one said a word. It was broken by the voice of Elvis singing some song about the rain on his shoes. They laughed as discreetly as possible given the circumstances.

They all stood there for a moment more, listening to the water splashing over Elvis and wishing that they could detect the smell of soap just one more time.

***

After talking about the situation and taking a vote, the group decided to stay in the panic shelter for a week.

After sunset, they climbed the ladder to the surface and opened the hatch cautiously. As soon as they'd cleared the storage area and the rest of the store, each of them went about the tasks they'd been assigned to by Richie. Mostly it was a gathering of supplies, but there were a few things that needed accomplishing to ensure their safety. Richie took those upon himself.

The first thing was to clear the blood they'd spread throughout the store during Amanda's rescue. Richie cleaned all of the areas with paper towels and water, afraid of using a cleaning agent in case a smell remained. The second task would be to transfer the charred bodies they'd left from the entrance area to the back of the building. If someone found them, they might go looking for what the dead men had fought over.

It wasn't likely that they'd be discovered, but they didn't need surprises upon their exit. Richie did all of the toting by hand, wrapping each man in a blanket and carrying them over one shoulder. By the time he was done, his body was screaming at him to stop all of the exertion. He wouldn't, though. Too many ideas were running through his mind.

He continued his work until the night was close to done. The final job would be to find a way to lock the mechanism that held their hatch in place. Upon examination with a penlight, Richie found this to be the easiest thing he'd approached all night.

There was a clasp on the handle that opened and closed the doorway from below that lined up with a thick slot. He had only to find a good padlock to make the shelf immovable. It was almost laughable.

He walked the store, grabbing a new shirt and shorts as he went, looking for the section where the locks would be on display. He found it in a short time and picked out a few different sizes to try, just in case the clasp was too small or the fit too sloppy for his taste.

He was walking through the camping section of the store with his newfound wares when he spotted a display sporting a picture of an outdoor shower bag. He picked the thing up and looked at it for a moment. It would be a real treat to have an actual shower and the vinyl case looked small enough to take with them when they vacated the place if it worked well enough. Either way, they'd each have a shower on that night.

Richie thought about his preparations as he walked back toward the storage area, going over everything, check marking a mental list to make sure that he hadn't forgotten anything. Something was definitely nagging at his subconscious mind as he walked.

He'd done everything they'd talked about. They had already set all of their possessions down into the shelter and cleared any sign that they might have taken up residence. He'd carried all four bodies along the width and length of the store to-

Wait, he thought, was it four or five.

Richie had come to the door of the storeroom and dropped everything in his arms at the front of it. His eyes were closed as he tried to remember exactly how he'd done the carrying. Why would there have been only four bodies when he knew they'd put five of them outside? Realization was close. He thought harder.

There were only four. Why?

"Feeders," he said out loud, startling himself.

He began to look for the others, scared to death that he wouldn't find them. If the local branch of Canadian Cannibals had paid them a visit, why would they stop with the cooked meat outside.

Bail had told them that the feeders didn't like dead offerings. That meant they might go looking for more food. Richie pulled the pistol he'd been carrying from his waistband, cursed himself for not bringing the coach gun instead, and kept walking the aisles, looking for his friends. Richie tried to remember the duties he'd given them, where they would be, but couldn't. His mind was racing.

Aisle after aisle proved empty. He cleared each one with his weapon aimed low, but was sure he was going too fast for his own good. He kept his finger outside of the trigger guard on the pistol to make sure he didn't accidently shoot one of his group. More aisles. Empty. Nothing. *Jesus.*

He wanted to shout for them, knowing that they would all come running, but didn't dare. If there was someone in the store, if there was more than one of them, alerting them to his position would be akin to suicide. He couldn't let that happen anymore than he could let someone be taken.

Faster. He moved faster, the corridors almost a blur as he moved from one side of the store to the other. He hadn't seen anyone, friend or foe, at the back wall, so he turned to the side when he came to a corner. He was sweating more now, becoming scared and worried. The darkness, though not complete, was stifling.

They're all dead because you didn't pay good enough attention, Richie.

More walls made of portable shelving hid him from everything and everything from him. Richie ducked in and out of the rows, now, searching every inch of the place from end to end. His eyes were drying out. He was afraid to blink, thinking he'd miss something, a person or a sign that someone had been there. He listened, but heard no one. Also, he noticed that it was getting hotter in the store. He checked his watch only to see that he was minutes from sunrise.

What could he do? He only had two choices. He could keep searching the rows until the sunlight flooded the place and burnt him to a crisp, or he could trust that everyone was in the panic shelter, waiting for him.

Maybe that was it. Maybe he was searching the store for ghosts. All of his friends were probably sitting on their cots, waiting for him to show up.

Nobody will be there. They're all dead because of you!

131

He ran, not caring about the noise he was making, until he was at the storage room door. He shoved through it, noticing in an instant that the pile of stuff he'd left was gone. He dismissed it and ran for the open shelf passage that would take him below.

He nearly dove for it, sliding down the ladder, the curve in his boots slipping along the vertical rails, his hands gripping loosely until his feet hit the floor.

He turned to see the lantern glow in the shelter. Buddy, Elvis, and Amanda were sitting there, looking at him as if he'd worn white after labor day.

"Got your stuff," Elvis said, holding up one of the locks that he'd already cut out of the casing, "Want to lock the door?"

Richie swallowed with an audible click and smiled, sweat still soaking his face, and climbed the ladder to close the door. The stretch his mind had just gone through seemed to shrink back to a normal shape. He'd overreacted, surely, but what if things had been different? What would he have done.

"Closing the door!" he shouted as he pulled a barrier between his group and the day.

***

"So, why didn't you just check here first?" Amanda asked Richie after he'd told them why he'd been so excited.

"I lost it a little," he admitted, "I didn't even think of checking the shelter."

"He's a little slow," Elvis told her, smiling at his joke as he picked at the strings on his guitar.

"Well, whether he's slow or not isn't really in question," Buddy said, adjusting his glasses, "The real question is what do we do about the flesh eating Canadians outside?"

"Nothing for a week," Amanda answered.

132

"I kind of have to agree," Richie added, "As long as we have supplies to last us, we don't have to leave this room."

"True," Buddy admitted, "But we might want to come up with something before the week ends. If they decide to camp out and wait on us, it might be a little hard to sneak out once we're done here."

"Yeah," Elvis agreed, "I don't want nobody eatin' me."

"At least it's a Canadian group of Cannibals," Buddy pointed out.

Everyone but Richie furrowed their brows at him.

"They're bound to be polite."

"Still don't want nobody eatin' me," Elvis said as they all snickered.

They were in agreement on that point. Cannibals were a frightening concept, but an even more frightening reality. Richie, Buddy, and Elvis had run into a group of them in the States and had been able to get past without incident, but Amanda was hit closer to home by the situation.

Her husband had been shot and eventually killed by one of these feeders. Richie wondered what she would do if she came face to face with one of them.

After seeing what she had done to rectify the Bail situation, Richie doubted that their girl would just curl up and surrender. He had a deep respect for the woman's toughness.

All of them were tired from the night of activity so they laid down to sleep, secured by the well locked secret entrance to their room.

Each person lay on their backs at first, staring at the ceiling and listening to one another's breathing, but soon Elvis was snoring and Buddy had turned on his side and fallen to sleep. Amanda was the next to go, her breath slowing until it was relaxed and deep.

Richie lay awake for a long time, scolding himself for the mistake of falling into a routine of working, of losing the focus he'd always prided himself on. He should have noticed that they were one dead man short from the moment he'd gone to move them. It was a slip that could easily have gotten one or all of them killed and he swore that he wouldn't repeat it.

The day wore on, but he slept little, no matter what comfort he'd been blessed with. At some point in the night, he woke to see Amanda propped on one elbow staring at him. She looked concerned.

"You were having a nightmare," she told him, "Are you okay? Need to talk about it?"

Richie shook his head and laid back again. He couldn't remember dreaming at all and talking about nothing would be a waste of time. Out of the corner of his eye, he saw her head fall back to the pillow.

Soon, he dozed off again, but he continued to move in and out of waking. Rebuking himself would accomplish nothing, but he continued out of a masochistic need for self-punishment.

They're all going to die and it will be your fault, Richie.

Fuck you.

Yeah, fuck me.

***

They lived like rock stars for four days. They ate when they wanted to, as much as they wanted to. They took lengthy naps during the night time and slept completely through the days. Richie had grown fond of drifting off to the sound of Elvis' guitar. They were truly clean for the first time since any of them could remember, taking daily showers under the outdoor rig that Richie had found.

Buddy read books as if he'd never read again, devouring whole novels in a sitting. Elvis played guitar until the strings made deep impressions in his fingertips. Amanda paged through old magazines they'd found by the stack and told them stories about magnificent shopping trips she would have gone on if she'd known that the world would go to shit so soon. Richie enjoyed reading well enough, but chose to draw instead.

Once upon a time, in a place no one would likely ever see again, Richie was a slave to the business world. He made it to work early, five days a week, and left long after his shifts should've ended. He dressed well and performed well, and surely would've been able to climb the fabled ladder that led, not necessarily to the top, but somewhere high in the middle. He was the type of employee that most companies searched for and never found.

In the evenings and on weekends, though, Richie loved nothing more than to sit in his most comfortable easy chair, facing a horizon filled with pollution and partially built condominiums, and draw the world into beauty.

He'd sketch the buildings as if they'd been long finished and the sky as if it were clear of contaminants in a sunset that was remarkable only to him. He would dig further into the pictures outside of his windows, finding an empty patio upon which he would add furniture and elegantly dressed party goers. He would find the beauty in a woman walking along the sidewalk in the rain, her umbrella broken in spots, and change the beauty of imperfection into the refinement it deserved. Richie loved to change the way the world looked with nothing more than a graphite pencil and recycled paper.

He did this often in his old life, most nights in fact, but he'd not drawn so much as a doodle in the time that he, Buddy, and Elvis had been on the road. This time they'd been given, this time they'd stolen from the hands of maniacs, gave him the chance to feel the way he'd always loved to feel and he was taking advantage. He drew everything and more in those four days, allowing the others to look at what he'd made from time to time. He only let them see when asked, but he hid back one drawing adamantly.

135

Elvis had been sitting cross-legged on his cot, the blanket he'd been using neatly folded at the foot of it, with his guitar. He was watching the fingers of his left hand as they traveled up and down the neck of the instrument with a quiet smile on his face.

His hair was gone, but Richie saw things as they could be, better than they were, so he drew a few strands falling across his brow. Richie let his pen change all of the qualities that were wrong, let it mark in details that could've never existed.

His eyes would glance at Elvis once in a while, more to see if he knew that he was being drawn than anything else. He'd never done this before, drawn the perfection inside one of his friends, and it hurt a little to look at the thing once he'd finished.

Richie made Elvis beautiful, as he'd always seen him, and it broke his heart. Some might have thought that making Elvis beautiful meant taking away the facial features forced upon him by the Down's Syndrome he'd been born with, but that wasn't the truth of it at all.

This picture of Elvis was much more lovely than what he would be if Richie had drawn him to look like everyone else in the world. It was his friend, sketched on the thirty-fifth page of the pad, looking exactly like he had on their last easy day in Miami. There were no cuts on his face or abrasions on his knuckles. His hair was a bit longer in real life on that day than what Richie had drawn, but it was really *him*. He was beautiful.

At the beginning of the fifth day they decided to leave the place upon waking. Everyone knew that it was time, but no one had to say what they were all thinking. They would miss this short break from the world outside.

***

Calgary, AB
April 8, 2021
9:12 PM 94*F

In the western region of Canada, the sun had set and night swallowed the earth along with everything that lay upon it. All was silent, most of the people and almost all of the animals being long dead, and few sounds would be made until dawn returned to burn things that were nearly beyond burning.

A fire had been started two nights before at a department store where much death had been brought. The concrete shell of the place, though singed by the heat of a blaze that had burned through all of the night before, remained intact.

A door opened on the ground, dragging the remains of an aluminum skeleton slowly along it's track, and a person climbed to the surface of the place. The person seemed shocked for a moment, said something to those following him, and stood waiting.

The surprise left him, almost before it could register, and he went about the task of helping his companions out of the hole in the ground. Each of them took the time to look at the damage that had been caused as they hid, their ignorance of the goings on evident in their postures and the looks that they gave to each other. Soon, though, they joined the first to come out and left the shell. There was nothing they could do about this ruined place.

Three men and a woman walked north and west along a seldom marked highway. Sometimes they walked in a cluster, seeming to draw strength from one another. Other times they walked in a single file to be isolated within themselves.

When they spoke to each other, it was quiet and careful. They were in sync in some internal way that told them what they needed to do and when they needed to articulate.

To an outsider of the group it would be considered odd, possibly even eerie. Few beings learned how to be with people void of the complications that come with most relationships. The common goal they shared, survival for their group at any cost, set them apart from the rest. Even the newest addition to their circle had caught on quickly and become one of them without knowing it.

One of the men led them naturally without ever having been elected to do so. The other two would surely die for their leader as he would die for them. The woman was becoming a sort of glue that would hold them together in a way they hadn't been before. Without her to reinforce the union they'd already created, it was possible for their foundation to crack. With the addition of her presence, the foundation had been made stronger than ever before.

They walked until they found the next place to be. They walked until someone tried to stop them. They walked.

Chapter 4

Elvis was humming softly as he used Richie's battered pocket knife to whittle a small chunk of wood away to nothing. He'd gotten in the habit of doing this, recently, and showed no signs of stopping his exercise in destruction.

Amanda watched him do this as they walked, wondering how he could do such a thing while moving. Elvis didn't notice her curiosity, so she didn't bring attention to it. They were in a quiet time, right now, and she had no urge to change that.

Richie and Buddy were walking side-by-side, Richie holding this coach at the ready. This was Richie's new habit, one he'd started just after they'd left the panic shelter, and though Buddy understood his reasoning, it made him nervous. He said nothing to Richie about it. Certain things put people on edge. Being anxious was a part of life these days. It could only be accepted and lived with.

"Time?" Amanda asked, breaking the silence.

Richie looked at his watch, blinked twice to get a better focus on the darkened face, and told her that it was just after two in the morning. Amanda thanked him. They kept moving along the road, their steps making muffled taps on the surface.

The silence returned. The night seemed thicker, somehow, but Richie knew that was his imagination. The temperature was dropping as they moved north. It was down to eighty-six on the surface at night, which was a major improvement on their situation with every mile they traveled. The days were still lethal, but the nights were definitely getting better.

Elvis, Buddy, and Richie had learned to doze while walking. It was an easy way to move through the night without thinking too much about it. Richie had been going in and out since their first hour on the road.

It wasn't like sleeping, not really, but more like a liquid daydream where everything took on a fuzzy aura. His eyelids fell, but didn't quite close. Amanda, who hadn't quite gotten the hang of their version of sleep walking, noticed the time pass while the others did not. There were moments, like this one, where she cursed herself for not finding her own watch at some point.

Amanda asked the time again. Richie was patient, didn't mind looking at his watch a hundred times in a night if it put someone at ease, and did so without paying much attention. It wasn't a big deal. He didn't even have to wake up much.

"It's two-ten," he told her from his blanket of walking slumber and yawned.

Amanda stopped, frozen in her tracks. This made the others take note and stop also, but with less fear in their eyes. Richie looked at her expectantly.

"What's wrong?" Elvis asked her, voicing everyone's question.

"How long ago did I ask you what time it was?" she asked, her voice trembling.

"I don't know," he answered, watching Elvis wipe the sweat off of his face with a red bandana.

That's odd, Richie thought, He hasn't been doing that lately.

"It's been a while, right?" she asked, "Tell me I'm not crazy here."

"It *has* been a little while," Buddy said, "What time was it the last time?"

"He said that it was a little after two," Amanda answered him, fear growing inside of her, "And it's getting hotter."

140

"Shit!" Richie said, looking at his watch, the thin hand that ticked away the seconds holding at three after the hour, "It stopped!"

They all stood there for a minute, though it felt like a year. It was close to dawn and they hadn't realized it.

They were less than sixty days from their destination. They'd survived for more than three hundred days by paying attention to everything around them, but the most important thing to know was the simplest thing. It was the thing that would've definitely killed them if not for Amanda's need to know what time it was. It could still kill them if they didn't get moving. When would the sun rise?

"Run!" Buddy shouted, "We gotta fucking run!"

They ran, though not as quickly as they might have been able to do a year before. They searched the sides of the road, praying for a house or gas station to enter their vision. They didn't say anything, too busy using the energy to run.

All of them felt the bundles on their backs gaining weightt, shuffling back and forth with their strides. The sound of the contents of their rucks served as a cadence.

They looked from side to side, not knowing how long they had to make it underground. They felt the temperature increasing, but didn't know if it was due to the exertion, or if it was the day closing in on them.

More speed. They needed more, just to make it to where ever they were going. The fear helped, dumping adrenaline into their blood streams as they went.

Richie cursed himself. How could he have slipped like this after so long? He cursed the watch for letting him down, cursed it for doing what everything does sooner or later. He didn't have time to hate himself, just now. He had to run, had to find a place for them.

They're all going to die! It's your fault, Richie! If you're lucky, you'll die with them!

Shut up!

"The right!" Elvis shouted, pointing out a squat structure against the side of the road.

Richie judged the place to be about a mile away. It would likely have shelter, as all of the buildings they'd found in the area so far were built over basements or shelters of some sort. He picked up speed, hoping to get there first, in case something was amiss. He pulled ahead of Buddy, really starting to feel the effects of the running. *Please God,* he thought as he started the last half mile.

The heat was becoming unbearable. They'd taken too long to get this far. If Richie had realized the time, they'd have picked up the pace. It was his fault if anyone got hurt or died. It would be on him to make this right.

When he reached the front entrance of the place he almost kicked the door in without looking inside first. He stopped for a brief second, the need for caution overwhelming his own need to get everyone under cover. The place only had two rooms from the look of it and was empty, but there was no sign of an entrance to a cellar.

He could have wasted more time if he'd try to enter it. He ran away from the front door, making his way down the near side of the house and still saw no cellar door. He moved around the back, hoping against hope, wondering if they could survive in the house if it had no basement.

"Over here!" Buddy yelled, only ten or fifteen feet away from Richie. He'd gone down the other side of the place and had found the door.

"Okay," Richie said when he reached the door.

"Gotta pick it?" Buddy asked, still catching his breath as their other two friends joined them.

142

Richie nodded, shedding his pack. He thought about breaking the lock with the butt of his shotgun, but didn't know if it would release under the assault or not. None of them carried a crowbar due to the weight and they didn't have time to find one. He hurried through his pack, looking for the picks.

He had a bad moment when the tension wrench slipped out of his fingers and fell to the charred ground, but Elvis was there to pick it up and hand it back. Richie went to work on the lock, trying to take his time, trying to feel the thing out. His friends didn't urge him on. They knew that he had enough motivation.

"It's gettin' real hot," Elvis whispered to himself. He didn't want to rattle Richie, but he couldn't help but say something.

The tumblers on this lock were loose, the key hole wiggling under his picks. He didn't have time for finesse, so he began raking the pick across the tumblers and adding tension to the lock. More tension. Rake faster. The sweat from his forehead was running fast into his eyes as he worked. The heat was almost unbearable. They needed to get in.

"Come on you cock sucker!" Richie finally shouted in frustration and yanked too hard on the tension bar, snapping it in two.

He stared at the remnant of the tool held between his index finger and thumb. His eyes were wide and beginning to fill with tears.

"Fuck," he whispered, pulling the pick from the lock, "Oh fuck."

It was Buddy who noticed that the lock had come partially free when Richie pulled the pick out of it. He reached for the body of the thing and yanked it downward. The lock popped open.

"Shit," Elvis said, laughing, "Get in!"

They pulled hard on the doors, getting one of them to open on the first try, and began squeezing into the space they'd opened. Amanda slid in easily, followed by Elvis. Buddy dropped into the opening and had to wiggle his way in. Once Buddy was clear, Richie dropped into the doorway feet first and began to tug the door back into place.

The damned thing wouldn't come easily from this position. He had to get back out and kick the thing until it was nearly closed. By now the heat was so bad that Richie felt the burning on his bare skin. Finally, he was able to get into the doorway and pull the door almost back to closed. It was jamming with a few inches left to go. Richie pulled as hard as he could on the handle, but the door wouldn't budge. He'd have to push it open part of the way to get it to slam shut. He braced his feet on one of the top steps before using his shoulder to open the door part- way.

Just as he was about to slam the thing home, two things happened. First, a bead of sweat poured into his right eye, stinging badly, and causing him to close it, leaving him with just the left. The second thing was sunrise.

Richie saw it for the briefest of moments, thought that it was beautiful in the back of his mind. It was pure and strong in a way that it had never been when people could gather to watch.

He felt the first ray of the day's light hit him full in the face. He fell, screaming, as the door slammed shut, blocking out the sun.

***

Richie woke up to the sound of birds chirping and the warmth of the sun on his face. He struggled away from the light, falling out of bed and onto the hardwood floor. He was tangled up in the sheet he'd pulled over himself when he'd gone to bed, so it took him a moment to get out of it and stand. He was amazed at what he saw.

It was his apartment, the studio that overlooked his imperfect horizon. He was at home and safe. He spun, slowly, around. He took in every detail of the place.

His head was killing him and it hurt more when he looked into the light, but he really was home. Dishes were in the sink. The drapes hung partially open allowing natural light to flood the place. The glass of water he'd taken to bed still perched on the nightstand.

"Is this real?" he asked the room, "Is this home?"

The place answered with silence. He could actually smell things in this place. None of them were charred burnt things. They were the smells he'd taken for granted in his life, but he smelled them now.

There was the scent of the oil soap he'd used to clean the floor so many times. He smelled the sweat left behind on the bed after his nightmare. He took a deep breath and held the odor of the left over take-out he'd brought in and forgotten to put in the refrigerator.

Richie smiled. This was real. *Wasn't it?*

He walked around the efficiency apartment, touching the curtains to feel something soft, touching the back of his favorite chair. He felt the coolness of the material because no one had sat there in a while.

He listened to the refrigerator humming off and on, the compressor cycling to make things cool and good. He walked over to it, opened the door, stood in front of it. He felt the air rush out at him and basked in the simple coolness of it. Had there ever been such a feeling as this? Had there ever been a lovelier word than "cool"? It was made even better due to the fact that the sun was warming his apartment a little too well. It was getting hot in there.

Richie almost laughed at the idea. In his dream it had been *really* hot. It had been so hot that it was dangerous. He was so glad to be awake now.

145

"Get some water! Oh Jesus! Look at his fucking *eye!*" a voice shouted from nowhere.

Richie looked around the empty room for the source of the sound. Had he left the radio on in the bathroom, or something?

He went there, to the bathroom, and saw that he had, indeed, left the radio on. That was kind of a weird thing to hear on the device, but he dismissed it. Who knew what people would say when they had their fifteen minutes of fame?

He closed the door, walking naked through the place until he reached his chair again. Richie picked up his sketchbook and sat down on the cushion without putting anything on his body. He usually slept in sleep pants or at least sweats, but he'd been nude upon waking, so he went with it. It was strange, though, because he usually liked to wear something comfortable when he drew.

Weirdest dream ever, he thought, deciding to draw the last thing he remembered from it. Richie closed his eyes to concentrate on an image.

He immediately saw Amanda (who's Amanda? Do I know an Amanda?) covering one of his eyes with a wet bandana, telling him that it would be okay if he just held on it'll be okay jesus buddy look at his skin it's burnt and we can't do anything for it we need burn cream or something elvis get me-

Richie opened his eyes, now seeing with both of them. His headache was getting worse. It was one of those that you got from looking into the light for too long. It was like a spike was being driven into his left eye. He stood, leaving the sketchpad and pencil on the table beside his chair, and went back into the bathroom to check for some Excedrin or something to kill this headache. The radio was on again, for some reason. Hadn't he just turned that off?

"We can't leave until he wakes up," the radio broadcasted, "We'll just have to hope nobody comes."

Richie kept listening to the voice. It was familiar. He thought it might be one of the people from his dream.

"*They* live here Buddy! If they come back, they'll kill us. We have to take him somewhere else."

"Where? Where the fuck can we ta-"

He turned the radio off, almost threw it against the wall for good measure. The voice, one of the voices, sounded like Buddy, but a Buddy who'd started smoking three packs a day. His throat sounded like it was full of gravel. It couldn't have been him, though. How would Buddy get on the radio?

Richie looked at the medicine cabinet, thinking that he would have to open it to get something for his head, which was pounding like a real bitch now. It was getting so bad that the vision in his left eye was blurring. The eye, itself, was even beginning to hurt.

He rubbed at it, looking in the mirror at his short, well styled blonde hair and clean shaven face and his roughly shaved head and thin patchy beard. He closed his eyes again, turning his head from the mirror. He was seeing things now. When he opened his eyes his reflection was normal again.

"It must be the headache," he told his mirror image, pulling the mirrored door open and reaching in for a pill or two.

That would do the trick. He'd take a couple of Excedrin and life would be good again. Maybe he would go back to bed. Maybe he could catch a nap and rid himself of this horrible (sunburn?) headache. He closed the cabinet and the mirror was in front of him. His reflection was gone. In its place was his friend Elvis, leaning down close to his face, telling him to *be quiet don't make no noise cause buddy says they might be comin' he's gonna help amanda make em go away but we got to be so quiet be okay richie just-*

147

Richie turned away again, stumbled out of the bathroom and into the main room without looking where he was going. His eye felt like it was going to fry in the socket and he just wanted the headache to go away.

All of the things he was seeing and hearing reminded him of the dream, but that was a very odd thing. He didn't normally remember his dreams. He'd told Amanda that when she asked-

What in the hell was going on? Was he still half-asleep or something. His mind was mixing things up between the world of dreams and the one of waking. Amanda had been a figment of his imagination, part of the dream.

Bed, he thought, I just need some sleep.

Richie lay down in his full size bed, lying flat on his back for some reason. It wasn't comfortable. He liked sleeping on his side (*They're carrying me*) or stomach. He tried to turn, but was restrained by nothing more than the air. He tried to sit up and couldn't. He'd just have to sleep like this. It must be the headache. It was getting better now that he was laying down. He'd just have to ride it out and everything would be fine. If not, Richie would go straight to the doctor.

What time was it? He'd have to check and see because the doctor's office wouldn't open until nine or so. He raised his wrist a few inches from the bed before he remembered that his watch had stopped (*we need to pick up another watch*) in the night. They sold batteries for them (*we'll have to get a pocket watch if we can find it, the kind that doesn't need a battery, the kind you have to wind every day*) at the drug store. He'd have to replace his.

"We need to stop and take a break. He's too heavy to keep going all night," a voice said.

"We can stop here for a little while, but we can't stay the night. We have to get further away from them," another voice replied.

148

The fucking radio was going crazy today. Any other time it might have been amusing, but he just didn't feel good at all. He was starting to shiver in the coolness of the room.

He felt like he was being carried, the ceiling becoming the sky from time to time, but it had to be a dream sky. He could see stars and the moon, but it was daytime. He'd just woke up and it was morning. His head was killing him and he really wished it would just go the fuck away.

"He's going to die if I don't go out and find some kind of antibiotic, Elvis. We can't all go. You've got to stay with him for me. He's going to be your responsibility. You take care of him"

That was probably the goddamned radio, again. He wanted to get up, go in there, and smash the thing to pieces but he couldn't get up because (*I'm hurt really fucking bad and I need to wake up so that I can tell them not to get penicillin because that'll kill me faster than the injuries*) his head was killing him and he just wanted (*Wake the fuck up! You're going to die! Wake the fuck-*

***

"Up!" Richie yelled, suddenly, just as Buddy was clearing the exit of a basement that Richie wouldn't have recognized.

"What?" Amanda asked, turning back toward Elvis and Richie.

"No," Richie choked out, "No fucking... I'm allergic. No pen... Shit!" he screamed, the pain in his face and eye like being stabbed over and over.

"Calm down, man. I got you. I hear you," Buddy told him as Elvis soothed his face with the damp cloth.

"No pen-"

"No penicillin, Richie. I got it," Buddy said, thanking God that Richie had come awake in time to tell him *that*.

149

If he hadn't, they would've surely used it to try saving him. He'd have died in minutes.

Richie nodded a shaky nod. His good eye turned toward Elvis and then back to Buddy. Only part of him knew what was going on. The other part, the frightened one, wanted only to sleep, to dream and be so cool like he'd been in the fantasy.

"Elvis is going to stay with you. He's going to take care of you while we go get you some medicine," Buddy told him, taking the rag from Elvis and soaking it again, "We'll find something for the pain. I promise."

"The lock... The lock piiiick! Oh God it hurts, man!"

"I know Richie. We'll take care of all of it. Sleep man. Just go back to sleep."

Amanda shook her head at Buddy. She pointed to the food and water that would be left behind for Richie and Elvis before pointing to Richie. Buddy nodded. He reached for one of the water bottles and spun the cap, putting it close to Richie's lips.

He was nearly out again, his good eye closing. His bad eye would never open or close again. Buddy looked at the blistered skin on his friend's forehead and left cheek, where the sun had caught him the worst, and cringed.

There wasn't much they could do for him until they found what was needed. Amanda had taken care of some relatives and knew more about medicines than the rest of them, so it was up to Elvis to care for their injured.

"Drink this, Richie. You got to drink," Elvis said, taking the bottle from Buddy.

Richie drank, but refused more than a few swallows. He hadn't drunk much in the last two days and that could be just as bad for him as the wounds. Elvis was persistent, though, making him try again and getting a little more in his stomach. When Elvis turned to Buddy, there was a smile on his face.

"I'll take care. You go. Just get back soon," Elvis told him.

150

"The King has spoken," Buddy said, turning to leave.

"Long live rock n' roll," Elvis imparted as they walked out into the world.

***

Richie stumbled along the road between the hellish world of reality and the quiet one of dreams. The two came together for him from time to time, but over the next three days and nights he began to know which was which.

Though he'd have rather dreamed all of this away for eternity, he knew that his friends needed him in their world. He tried to keep a small piece of the dream with him at all times, but it was fading with the pain. Elvis had been the only one at his side during the worst of it, listening to his friend scream and consoling him when he woke.

Buddy and Amanda had come back just after sunset on the next night. They'd found a small grocery store with a pharmacy attached. They started him on Vicodin for the pain, which didn't do as much for it as Richie would've liked, and vancomycin to treat the infection that had probably already set in. They couldn't be sure how bad it was, so only gave him four of the antibiotics throughout the night.

Elvis was always with him, forcing water down his throat and trying to feed him when he was awake, giving him his pills at the right time. Now, instead of a damp cloth, Elvis was spreading aloe over his wounds, carefully, and making sure that his injured eye was clean and clear of contaminants. Amanda had tried to take over the duty only once, and Elvis had balked.

"You need rest, honey," she'd said to Elvis.

"I get rest. You leave us alone," he'd stubbornly demanded, "I can take care of Richie."

"You can come right back, after you sleep."

151

Elvis had simply looked at her, deciding that the subject was closed and that he didn't need to say anything more. She didn't get angry. She didn't try to help him again.

There were times when everyone would be quiet, eating or drinking, and Richie would say something unintelligible. Amanda and Buddy would try to get closer and Elvis would wave them away. He'd tell them that Richie was in his apartment and talking to the radio. They would agree with him and back off, knowing that Elvis had made the decision to bring their friend back by himself.

"He listens," Buddy told Amanda when she asked why Elvis was acting this way.

"No he doesn't. He won't sleep. He won't eat if Richie won't. He's obsessed."

"I told him that Richie was his responsibility. He listens. Elvis won't leave him until he gets better or dies."

Richie was awake on the fourth night, finally able to sit up and eat voluntarily. He took small sips from a water bottle and got used to the idea of only having one eye. Elvis was there with every request, giving Richie the things that he needed and talking about his old apartment, asking questions about where he'd been in the dream.

It was as if he were trying to ease Richie back in to the world of the living. Richie was thankful for that. He'd been mostly gone during those three days, but was coming back quickly. His eye was gone and his face was a mess, but he would live. When he asked what had happened after he fell, Elvis allowed Amanda to tell him, finally relinquishing his responsibility.

"You fell hard and the door closed. We couldn't see anything until Buddy found the lantern. When he turned it on, we figured out that we hadn't made the best choice of lodgings for a long term stay. There were supplies in one corner of the basement and sleeping bags piled everywhere," Amanda said, as if she were setting a scene.

Her voice became mechanical, almost emotionless, as she explained their plight. Richie wished that he'd heard her talk, been able to listen to the way she'd told stories, before all of this.

He was indebted to her. He knew that. The woman had gone with Buddy, into a dangerous world, to find the drugs needed to keep him in the land of the living. In a way, she'd become as close to them as they were to each other in these past months.

"I saw some bones on the floor. They looked like somebody had cracked them to get at the marrow and I knew who's house we'd managed to invade. Cannibals."

"You're," Richie started, "You're shitting me."

"She shits you not, my friend," Buddy added.

"So we had to get you and us out of there as soon as the sun set, but we had to figure out if you were even going to live first. I've never seen someone get burned like that," her voice fell into normal tones again, "I saw this kid get sun burnt one time on vacation. He got burnt so badly that these big watery blisters came up on his back and that's what it looked like. Jesus, Richie, I can't believe you're alive."

Richie nodded, thinking of the way he'd lain on his back in the dream, unable to turn over. He must have stolen the feeling from his real body and incorporated it into his delusion.

"How long?" he asked her.

"We carried you for most of a night. Elvis remembered some TV show where these people made a stretcher out of their back packs and we tried doing that, but they weren't strong enough. We had to rummage for conduit in that house we were under. Buddy's a slave driver. He barely let us stop to rest. We made a stretcher and carried you here."

"Thank you," he whispered.

"Fuck you, dude," Buddy interjected, "No thanks needed."

Elvis nodded and gave him the finger, one corner of his mouth perking up into a smile. Amanda saw this, turned back to Richie, and copied the gesture. Richie smiled, ignoring the pain it caused him.

"So this is how they say 'you're welcome' in Canada?"

Chapter 5

<u>**Carvel, AB**</u>
<u>**April 24, 2021**</u>
<u>**3:31 AM 81*F**</u>

The bandage over Richie's left eye was bothering him as he walked. He kept reaching toward it, trying to pull it away from his dead eye, forgetting that he couldn't see out of it any longer. Once the realization struck him again, he'd leave the patch alone for a while.

He wondered how well he'd get along as a half-blind squatter. At least he'd chosen a shotgun as his weapon of choice. There wasn't a lot of need for precision shooting, or even aiming, when you were firing buckshot.

They were traveling again, walking down the road in a loose grouping. Richie had given watch duties to Amanda. She'd taken their new find, a wind up pocket watch they'd scavenged from a pawn shop, and kept up with it religiously. She'd even started sounding the hour, telling them how far they were from the light of day. It was helpful, but somewhat discomforting.

Richie's need for Vicodin hadn't diminished much, but his ingestion of the pills had. He had to make sure that the tools he had left could be used without too much chemical dulling.

He *had* taken to slathering the aloe gel all over his burns whenever they started chafing against his dressing. The relief of the cooling gel was close to what he'd felt from the Vicodin, but it did nothing for his lack of sight.

Elvis had already started keeping an eye out for one of those pirate eye patches with the skull and crossbones painted on. Buddy, always the smartass, had started calling him "One Eye" and pointing to his own crotch when it struck his fancy.

"You're a dick," he told Buddy after one of these displays.

"Yeah, but you actually look like one, now."

"Nothing like a couple of apocalyptic survivors walking down the road making dick jokes," Amanda chimed in, "Gives me real hope for the human race."

Elvis laughed for a long time over that one.

"Good humor never dies," Richie said, tugging at the bottom of his bandage, earning a slap on the hand from Amanda, "It just changes location."

"Amen to that my one-eyed friend."

"So, you know that you're going to have to try shooting soon," Amanda told Richie.

"Yeah," he admitted, "I know. We just need to be in a safe spot."

"When you find one of those," Buddy added, "You just tell me where."

"You don't want to take aim with the wrong side."

"I'll stay on his bad side," Elvis said, causing laughter that he didn't understand at first.

"Never in life, Elvis, could you be on my bad side," Richie said, helping him along.

"I meant the bad eye side," Elvis clarified.

"It's not a bad idea," Amanda said.

"Let's just burn that bridge when we get there. Amanda, what time is it?" Richie asked.

"Just past three-thirty."

"House up ahead," Richie said, "Want to stop for the night?"

"Is it on the right?" Buddy asked with a grin.

"You never told em' how you kept the one eye, Richie," Elvis said.

156

"They never asked," he replied, slapping Elvis on the shoulder.

"I'm asking now," Amanda said, "I've been wondering about that."

"Saw a pretty girl driving by and winked at her," Richie said.

"Can you see this?" Amanda asked, raising her middle finger just to the left of his face.

"Low blow, woman," Richie remarked as his friends laughed, "It was sweat. It got in my eye and I closed it. I must've turned my head too."

"Jesus," Buddy said, "No shit?"

Richie shook his head. *None at all*, he thought but did not say.

They each hoped for such luck. Pain, something they'd all grown accustomed to, had partially saved their friend. The need, the instinct, to avoid it had allowed a man one eye with which to see when, by all rights, he should've lost both. Pain could help a person to escape, warn them not to get too close, and save their lives as easily as such a thing could end it.

***

Richie stared at the thermometer with nothing but sheer amazement. They'd slept the day away, ate when they woke, and exited their shelter for the night. It was all very routine to them after eleven months on the road, but something had been different about the air on this night.

All of them had felt it, right away. It wasn't nearly as hot as it had been just before dawn, which was normal, but it also wasn't as hot as it had been twelve miles south of where they stood, where they'd started out on the night before.

The cycle was easy to keep track of. Two hours after sunset was the warmest time of the evening, starting the night in the most uncomfortable fashion possible. Half way through the small hours, say around one, things cooled down to the nicest part of the night. By four things started to heat up again, leading up to a killer sunrise.

Lately, the nights were starting out in the low eighties, dropping down as low as seventy-six, and finishing out just over eighty again. Tonight, however, was turning out to be different.

"What's it say?" Elvis asked.

"Seventy-two," Richie said as if whispering a prayer.

"It's really happening," Amanda said.

"It is," Richie replied, "It'll be hotter on the surface, but not by that much."

"Let's get moving, before we all lay down right here. Man, I haven't felt air like this in...," Buddy began, but couldn't finish.

"Yeah," Elvis said, hitching the straps of his backpack further up onto his shoulders, "Don't wanna catch cold."

Their steps were lighter, more energetic than they'd been before. The group of them headed northwest, barely noticing the way the road was starting to elevate. Their packs were lighter than they'd been, too.

Supplies had been growing thin, but if their calculations were right, everything they had would stretch for at least a month. It made sense that they should travel lighter. They'd be able to find everything they needed once they found a town in Alaska to settle into. That was what all of this had always been about. That was the *plan.*

Richie thought of these things with growing unease. His mother had told him once that if he'd like to hear God laugh, he should tell him about his plans. The thought of it actually sent a chill down his spine.

He had to turn his head now to look left, and he did exactly that in order to catch a look at Elvis. The man had grown thinner than Richie thought was possible. He glanced back to the right, seeing Amanda and Buddy. Something

158

was wrong. It was almost like autumn outside and they were close to what would be their new home.

Something's wrong with all of this, he thought, we're too happy.

And what kind of a thought was that? How could you be too happy when everything was going well?

This is the dream, again.

Richie stopped, dead in his tracks, and turned toward his friends.

Are they real?

"Are you real?" he asked them.

"Shit," Buddy said, sounding exasperated and worried at the same time, "It's happening again."

"We're real Richie. We're here with you," Amanda said.

This happened before. It's not the dream. It's your life.

Suddenly, the coach gun was in Richie's right hand and aimed low toward Buddy's feet. Richie didn't know how it had happened or why he continued holding the thing once the realization had hit him. He had no intention of shooting his friend, but his finger was wrapped around the trigger all the same.

"Buddy, tell me. Are you real?" Richie asked, his left hand moving to the left side of his face.

"Brother, I'm real. We've been through this before. You just have to think through it, man," Buddy explained with slightly raised hands, "Put that thing away and think."

We've been through this before? We've been through this before. We have? We're going through it right now.

"Is my hair short?" Amanda asked, walking to him slowly and taking the hand he'd been about to use on his face into both of hers.

"Yes," he answered, needing to touch his injured skin to see if it hurt. That was how you could tell when things were real. If it really hurt when he touched his face, that would mean that this wasn't a dream.

"If it was a dream, wouldn't you give me back my long hair?"

It was as if she'd slapped him in the face, causing the pain he needed and proving things to him. He actually saw her hair for a moment, long and thick and beautiful in its own way, but he *knew* he was just seeing that because she'd said it. This was all real. He wasn't in the dream again.

"I'm sorry," he said, "I just..."

"We know, man. It's been happening once in a while. In a few hours you'll probably forget it again."

"It's a side effect of the drugs, Richie. In a few days you won't need the antibiotics anymore and it'll stop."

"You're sure? That's what it is?"

"Yeah," Elvis said, "It started right after the pills. We tell you every time."

"Shit," Richie said, "It's like Alzheimer's."

"Yeah," Buddy said, "But at least you get to meet new and interesting people all the time."

Elvis put an arm around Richie's shoulders, nonchalantly pressing downward on the shotgun's barrels so that Richie wouldn't aim it at anyone, and they all began to walk again.

***

"Antibiotics don't cause this kind of thing," Amanda whispered, looking at Buddy sternly, "They don't cause hallucinations."

"You don't know that. You're not a doctor and you don't know how all of this is affecting us."

"Maybe I'm not, but it's dangerous one way or the other," she said.

"He'll be done with them soon. We'll keep an eye on him to make sure he's fine."

"What if the burn did it? Have you thought about that?" Amanda asked, finally looking away from Buddy's eyes.

"It's the equivalent of getting like fifty sunburns in your *eye*, so I don't know, Amanda. What I do know is that my friend almost died and now he's alive. If he's a little fucked up because we had to play pharmacist, then he'll be fine soon. If he's fucked up for good, then we'll have to deal with it."

"But what if we need him and he locks up? Do you want to think about that? What if he gets Elvis killed? Or you?"

"He won't, Amanda," Buddy said, "What do you want to do, anyway? Leave him? We can't do that. I wouldn't do it and Elvis sure as hell wouldn't."

"No. I don't know what to do. I'm just scared of what could happen. Don't you get that?"

Buddy sucked in a deep breath. They were sitting on the top of the stairwell, just as he and Richie had done so many times, while the others slept.

He could hear Richie talking in his sleep. That was something new he'd picked up. It *was* scary to think that your best friend was losing his mind, but Buddy wasn't about to throw him to the wolves. He would help him through whatever this was. All of them would.

"You need to think about this," Amanda told him.

"You need to have a little loyalty. If it wasn't for that guy down there, you'd be long dead. All of us would."

She was silent, thinking that he was right. The problem came from the idea that he'd be fine in a few days. Richie was suffering delusions and a kind of short term memory loss that left him confused and afraid. He became self-destructive when these episodes hit, so much so that his burns were taking longer to heal than they should have. She hoped that things would change once they finished pumping him full of drugs, but, like Buddy had said, how could she know?

"I'm going to sleep. If you want to talk about this again, we do it *with* Richie. I'm not going behind his back again," Buddy said, taking the steps downward, "And if anybody gets left, it won't be Richie."

She watched as he disappeared into the shadow, angry with herself for being scared by that last comment. They wouldn't leave her to survive on her own. The man was just hurt and frightened for his friend. When she went down to sleep, she did no more than drift in and out for the rest of the day.

***

He could tell that he was in the dream, now. The sun was shining through his windows, a moat of dust particles floating lazily in a beam of light, and he was sitting in his favorite chair. He took a deep breath, relishing the safety of the sleeping world.

He closed his eyes, both of them intact and functional, and opened them a moment later to look around. His sink was full of dishes, not the ones that he'd actually had in his apartment, but a rag tag pile of mess kits that he knew were a transplant from the real world.

Benny was leaning back on one of his kitchen chairs, picking his teeth rudely with the tines of a fork. He was in the dirty ragged shorts he'd been wearing the last time Richie had seen him, but was otherwise clean and healthy. Richie watched him for a long time, grimacing at his manners, which had been awful even before the world fell apart.

"You know you can't stay here," Benny told him, "You gotta get back to those assholes you're walking with."

"Fuck off Benny," Richie said, "Where you been?"

"Dead," Benny replied, "Where you been?"

"Almost dead."

"Yeah. You're going nutso. You know that, right?"

"A little," Richie admitted.

"There's a way to keep it a little cool, but it won't ever be all the way cool again," Benny said.

He set the fork down onto the surface of the table and stood. Benny picked up a sketchbook that had been laying there along with a pencil. He brought it over to Richie and dropped it into his lap, disturbing some of the dust moats in the process. Richie's dead friend stood in a shaft of sunlight, looking down at him expectantly.

"Want me to draw you something?" Richie asked, turning to an empty page, "You always wanted me to draw Elvis' mom naked for you."

"Nope. I'm past all that goofy shit. I want you to draw something for *you*," Benny said, "Start with that chick you're hanging out with these days. And write something down on it for me."

Richie woke with a start, confused by his surroundings for a moment, wondering why he couldn't see anything on his left side. It all came back as he looked around the room at the sleeping forms of his companions.

His left hand went to his face, touching the tape and gauze that layered over his eye. He felt the healing skin with the tips of his fingers, pressed against it to remind himself that he was awake.

Is it the dream? a voice in the back of his mind asked.

It wasn't. He knew that, but there was always a hand around his wrist, pulling him back in. He didn't know if it was the medication that was doing this to him, or not, but he would soon find out. There had only been four pills left in the bottle when he'd rolled over and into a fitful slumber.

There *had* been dreams in that sleeping world. He couldn't remember them, but they'd been mostly bad ones. There had also been Benny. Whether *that* dream was good or bad would soon come to light.

This is not a dream, he told himself, in a dream the world wouldn't be like this. I would be back at home. Amanda would have long hair.

For some odd reason that thought always brought his mind back around. It took time, more time than he would like to give, but he always came back to that thought when the line between dream and reality blurred. He was thankful for that. If she hadn't pointed it out, he may not have been able to hold onto the idea so strongly. In a way, it was a miracle.

Richie rubbed sleep out of his good eye and stood among the sleeping bags and blankets. He searched the sleeping bodies around him until he saw Amanda's visage. Her hair was starting to grow out from the buzz cut unevenly, but it was starting to grow out. He thought of asking her to keep it short, to make sure it didn't grow in length past her chin, but he couldn't really make that request. He could only hope that she did. It was all that he could grasp.

He walked to the corner where they'd set their packs. He found his gear and began to search through it. When he found the sketch book, he began looking for a pen at the bottom of the ruck. Soon, he had one in hand.

He thought for a moment before opening Amanda's pack and rummaging through it until he'd found what he was looking for. Richie carried his things back to his make-shift bed and sat crisscross with the pages in his lap. Richie began turning pages, quietly looking through all of his creations.

He passed pictures of his friends, pictures of the shelter in which they'd slept, pictures he'd drawn from the memory of the horizon outside of his apartment windows. He could barely see the lines of any of it in the darkness, but he knew what each of them was.

164

When Richie came to the first blank page, he began to write. It took him a long time to do it, to make it small enough and still legible but when he finished, he'd written himself a short note on the top half of the paper and drawn a small picture of Amanda as she was right then.

He carefully pulled the page out, ripping the edge along the perforated line. He folded the page around the tiny letter and drawing, trying to be precise, needing the thing as miniature as he could make it. He worked up all of the saliva that he could manage and licked the edges he'd folded before pulling the wet ends apart.

Richie picked up the pocket watch he'd taken from Amanda's possessions and pressed the small button on top to open it, the attached chain dangling along the outside of his hand. He held his portrait up to the watch cover, considered, and turned the corners in before fitting the paper into the watch as if it were a locket. He nodded as he read the words to himself. He could use this. This would help.

He opened the clasp that held the chain onto the watch and slid the thing out of its loop. He'd find a piece of string, maybe, or see if one of the others had kept a necklace that was long enough and strong enough to hold the thing.

He hoped that Amanda wouldn't mind giving him back the duty of time keeper. She seemed to like being able to look at the clock, but he needed it more if he wanted to stay in the moment with them. He needed this reminder of reality.

"This is not the dream," he whispered, before reciting the words he'd been told to write down, "The night is real."

Richie put his things away. Richie laid back down on his sleeping bag. Richie went back to the dream for a while, but Benny didn't join him.

***

"I don't mind," Amanda said as she packed her things away and zipped the opening on her ruck.

"Thanks," Richie told her, the fingers of his right hand fiddling with the pocket watch hanging against his chest on a shoe-string Elvis had given him.

"Got to talk to you about something," Buddy said.

Richie looked up at him. Buddy was already on his way up the stairwell, but had turned to Richie. Richie nodded and followed him while the others finished stowing their gear.

The doors, heavy wood on rusty hinges, screamed in protest as Buddy pushed them open. The night was cooling, as it adjusted to the world of moon and stars. Both of them breathed deeply of the fresh air and walked a few feet away.

"Never saw the stars this clear back home," Buddy said as he looked up.

"Too many lights back then. End of the world can't be all bad."

"I miss things, though."

"We all miss things, Buddy."

"Remember sitting down to a table? Me, you, Elvis, and Benny would all go to that seafood place in Lauderdale for oysters."

"Southport," Richie said with a faint smile, "Great view from the back deck."

"Elvis would pile the horseradish onto his oysters and sweat the whole time he was eating."

"And Benny would have a mountain of cracker crumbs in front of him. That guy was awful to eat with."

They both laughed, before the moment could pass. Once it did, a sober look stole Buddy's face away from happiness. He looked away from Richie, blinked a few times, then met his eye.

"I'm sorry, Richie," Buddy said.

"About what? It wasn't your fault that Benny was a slob."

"I need to take your gun," Buddy told him, struggling to keep eye contact.

The sound of crickets. That was another thing Richie had been missing recently. He'd heard them in the dream, finding the memory pleasant. He focused on that for a moment before saying anything.

He didn't know if he was angry, or sad, or if he understood why Buddy wanted to take his weapon from him. He did. It wasn't something he was very fond of, but his lapses in grasping reality were unsettling.

"Amanda and I were talking while you guys were sleeping," Buddy said, "This *thing* that you're going through. We don't know if it's the drugs or if it's something permanent. I just want to make sure we're all safe, including you."

"You think I'm going to what? Just turn around and start shooting?" Richie finally asked, not sure whether he was angry or just curious.

"No, man. I just want to make sure we're all safe, like I said."

"You also said, 'including me', right? So what happens if I get caught in a fight with no way to protect myself?"

"It's just until you're done with the antibiotics, Richie."

"That's today, Buddy. What about tomorrow?"

"You're fucking dangerous right now, man!" Buddy shouted, losing his self-control unexpectedly, "Every time you have one of these fucking freak outs, you aim the coach at somebody! I can't risk it!"

Richie glared at his friend. He *was* angry now, but he didn't know if it was anger at Buddy or himself. He closed his eyes for a moment, trying to hold the fury at bay, trying not to say something that couldn't be forgiven.

"Fine," Richie said, "Get it out of my pack."

"You know I don't want to do this, but things have been getting scary lately," Buddy explained with an apologetic note in his voice.

Richie nodded. He *did* get the reasoning, but couldn't trust himself to speak any further on it. He walked away from Buddy, toward the road, needing a moment to himself. He held the pocket watch tightly and stared down the length of the road.

Is it the dream? he asked himself, wishing for a moment that it was.

To be in a dangerous world, unarmed and confused, was a frightening concept, one that he could barely grasp. Richie was afraid, not of what could happen to him as he walked down the road, but of what was going on in the back of his mind.

Could I actually hurt them, thinking that it was the dream?

He opened the watch, looked at the picture he'd drawn and the words that went with it.

"The night is real," he whispered.

***

Elvis walked to Richie's left at all times now. He would defend his friend's blind side and Richie was thankful for that. He wondered if Elvis knew what was going on. Did he know why Buddy was carrying the coach now, rather than Richie? It was possible. Elvis was perceptive.

"You remember South Beach?" Elvis asked him, not looking away from the road.

"Oh yeah," Richie said with a small smile. It was the first thing he'd said since they'd started walking.

"You remember the boardwalk?"

Richie's smile widened as the memory of that long stretch came to him. Elvis was smiling, too.

"The coconuts, right?"

168

Elvis laughed out loud at that. They were avid fans of the tourist walk along South Beach in Miami. They would find a spot at one of the beach entrances on warm days and just watch. It was always a kick to watch the travelers buy coconuts from the locals when they could have simply picked them up on their walk. There was always a guy with a shopping cart full of the things, selling them at ten or twenty dollars each and there was always a line waiting to buy them.

"And the necklaces and earrings," Elvis said, still snickering, "Coulda' bought the same stuff at the dollar store for cheap."

Richie and Elvis had always enjoyed watching the tourist's transactions. Buddy hadn't ever joined them on these little expeditions, not understanding the entertainment value of watching people buy random things. It would always be just the two of them and it was always good. Richie had almost forgotten such simple pleasures.

It was good to think about sitting in the sun, the warmth of it on your face, and people-watching with a friend who could enjoy it as much as you did. At the thought of the sun on his face, Richie reached up to touch his bandage, but touched the pocket watch instead.

"What are you guys laughing about," Amanda asked, "Secrets don't make friends."

"Just old times," Elvis told her, "Did you ever go to Miami?"

"Once," she said, "When I was in my thirties."

"Did you ever go to South Beach?" Elvis asked, looking at Richie to let him in on what was coming.

"Yep."

"Did you ever buy a coconut?"

Buddy looked over at Richie for the first time since their conversation earlier in the night and grinned. Richie gave the grin back, telling him that it was okay, that he could accept what had happened between them and that their friendship would remain as it had always been.

"I did, actually," Amanda said, her face lighting up in with reminiscent smirk, "From a little island guy with a shopping cart."

Richie's eyebrow raised and his smile changed to laughter. Elvis was trying to talk, but couldn't get anything out for his own chortle. Buddy shook his head and chuckled.

"What?" Amanda asked, confused and amused at the same time.

"You guys are such dicks," Buddy said.

"Takes one to know one," Richie told him.

The night wore on, the four of them walking without incident and talking to each other about old times. Richie made it through that part of the journey without falling into himself and was happy with the lack of daydreams.

He didn't think that they would ever be as happy as they once were, not in a world that had turned against all of them, but there were always memories to keep them together. They had enough good ones to cancel out some of the bad things, and it was obvious, to him at least, that they would be able to hold onto that. They would always have each other and the life before to get them through the one they were living.

They walked north.

<u>Chapter 6</u>

<u>DeBolt, AB</u>
<u>May 12, 2021</u>
<u>4:01 AM 80*F</u>

Changes in scenery were uncommon lately, as they traveled along I-43, and anything out of the norm was suspicious. Buddy had been the first to notice the latest change on the horizon and they decided to stop for the day before they got any closer to it.

The road was straight for some miles at this point and they could see for a long distance. The sight that greeted them at the end of this night was a monstrosity of a truck and trailer arranged to block both lanes of their road.

"How far?" Elvis asked as Buddy worked to jimmy the lock at the back of an oddly built service station.

"Gotta be about five miles from the look of it, but I'm not sure," Buddy replied as he fumbled with the deadbolt.

"You think it's anything to be worried about?" Amanda asked from a few feet behind them.

"I think we need to approach with the utmost caution," Buddy said.

"Are you going to be dicking with that lock much longer?" Richie asked.

"Do you want to do this?"

"He *is* better at it than you are," Amanda said.

"He is," Elvis agreed.

Buddy stepped back with a flourish and a cocked eyebrow, both of his hands pointing at the lock, palms up.

"Then be my guest, one-eye."

Richie took the tools from Buddy and set to work on the lock, grinning. He hadn't been allowed to pick a lock in quite a while and actually found that he missed performing the task. It could be tedious at times, but he'd gotten fairly good at it. It was also something from the old routine, much like keeping track of the time, and he felt a little more of his old self return when the lock twisted open straightaway. Buddy looked at him sourly.

"I loosened it up for you."

"Yeah," Richie said, "Same thing you said about your sister."

"Oh! Good one!" Elvis laughed.

"Bite me," Buddy retorted amiably.

With the door opened and the night close to its end they entered the gas station in a single file line, Richie in the middle due to his lack of a weapon, and cleared the main area. The doorway marked "storage" opened without manipulation. Richie and Elvis stood together outside of the stairway as Buddy and Amanda checked the place for inhabitants. None were found and they were able to set up camp in little time. They were in the middle of preparing the day's meal when the sound of breaking glass filled the area above them.

Buddy jumped to his feet, the coach in his hands instantly, and looked to Elvis. Neither of the men spoke as they started up the stairs. Amanda stayed at the bottom of the steps, her weapon at the ready. Richie pulled a pocket knife out of his pack, wishing for the weight of a gun in his hands. The storage room was silent, but for the movements of Buddy and Elvis on the stairs.

Richie waited, afraid to breathe as if the sound of it would tell some intruder of their location. He watched his friends disappear through the doorway at the top of the steps with frustration. *He* should be the one going up, leading the group into whatever lay in wait. *He* should've been the one in danger, the first man through the door, able to protect the rest of them as they did him. His

172

heart was beating too fast and his breath becoming too shallow. He knew what would happen in the next few minutes if he didn't calm himself.

Is it the dream? his injured mind asked as the room began to blur.

No! he shouted silently, grasping for the pocket watch and flipping the thing open to look at the message he'd left for himself. It was like leaving breadcrumbs along a trail into the woods. If he didn't look at it soon, the chance would be gone. *The night is real!*

It is the dream, his thoughts insisted, but he fought them, closing his eye and grasping the watch in his left fist, struggling with whatever this was as his friends searched for an enemy that may or may not be stalking them.

Amanda watched this struggle, knowing what it was without asking and began to nod. She knew what he was doing, knew that he had a chance, but that he may need something more than a picture to get him through it. She said nothing, hoping that Richie could hold on, praying for him to a God that might not be real or care to listen if he was.

She was amazed by the look on Richie's face, as it transformed from the scared frustration she'd seen time after time, whenever his fugues began, to the relaxed look of a man who'd pulled himself back to the world. His eye opened, showing an awareness of the here and now that she hadn't really expected to see. He was still with her. When he met her gaze, she didn't smile. She was too relieved for that.

"The night is real," he whispered.

I won this time, he thought, elated by it, but tired from the struggle. He would get better at it, maybe not come so close to losing himself the next time, but he would need the time.

The night *was* real and he'd convinced whatever part of himself that had been damaged of that fact for the first time. His victory was a small one, but it was a victory nonetheless. He looked at the palm of his left hand and saw the imprint

173

of the watch casing in his skin. He pushed out the breath he'd been holding and shuttered.

Elvis appeared as a silhouette in the doorway that stood at the top of the stairs. He looked to be uninjured, but Richie could tell from his posture that something *was* wrong. Elvis was breathing heavily and waving to them, trying to get their attention. Amanda ran half-way up the steps, listened to Elvis' whispering, and then ran back down to where Richie stood.

"We need bandages and water," she told him, opening up her ruck, "They have somebody up there who's hurt."

"Can't they bring them down?" Richie asked, perplexed, still recovering from his momentary ordeal.

"I guess not. Come on. We have to help."

Amanda quickly ascended the stairway, a pile of supplies in her arms, and Richie followed. His eye searched the opening at the top for some idea of what they were walking into. He felt the absence of his weapon, the pocket knife being a poor substitute for the shotgun he'd been carrying for so long. It was a useless feeling, but he couldn't shake it off. The door was open at the top of the stairs and he shuffled through it, trusting that his friends were protecting the area from threats. As he turned toward the front of the building, he saw the reason for which they'd been brought up.

***

A young girl sat in the corner of the store cradling the head of a grown man, both of them barefoot and clad only in dirty underwear. The man seemed to be bleeding from everywhere. The girl looked up at all of them, her filthy blonde hair barely hiding the tears streaming down from her wide blue eyes.

Help us, those blue eyes told Richie. *Please help us.*

174

Amanda was on her knees, checking the man for a pulse, trying to find a spot on him that wasn't covered in gore. She finally did, looking to Elvis who was on his haunches beside her, and nodded. The medical supplies were laying in a pile beside her and she reached into them for peroxide and gauze. Elvis handed her one of his many bandanas and she drenched it in a steady stream of antiseptic. Buddy was staring into the night, leaned against the frame of a large broken window with the shotgun held in both hands.

"Where in the fuck did *they* come from?" Richie asked.

"The truck," Elvis answered him from the man's side, "I think he broke the window."

Richie watched as Amanda swabbed the blood away from the stranger's actively bleeding wounds. She concentrated on the worst of them, smearing the stuff away from it to see if the blood flow could be staunched. Richie knelt down, noticing something about the man's lacerations that caused him to look closer. His eye widened. He looked up to Buddy, who had yet to turn their way. He looked back to Amanda who had seen the same thing he had.

"We have to get them downstairs," Richie said, already pulling the unconscious man partway off of the ground, "Help me, Elvis."

"What is it?" Buddy asked, finally turning from the window.

"Bites."

"Bites? What do you mean?"

"They aren't cuts, Buddy," Amanda told him from the floor, "The blood is from bite wounds."

"Fuck," Buddy said, turning back to the broken window's frame, "Hurry it up."

"Honey, you have to come with us," Amanda told the girl, "Is that your dad?"

"No," the kid admitted, "But he's my friend. He brought me with him. They were going to eat us."

175

Richie heard all of this as he and Elvis carried the man down into the basement and felt his stomach tighten. Bite marks meant cannibals. The girl had probably been one of their future meals and she was with them now. The feeders wouldn't be far behind.

"Get that kid down here!" Richie yelled up at them, "We need to get locked up!"

They lay the man onto a blanket, knowing that they wouldn't be able to use the thing now that it was covered in blood. It couldn't be helped. The man had bites all over him, including his upper back and shoulders, and the blanket would actually help to stop the bleeding from those.

Elvis ran back up the stairs as soon as they laid their passenger down. Richie stayed with him, waiting for his friends to join them. Soon Amanda was coming down with the girl in her arms. Richie tried to figure out how old she was and could only guess that she was between eight and twelve.

"We've got company!" Buddy shouted from upstairs, his voice straining.

"Stay with them," Richie told Amanda, before running to the top of the steps.

He flipped open the pocket watch, the lines of his drawing showing above the face of the clock, and saw that it was close to sunrise. Surely even *these* crazies wouldn't risk being caught out in the sun, but he couldn't know for sure how insane they really were. The sound of a pistol firing burst through the room above just as he reached the landing. Once outside of the basement, Richie slammed the door shut and ran to where he thought Buddy and Elvis would be.

They were there, shooting out into the shadows at running forms through the broken window. Without hesitation, Richie picked the coach gun up off of the floor where Buddy had set it before opening fire. Their targets were too far away to hit with the coach, so Richie fled to the door through which they'd entered. The entrance was still closed, but not locked, and he saw the doorknob turning just as he got to it.

Richie posted himself with the shotgun aimed at the doorway, both hammers cocked and ready. He hoped that there were shells in the breech, but didn't have time to check. When the door swung open Richie fired one barrel into the center of the opening without consideration, shoving a man back through it. A second man filled the doorway, his form thick from eating too well on his fellow man. Richie emptied the second shell into his midsection.

With the door cleared, Richie kicked it closed and ran the bolt. He turned to look for his friends, still hearing pistol fire, and ran to them. He was out of ammo because he hadn't been the one carrying the coach. Buddy would have more shells in his pockets.

He wiped sweat away from his brow, trying to protect his good eye, as he came upon them. Their pistols fired, one after the other, scattering bullets among the six or seven runners coming at them. Richie counted fallen bodies and saw that they'd taken out six men, so far. They were more than halfway through this if the assault was limited to those they'd already seen.

"Shells!" Richie yelled, noticing the temperature rise in the room.

"Right cargo!" Buddy directed, taking a bead on one of their assailants and shooting him down.

Richie pulled a handful of the twelve-gauge shells from the big pocket on Buddy's shorts and put two into the coach. The others he shoved into his own pockets as he moved. He cocked the hammers on the weapon and turned back to the entrance, the barrels propped on his left forearm. No one seemed to be coming from that direction, possibly weary of what'd happened to the last two that had, so Richie went back to the window.

It was getting warmer by the second and they would have to get down cellar as soon as possible. Richie wasn't eager to get another dose of daylight.

"Downstairs!" Richie shouted, taking a position at the window, "I'll cover!"

Buddy began to back away from the portal, firing the last few shots in his clip into the scattered group of runners, as did Elvis. The cannibals were running straight for them now, not bothering to dodge fire. Richie took aim on the closest as he began backing toward their sanctuary, and squeezed the trigger, taking the man down with a chest shot. Another came at him, almost at the window now, and he fired again. Another body fell, bleeding, to the ground.

"We're in!" Elvis yelled, holding the door halfway open for Richie, who backed into the doorway as he reloaded.

A shirtless man leaped through the window just as Richie closed the breech on his weapon and ran at them. Richie pointed the shotgun at his face one handed, and took off most of the man's head with both barrels, the weapon almost jumping over his shoulder. They closed the door, sliding the bolt on their side just as the sun was beginning to take the world again.

***

Day became their guardian. The sunlight was all that kept them from another confrontation with the feeders. This was a difficult concept for them, but they took advantage of it just the same.

Amanda and the little girl, who'd introduced herself as Abby, were in the business of disinfecting and bandaging wounds. The man's name was Dylan, but that was as much as Abby could tell them about him past the fact that they'd both been imprisoned by the group of feeders. Richie and Buddy tried to come up with some type of strategy, some way of circumventing the cannibals, but were coming up short. Elvis, who could be counted on for fresh ideas, had nothing to add.

"We don't know where they are. We don't know how many there are. We're fucked if we go at them head on. We're fucked if we run. Can you think of any other scenarios?" Buddy asked.

"Not until *he* wakes up," Richie answered, pointing at Dylan.

"*If* he wakes up."

"Abby can't tell us much about where they were being held. If she could, we might be able to plan," Richie said, circling the edge of the pocket watch with one finger before opening it to check the time, "And we have to sleep."

"You can sleep right now?" Buddy asked rhetorically, "Go ahead. Be my guest."

"All I'm saying, Buddy, is that if we don't sleep, then we'll be useless no matter what happens."

"Richie's right," Elvis said.

The three of them sat quietly, all trying to think of something. Elvis looked as if he might fall over and sleep whether he wanted to or not, soon. Richie wasn't far behind him. The wealth of possibilities was staggering, but they all ended in basically the same way. They were probably outnumbered and would all die no matter what they did.

"At least it isn't a surprise," Buddy said, "At least we know we're walking into a shit-show."

"Understanding is still understanding," Richie added, "Even if it's vague understanding."

"Fucking Confucius," Buddy remarked, shaking his head.

"We could try charging them. Use the element of surprise. That's worked for us in the past," Richie suggested.

"That won't work," an unfamiliar voice declared with a grating rasp.

They all looked over to the man they'd rescued, but said nothing. It was obvious that he wasn't finished. They hadn't even realized that he was awake.

179

"There are too many of them to run at head on," Dylan said, "Have to be at least twenty of the fuckers."

"We put down quite a few before we could get down here," Buddy told him, "Maybe we evened the odds out a little."

The man shook his head, tried a laugh but lost it, and began to speak.

"I could only get Abby and myself out of there because they were getting ready to come after *you* from behind the trailer. Their camp isn't too far from there. They don't know how many of you there are, yet, but that doesn't matter. Even one live man is a meal for the whole group of them.

"They also know you have a woman with you, which makes it that much better. You get what I'm saying here?"

Richie nodded, seeing the problem with a head on charge. Buddy just looked on, his face tense with thought.

"What if we just fight like we did before?" Elvis asked, suddenly.

"The King has spoken," Buddy said.

"Wait. Give him a chance. What do you mean, Elvis?"

"We use the cars."

Richie's eye widened. He smiled at Elvis, patted him on the shoulder. Buddy looked perplexed.

"He means flanking, like when those people tried to steal our gear. It's actually not a bad idea."

"You don't think that's a bad idea? If they have anybody watching, we're dead anyway."

"I don't mean what *we* did," Richie said with a grin, "I mean what *they* did. The feeders have to be underground somewhere, or they'd all be dead and we wouldn't have anything to worry about. That means they'll have to wait for things to cool off after sunset, just like we will."

Buddy nodded, starting to see where Richie was headed with all of this. He saved a grin for Elvis, too, the King, who might've just saved their asses.

"Hope you three know what you're doing," Dylan offered, before drifting back to sleep.

Chapter 7

DeBolt, AB
May 12, 2021
8:27 PM 102*F

They were out earlier than they usually would have been, the heat much more intense than they were used to. They took their designated positions near the tractor trailer.

Buddy was getting ready on the left side of the road, counting his ammunition and loading the two spare clips he kept for the nine-millimeter. Elvis was doing the same with the revolver on the right side. Richie knelt in the space where the truck and its trailer were connected, readying the rifle that had been involved in a similar operation not so long ago. Richie counted out spare shells for the coach, knowing that some close work would be in his near future.

Buddy had balked earlier at the idea of Richie packing guns during all of this. Yes, he'd done well when they were under attack, but what if they were in the middle of a major fight when he fell into one of his lapses in reality? Amanda had actually been the one to speak for Richie, which surprised everyone, including Richie.

"He fought one off while you were upstairs, Buddy," she'd persisted, "I watched him *will* himself through an attack before he came to help you."

"How do you know he won't lose the next one?" Buddy had asked her, his face reddening as he spoke of Richie like someone who wasn't there, "I don't want the risk."

"Well, let me put it this way, then," Amanda started, "If you don't let him help, we're all going to die. How's that?"

Buddy had nothing to say in return.

"Then it's settled," Amanda declared, going back to Dylan's side.

Richie ran all of this through his mind, trying to pick what he wanted from it. He hadn't known that Amanda was paying attention as he fought for his lucidity, but was glad she had. Otherwise *he* would be the one staying back in their shelter to care for Dylan and Abby as all of this went on. He was thankful for the fact that the man and child would be safe from danger, but wished all of them could just hide out.

Maybe the feeders wouldn't even show. It was a possibility, but not a likely one. They'd be back and it would be soon. He and his friends would have to deal with that.

No one spoke. No one moved. It was up to Richie to give them a signal and he wouldn't give it until he saw a target. That's what these people were to them now. Targets.

"The night is real," he told himself, as if he were trying out some kind of preventative maintenance to keep the attacks at bay, "The night is real."

Richie watched the horizon while the others watched the open land to their right and left. Something told Richie that the feeders would stay to the road, just as he, Elvis, and Buddy always did.

Being off the road, no matter how far, invited hazards that didn't exist on the pavement and hazards were something to avoid in the days where medical care was a thing of the past. Even the freaks had to know that. They were once normal people before they'd let themselves be driven to do things unimaginable in order to survive. Richie made a headband out of his bandana to keep the sweat from running into his eye.

The sound of running feet echoed through the world. Richie looked around, frantically for the source, but couldn't see it. There had to be someone close, or else the thudding would've sounded less concrete.

He saw it, the person that was no longer a real person, coming down the road in a sprint. Behind him there were eighteen more sets of feet. Some had guns, but the rest were armed with blunt instruments, mostly baseball bats. The ones with guns seemed to stay back while their counterparts ran dead toward them. It was time.

Richie let out a whistle, just loud enough for his friends to hear, and fired the first rifle shot into the shoulder of the lead runner. Another round hit the man beside him in the stomach. A third went down. Then a forth was in Richie's sights. Down he went, a spray of blood coming from his neck. Richie fired again, missing one of the club bearers and shattering the windshield of a Chevrolet pickup that wouldn't ever be used again. He took deep, calm, breaths firing with each exhale and willed himself not to get excited. That was the key to staying in control right now.

One of the gunmen had taken aim at the area he was in and fired a three shot burst into the trailer beside him. All of them would probably be bad shots due to the tremors associated with eating human flesh. He didn't really understand the sickness side of it, but he hoped to take advantage. Richie fired back at him, hitting a man to his left instead, before taking aim at another runner.

By now, he knew, Buddy and Elvis would be getting close to where the gunmen were. If everything worked out and he was able to keep all of them busy, his friends would be able to get close enough to complete what they'd planned.

Richie kept firing, hitting more bodies than he missed, but the charging feeders were getting close now. They'd started ducking behind the dead vehicles to avoid gunfire. There were six gunmen left, all of them firing on Richie's hide, but none of the shots had gotten close to him.

He paid attention to the front runners, trying to count them as they appeared between the cars on the road. He guessed that there were still five of them out there, creeping toward him. He sent a few rounds toward the gun carriers and dropped one of them. Soon, the gunners were firing his way out of pure frustration, hampering their own people.

The sound of pistols firing seemed to double for a moment, telling Richie that his companions had rounded upon the enemy. He dropped backward with the rifle, laying below the line of the rig and began firing low along the asphalt. He didn't aim at any one area, spreading the ground level projectiles evenly across the road, mostly looking to kick up asphalt and shrapnel. He didn't see much movement, but wasn't really expecting a great deal. He was, after all, playing as a distraction while trying not to get himself killed.

Richie lay on his left side, hoping to keep his good eye safe from intrusions. Firing the rifle like this wasn't easy. It was, in fact, quite painful. The recoil of the thing, though minimal, was trying to turn him over on his back. All he could do to counter it was to keep his right foot partially planted behind his laying form. He stopped firing for a moment to listen.

***

Elvis was out of breath, possibly due to not being ready for the increased heat in this earlier darkness, but kept running in spite of his condition. When Richie's shooting had dropped, the rounds no longer whizzing above the vehicles he was hiding near, he and Buddy were supposed to round on the enemy and face their backs.

He could see them, now, twenty feet or so from him and knelt behind a Ford Tempo that reminded him of the one his mother had been so fond of. He smiled a little at that, before he began firing on his targets.

There were twelve men back here, quite a few more than Richie had seen, and they were taking turns pot shooting at the tanker truck. Elvis didn't take

185

the time to count runners, because they would be Buddy and Richie's problem. He just had to take as many of these enemies out as he could, before joining his friends.

Elvis took his time, using the sound of Richie's rifle to cover his own shots. Three were down, so far, and he'd only used four of the loaded bullets. He kept firing on the feeders that had guns, the men not even noticing that their comrades were falling beside them. It was a great stroke of luck for Elvis, but he didn't get overconfident. He would fire off a round, then hide for a few seconds behind the engine block of the Tempo.

On his sixth shot, the revolver clicked rather than roaring, and he looked at it for a moment. Hadn't he loaded all eight chambers? He pulled back behind the vehicle again, flicked the carousel out to check the loads and found that there were, indeed, two more cartridges in the gun. He whipped the thing closed, aimed the pistol at the nearest man, and squeezed the trigger eight times without it firing. Something was badly wrong with either the ammunition or his weapon. He was still safe, still undetected, so he took the time to drop the unused shells into his palm, reload the gun, and try firing again. Nothing.

Elvis looked down at the weapon, cursing it for being so dependable up until now, and thought about bolting back to where Richie was while he still had a chance. He was turning to do that very thing when he saw a discarded handgun on the pavement, laying not six feet from where he was crouched. He'd have to come out of hiding if he wanted the thing and that would be dangerous and scary as hell to boot, but his friends were counting on him.

Buddy would be getting ready to start firing on the middle range of their attackers once the last one ran past him, but he wouldn't be able to do that if Elvis couldn't clear the shooters from the equation. He decided to go for the weapon, decided that being able to help was worth the risk.

He ran, still crouched, to where the weapon lay on the ground, too far out in the open to be grabbed without being spotted. He counted his steps, a habit he'd gotten into during their long journey, and figured he was three steps away when something struck him high on his left leg, driving him to his knees. He didn't stop moving toward the gun that he'd decided was his now. He reached for it, grabbed the thing, and turned toward the grouping of men that had been shooting toward the truck and, in turn, his friend.

Elvis fired the weapon at two men, one of them had actually been the one to shoot him, and dropped both of them. He crawled to cover, unable to stand with his new injury, let alone run. He put his back against the passenger side wheel and tried to catch his breath.

He reached down with his free hand to check the wound and it came away wet and warm. The blood was really pumping out of the hole in his thigh, but he hoped that it wasn't as bad as it seemed at the moment. Elvis fought his way into a crouch, the pain taking over his senses for a moment, and turned to fire on whoever he could see.

The moment his head popped up over the hood of the car, gunfire littered the opposite side of the Tempo. He dropped quickly, knowing that he'd given himself away. All he could do for the moment was wait, and hope that someone gave him an opportunity to return the fire.

***

Buddy was starting to get worried. He knew that Elvis had taken a risky position, but if everything went as it was supposed to, his friend would've been able to pick off most of the shooters without putting himself into any real danger. That's the way things were *supposed* to go, but the shooters were still shooting. That meant that Elvis had run into some kind of problem.

187

"Stay or go?" Buddy whispered over and over, his legs tensing to raise from his position and go to Elvis'.

He waited for a moment more, thinking that if he ran to Elvis that he'd be leaving Richie to his own devices. Richie was still sending out rounds, though, which told Buddy that he was fine for the moment. It was possible for him to run close to where Elvis was, check to see that everything was alright, and get back before blowing their plans to shit. The decision wasn't an easy one, but it *was* an obvious one. If something had gone wrong on Elvis' end, that would mean failure of the plan, anyway. Buddy ran.

The cars made good cover, each of them nearly touching the one in front of it, so he remained undetected as he made way to the opposite side of the road where Elvis should be. He saw the problem within seconds. Half of the shooters were firing on Elvis' position while the others continued their assault on Richie's.

Buddy knew that Elvis was being held at bay by the men, but not whether he was hurt or not. Rather than running for Elvis, Buddy decided to lay down some cover fire, using his pistol to take out three of the men that were shooting at Richie in quick succession. All but two men turned to fire on Buddy. He ducked down, waiting for Elvis to open fire.

Nothing came from Elvis' side of the road for a few minutes. Bullets ricocheted off of the trunk lid that lay open over Buddy's head, the sound of the things deafening him for seconds at a time. He laid down on his stomach, began firing at the feet of some of the feeders. One went down, but not before emptying his weapon toward Buddy and succeeding in scaring him half to death. He didn't feel any pain, so decided that he hadn't been hit by the onslaught. He continued to fire on them, reloading, and firing again.

Buddy didn't notice that Richie had stopped triggering.

***

Richie stayed on the ground with an empty rifle at his side. He tried to keep the same posture, one leg splayed behind his twisted body, an arm under him holding the coach gun. He knew he'd gotten the bulk of the runners, but didn't dare believe he'd gotten them all.

Gunfire was still punching the broad side of the truck and Richie hoped that it was holding their men to cover as much as it was him. He waited, breathing shallowly to give the illusion that he was dead. If the constant bang of the weapons downrange didn't stop soon, he'd have to accept the fact that his friends were either injured or dead. He'd know that their plan had failed.

For the moment, though, he kept hold of himself, tried to appear injured or dead, and readied himself to use the coach on anyone who showed up. It wasn't long before someone did.

Muddy black boots appeared at the corner of his vision, creeped in through the barely open lid of his good eye, and slowly walked toward him. There was only one in sight. This didn't alarm him, as the coach was good for close work and he'd be able to surprise a single man easily. It would probably work for two, as long as he fired one shell at a time. Three would be a tremendous problem. He could only hope that if there were three left, that they were even worse at all of this than he was.

His heart raced, adrenaline dumping into his bloodstream, as a second pair of boots joined the first. Richie's hand was gripping the handle of his weapon so tightly that it hurt.

Pain. Pain would help him to stay in all of this. He knew that stress brought the attacks on, which would be much worse than usual for him just now, but pain would keep him awake. He squeezed the handle tighter, feeling his hand cramp. His finger was wrapped onto the trigger of the gun and he was ready to use it. His vision, though already limited, began to fuzz around the edges.

The first pair of boots was close now, inches from his face, but the second had stayed back a few feet. Richie thought the second man was a little too far away. If he'd get just a foot closer, Richie would be at the advantage. He soon realized that the ideal was not going to happen. He would have to go at them as they were.

Richie breathed deeply, trying to keep his mind and body under control. He felt a tremor in his left shoulder, wondered how long he'd really been laying in that position, and suddenly lost sight of everything in front of him.

The world changed. One moment he was looking at the badly abused pavement as two men stalked toward him, the next was filled with the image of his bathroom mirror. He was glaring at his own reflection, the old version of him who'd been clean, civilized, blind, even with the possession of both eyes, to the way things would soon be.

"No!" he shouted at the mirror, "Not this!"

His fists balled, the impotent way his mind seemed to function provoking a rage in him. He couldn't be here now. This was the dream and he couldn't let this happen. Desperation was the only true feeling in that moment.

The mirror disappeared, his vision changing to the one-eyed focus, and he saw the boots flash in and then out again. The mirror. The pavement. His reflection. Two worlds were mingling in his vision, creating a sickening double vision that left him nauseated and confused.

Richie pawed for some grasp on reality as the mirror solidified, but felt only the radio from his bathroom in his right hand.

He looked at the object he'd picked up from the dream counter with a stumbling idea forming in his mind. The next moment was filled with the sound of breaking glass as he pulled back and threw the radio against the mirror.

"The night is real!" he shouted as the glass shattered, revealing the real world at the very last second in which survival could be had.

Just as one of the boots raised to nudge his shoulder, Richie spun toward its owner, his leg becoming trapped below the rest of his body, and fired one barrel into the man's stomach. He pointed the unspent barrel at the other man, who'd been badly caught off guard, and put a shell into his chest. Both went down, but neither was dead.

Richie scrambled for the dropped weapon from the first man, an aluminum baseball bat with a dented barrel, snatched it from the asphalt, and clubbed the first man quickly. The second man was pulling himself away, his own weapon still in his hand. Richie bludgeoned him with the bat, leaving him as dead as the first.

The aluminum bat fell to the pavement, discarded so that Richie could reload the shotgun and go to his friends. The bandana he'd tied over his forehead was drenched with sweat, but still working to keep his eye clear. His hands were shaking marginally, but that would not stop him from running.

***

Elvis was bleeding badly, so badly that he didn't know if he could move at all. His leg was a blaze of agony and blood. He was having trouble staying aware of what was going on, couldn't be sure if he was even still being targeted by their enemies. He was growing desperate. He didn't want to shout for his friends, couldn't even be sure that he had a shout left in him, but he didn't have much of a choice. He knew that his shouting might make the feeders aware that there was at least one more of his group in the area, but he would need help soon no matter the cost.

"Buddy!" He yelled as loudly as he could manage, "I'm hurt Buddy!"

No one responded. Elvis was sure that the gunfire was louder than *he* could be. He wanted to close his eyes. Elvis was tired and hurting and nothing would be more pleasurable than to just shut the pain out.

He glanced down at where he was sitting, noted that there was a sizeable puddle of blood beneath him, and laughed. He looked to his waist, thinking that maybe he could tie the leg up with his belt, but he'd stopped wearing a belt long ago.

He laughed again, before tears began to fall down his cheeks. He wished for his friends, wanted to talk to them one more time. He shook his head at how stupid he'd been. His eyes closed.

"Elvis has left the building," he whispered as he coasted away.

***

"Two more left," Buddy said to himself, "Got all but two."

He was out of ammo, having left a clip behind when he'd made his run, and didn't know what to do with the *nothing* that he had left. He thought about trying to go back, but wasn't sure if he'd be able to get out from behind his hide in a secretive fashion. The shooters were still pouring their guns out on the vehicle by which he hunkered, and even two men shooting was enough to make him think twice about making a run for it.

"Fuck," Buddy said, "What now?"

Richie answered him with soft quick footsteps. Buddy looked for his friend, noticing the form running down the center of the road, using the lack of

192

attention that the two men were paying. He was closing, the coach in hand, and would be upon the last of their attackers soon.

Buddy, hoping that he could keep them looking his way, untied one of his boots and yanked it off. He threw the thing behind him, toward the cannibals. They took the bait, turning at the movement and continuing to spend what seemed like an unlimited amount of ammo.

Buddy stayed in his crouch, hoping to hear the coach roar. When he did hear the gun, fired twice behind him, it was the last weapon fire of the evening.

"Elvis!" Richie yelled, "Buddy!"

"Here!" Buddy shouted, immediately thinking of homeroom attendance in high school.

"Elvis!" Richie hollered again, "We're clear!"

There was no response. Buddy rose to his feet, his legs turning to pins and needles as he let blood flow to them again. He pointed to where Elvis was hiding. Both Buddy and Richie ran to it.

Their friend came into sight a little at a time, his feet splayed out in front of him. They could see the blood on the ground as his midsection came into view. When the rest of Elvis was revealed, both men fell to their knees beside him, Buddy feeling for a pulse.

Richie watched him, his vision blurring. Buddy began to lightly slap his cheeks, repeating his name over and over again. Richie knew, almost without checking, that Elvis was gone. The blood on the ground, too much blood, was the dark red of arterial blood. The pale peaceful look on his face would be the one that Richie tried to keep out of his mind for the rest of his life.

"Fuck me," Buddy croaked, "Jesus."

Richie didn't speak. Words wouldn't do justice to what he felt just now. He touched the pocket watch against his chest and wished that this was the dream instead of a dreadful reality.

"We need to bury him," Buddy said, "I don't want to leave him in the sun, okay?"

Richie nodded, still unable to speak. They would take care of their friend as best they could. They would protect him from the sun.

***

They spent most of that night digging. They had one small spade that Buddy had always used to bury rats and Richie's pocket knife. Mostly they loosened the dirt with their tools and scooped it by hand. It was hard work, but they were determined. By three a.m. the grave was mostly dug, a copious pile of soil standing just to one side.

Amanda came to them from time to time with water, a steady stream of tears mapping clean streaks through the dirt on her face. She stayed away for the most part, tending to Elvis as best she could.

Amanda cleaned his face and hands, making sure to wipe away any trace of blood that she found. There was a lot of it under his fingernails and she'd had to borrow Richie's pocket knife to scrape them. His clothes were dirty, one side of his shorts terribly matted with his life's blood, but they had none to replace them with. She never broke down during the task, but there were times when she felt her heart break open for her lost friend.

Richie wished that he'd learned some song from Elvis that he could sing or hum, but he hadn't put in the time to do such things. Elvis was supposed to always be there. It was an unfair world that had taken this man from their company and he cursed it for such cruelty. There had always *been* Elvis, therefore there should always *be* Elvis.

Buddy stayed silent. The others couldn't read his thoughts, but Richie had known Buddy for a lot of years. He knew that guilt would be the primary

194

emotion as it was for Richie. Either of them could have done something different or predicted the way it would all happen. Either of them could have saved their companion, their brother, if they'd just thought a bit harder. Hindsight, as always, is 20/20.

When they laid Elvis into his grave, just a hole somewhere in Canada, neither of them cried. They said very little as it would be impossible to express the depth of this loss. The dry dirt spread across Elvis' chest with each handful, both men reluctant to scoop the soil onto his face. When, finally, there was no choice, Buddy was the one to cover Elvis' features. When they'd enclosed him completely, Richie let out a sob, a wretched one so full of pain that Buddy could no longer hold back his own tears. Such loss could never be expressed through anything less than the weeping of men.

It only took them an hour to finish burying Elvis, who had walked this earth with them for so many years. It was such a short time that Richie couldn't believe that they were finished. He looked around them, hoping for some way to mark his grave appropriately. Nothing stood out.

"Can you draw something in the dirt?" Buddy asked quietly.

"It won't last for long."

"Nothing ever does."

Richie nodded, sitting down off to the side of the grave and picking up his pocket knife. He began to draw.

Buddy watched him, reluctant to leave before the job was done. He saw what Richie was making for Elvis, his tears darkening the soil from time to time as he carved the image into the earth. Buddy smiled, knowing that it fit, knowing that Elvis would laugh about it from where ever he was now. He added some of his own water to the soil.

The two men, who once were three, walked away from a freshly turned mound of earth. If you saw the area from their level you might be able to make

195

out the image that served as a gravestone for Elvis, but you would know immediately if you saw it from above. An acoustic guitar, more detailed than you might have thought was possible, was painstakingly etched in the ground along with the name "Elvis".

***

Goodwin, AB
May 15, 2021
9:46 PM 80*F

Buddy and Richie walked with the ghost of Elvis down a two-lane road still many miles from the border that separated Canada and Alaska. Their eyes were always searching, looking for threats, looking back for the friend they'd lost, and searching again.

Both men were scarred, one who now only had one good eye and a ruined patch of mottled skin on the left side of his face, the other with a thick burrow that went from the middle of his left cheek to his jaw line. Buddy hadn't felt the graze of the bullet when it'd found him, but he would always have the reminder of the battle, and the loss, etched into his skin for all the world to see. They shared one other scar, but it was upon the earth rather than flesh, a small plot where a good man lay, protected from the rays of the sun.

They were quiet company for the others. Amanda, Dylan, and Abby stayed behind them, allowing plenty of space for the grieving men. Amanda was one of them, had become close with their fallen friend, but still she remained an outsider to the true friendship the three men had shared. She held nothing against them for that fact. No ill feelings existed. She understood the depth of their love for one another, brothers in truth rather than blood.

Amanda's night was spent hand-in-hand with Abby. She did her best to keep the girl moving without much complaint. When her tears came from time to time, they were silent and not fretted upon.

Dylan was quiet and brooding, but required nothing from the others, so nothing was offered. Abby looked to him once in a while with a shy smile. He returned it each time, but looked pained as she glanced away.

Richie's mind wandered from the road, slipping along the cracks of sunlight in his mind. He thought about the last sleeping venture he'd made into the dream, finding Benny in his quiescent world. Would Elvis haunt him now, waiting at his kitchen table with a beaten guitar in hand?

It was peculiar that he saw Elvis that way now. He hadn't even known that his friend could play the instrument until recently, but it had become a descriptive part of his picture of the man he'd called a companion for so many years.

Buddy tried not to think at all, letting his thoughts slide into the night without consideration. He and Elvis had spent so much time together in their former lives, more than Richie had spent with either of them, and there was a void that could never be filled traveling in the dead man's place.

His own mortality did not concern him. As far as Buddy was concerned, they were all a blink away from death, but Elvis was meant to be different. Buddy would've rather been the one to pass on. Who knew, though? Maybe his time would come sooner than later. Oddly enough, he was comforted by the thought.

The night, as it always had, wore on. Time was checked. Worries were had. Conversations were left in the dust that lay alongside the asphalt. They shuffled through the night on the way to the countless ones that would proceed from it.

Searching for the Border

Chapter 1

Watson Lake, YT (Root Cellar)

June 30, 2021

7:12 AM 214*F (Surface)

"We're going to be in trouble soon," Amanda said without raising her eyes from the pouches of dehydrated food.

Buddy nodded without saying anything in response. Amanda had all of their supplies laid out on the basement floor, the meals standing on their wide bottoms in neat rows of five. He counted twenty. There were five people traveling in their little group, and they'd been unable to restock their food stuffs for the last two weeks. There had been service stations along the way, but no bigger stores that would provide them with anything of use.

Amanda pulled three packs to the side and began stowing the rest equally among the packs. Her mouth was set in concentration as if she might be able to find a way to multiply the food by the sheer force of her will.

"Richie," Buddy finally said, "How far?"

The floor where Richie sat was covered in loose sheets of the atlas he'd been carrying along with a small booklet describing the main route to Alaska. He looked up to Buddy with his good eye, the other covered by a makeshift patch, and shook his head.

"Give me a few minutes. I need to check the legends."

Dylan and Abby were in the process of laying out sleeping bags and setting their water to cool. Water was still easy enough to get as they wandered by lakes on a regular basis, but water alone wouldn't keep them alive. Richie had heard once that a person could live for quite a while without food if they had enough to drink, but living wasn't the only thing they had to do. Even if they tried to stretch the meal packs by rationing, the five of them would progressively grow weaker, no matter their level of hydration.

There hadn't been any rats to speak of recently, either. That was something of concern. Why had they been so plentiful south of them and so sparse in the north? Was it because there hadn't really been that many of the things this far north to start with, or had they been killed off somehow? Richie and Buddy had discussed various theories on the lack of rodents in the north and had decided on their previous elimination being the most likely explanation. It wasn't a satisfying idea.

"If I have to guess a distance," Richie admitted, "We're about 600 miles away."

"Shit," Buddy replied.

"Yeah."

"How long will that take us?"

"One hell of a lot longer than we have supplies for," Amanda interjected, "We need to figure something out."

Buddy ignored her. Richie agreed with her. Dylan and Abby walked over to where they were sitting and took a seat of their own. No one spoke for a moment, allowing Richie time to do the math in his head.

"Since we've been getting a couple of more hours at night lately," he began, "we can get up to twenty miles a night, give or take. I think we could make it to the border in thirty-five days."

"We could ration the food. Split one pouch between everybody," Dylan suggested.

"If we do that, we're not making twenty miles a day," Amanda argued, "We're malnourished as it is. If we start eating even less..."

"Yeah," Richie agreed, winking his one good eye at Abby. The girl giggled at his gesture.

At least somebody gets some enjoyment from my mutilated face, he thought.

"Well, we've listed our problems out. Got any solutions?" Buddy asked.

Each of them, including Abby, shook their head.

Richie looked around the group at the long faces, but could glean nothing from them. He missed Elvis, who always seemed to spit out an incredibly unique idea when they needed it the most. He was gone, though, and wouldn't be providing resolutions for their daily problems anymore.

They'd been taking food for granted. Richie knew that, but didn't dare say it aloud. There had always been food, at least enough to keep them alive and moving, therefore there should always be food. It was a dangerous way to think, but they hadn't known that at the time. He'd thought of their supplies as a constantly replenishing thing that they just had to work a little to find. Recently, though, working to gather food was proving to be a fruitless task.

"We need to eat while we can," Richie said with finality.

"One pack each," Buddy allowed, "But we can't keep that up. Day after tomorrow we go down to half a pouch each. We need to stretch it."

Amanda looked as if she were ready to debate the matter, as she'd done with Dylan, but seemed to reconsider. She said nothing, knowing that Buddy was right.

"What I wouldn't give for a cheeseburger," Dylan said before adding water to five pouches of dehydrated food.

***

Richie was thinking more and more about the cannibals. The "Feeders", as they'd begun exclusively calling them, had been an obvious danger from the very beginning, but Richie had accepted them without much contemplation. They were there. That was all.

Now, however, it was different in his mind. He thought about their past luck with finding food. Supplies had just been in their path without much consideration, though now that was changing. Had the people who'd resorted to feeding on their fellow man had a different kind of luck in that department? Had it been much harder for them to find food than it had been for Richie, Buddy, and their group? Were they just driven so crazy by hunger that resorting to cannibalism had seemed a necessity to them? Questions. There were always questions.

Richie supposed that there were just some people who wanted the meat that couldn't be obtained by killing rats, if they'd even thought of or come in contact with the animals that had been such bountiful fair in his own experience. It was also possible that they had been mentally unstable from the start, ready to do things in order to survive without worrying on morality. The thought was a disturbing one but a definite possibility.

He was in the dark, now, laying on his back with the pocket watch held loosely against his collar bone by the fingers of his right hand. Richie hadn't felt so compelled by the dream in recent weeks. His mind was clearer than it had been since the confrontation he'd had with the sun. The skin around his left eye had healed well, wasn't so painful to the touch as it had been, but the scar would always be there. The burned eye was dead and black in the socket, something he'd never heard of happening to anyone before, and was useless to him now. Half blind, however, was preferable to being completely sightless. He tried not to complain.

The strange thing about the condition, to Richie at least, was the ghost of vision that crept into his brain from time to time. He would be walking along with his group, looking at the road ahead or something that decorated the side of it, and would somehow see two things at once. His good eye would register the actual scene before him. The empty eye would see the world as it had once

202

been, a tree on the side of the road that bore lovely green foliage to his left and a sparsely littered waste land to his right. It was unnerving.

He'd mentioned the thing to Buddy once, without thinking much of it, and Buddy had chuckled. His friend wasn't cruel, but the sound of the laugh had been similar to cruelty before he explained himself.

"I know it's not funny, one-eye, but I have to admit that I'm jealous."

"Of what?"

"Of being able to see anything that hasn't been burned to shit by the ever loving sun."

"I'm not really *seeing* it, Buddy. My mind is playing tricks on me," Richie explained defensively.

"Want my glasses?" Buddy asked, pulling the things off and showing him the spider web damage in one of the lenses, "It's kind of the same thing. You get to see some crazy version of a live tree and I get to see like twenty dead ones on one side. I'll trade you."

"Only if you take a good long look at the day, dick," Richie mumbled with a grin.

"Good point," Buddy said, "It's like losing a hand, though."

"How so?"

"Haven't you ever heard about a person who loses a limb going bat shit because the hand that's gone won't stop itching? Imagine always having an itch that you can't scratch."

"That would suck."

"It would, but you are in luck, my friend. Your shit doesn't itch too much."

Richie stared up at the ceiling, trying not to think about amputees and cannibals. The two seemed to be too easily integrated into the same thought.

If you had to pick a limb to chop off for dinner, which one would you choose? Richie's dark thoughts taunted.

***

The day gave way to dusk at 7:15 p.m. and complete darkness covered the earth within thirty minutes. Richie and his group were awake long before the sun fell to sleep, but they were careful not to leave their hide until well after dark. Two hours after sunset, they emerged from the cellar as quietly as they could, one man exiting a few minutes before the others to clear the area. No threats were in the vicinity, as far as any of them knew, so they began their walk, moving in the direction that would lead them into Alaska within two months if all went well.

The man watching them, a quiet and pleasant man in the world before the night became their time to wake, didn't follow them immediately. He waited for them to get into their pace, to find the comfort in their journey as they did each night, before tracing their steps along the side of the highway. He made very little noise as he traveled.

He had no one to talk to, so that wasn't a risk, and he wasn't in the habit of conversing with himself or any voices that might have been rambling inside of his head. His silence was one of choice and necessity. He didn't want any of them to know that he was there until he was ready to reveal himself.

The follower walked with a limp, favoring his right leg, but it wasn't always noticeable. He could control the weakness in his knee and ankle quite easily if that was his preference. As with most things on this walk, it didn't matter. He could rest the muscles in his lower leg a bit from time to time. If he really wanted to, the man could rest for the whole night in a freshly dug den and find his quarry still on the same path. They weren't navigating a complicated route.

He adjusted the shoulder straps of his backpack, the contents rustling inside with the sound of crinkling plastic, and gripped the short spade loosely in his right hand as he would've a cane. He reached down to his bandaged calf to be sure that the binding was secure.

Faint blood stains showed through along its length, but he felt none on his fingertips. The man turned his head in either direction slowly to crack the vertebrae in his neck with an audible pop. He breathed deeply to calm the tremors that rolled through his body.

Once he was ready, he followed the group of people along the road.

Chapter 2

<u>**Rancheria, YT**</u>

<u>**July 3, 2021**</u>

<u>**9:42 PM 78*F**</u>

A service station, this one bearing a startling resemblance to the truck stop where Amanda had joined their group, loomed in the distance. Buddy had spotted the great hulk and had pointed it out to Richie with a scathing remark about his inability to see things on the left hand side. Richie, who had heard almost every possible version of the term "one-eye" by this time, gave him the finger without retort. Buddy laughed, though without his usual gusto. They'd been on half rations for the past two days and the gnawing in their stomachs had begun to irritate them.

"Can we just hope that there's some kind of food in there?" Amanda begged, "I don't think I can take Buddy's shitty jokes on an empty stomach, anymore."

"At least he's got jokes," Dylan added from behind them, "I can't seem to find any humor on this fucking road tonight."

"That's because you're still new," Richie explained, "If you were a veteran of the group, like myself and old Peggy Sue here, you'd find humor in all sorts of fucked up shit."

"We're going back to the Buddy Holly jokes?" Buddy asked with a roll of the eyes.

"Better than nothing," Abby suddenly added, stealing a laugh from all of them.

"Do you know who Buddy Holly is?" Buddy asked the kid.

"I thought it was you."

"Shit," Buddy said with a wince, "How old are you?"

"Almost ten," she told him with a smile that warned of wisdom beyond her years.

"Yeah. Ten going on twenty-eight," Amanda said with a smirk.

Dylan, whose voice hadn't been put to use nearly as much as the rest of them, laughed heartily at that. The older man shook his head at the girl and put a hand on her shoulder as a father would his daughter.

Richie had noticed the way Dylan treated the child and was impressed by the man. He'd risked his life, and nearly lost it, to get the girl out of the cannibals' camp and seemed to take on the role of a father as easily as Amanda did the role of a mother.

Richie was curious about the possibility of garnering a small family, one made up of complete strangers, in this new world. Would it be possible to find that kind of happiness?

They kept moving at their constant pace toward the truck stop, their hopes not raising as high as they would've even a week earlier.

***

They scattered amongst the aisles of the place with no real enthusiasm. It was obvious to them that they weren't going to find much, if anything, and their mood was a dour one.

Richie was looking for the store room, as was his usual habit. It was obvious that the shelves would be emptied first. They were the first place that anyone would scavenge for supplies, but the store room could be overlooked by average looters. He found a door marked "Private" and twisted the knob. Locked.

He dropped to his knees, his pack on the floor beside him, and fished out the pick set that had aided them for so long. The tension wrench that had come with the kit had been broken in the lock of a cellar that he barely dared to remember, but Buddy had fashioned a replacement from a precision screwdriver.

The new tool actually seemed to function more smoothly, allowing Richie to use his palm rather than just his fingertips. In a moment, the door was swinging open on protesting hinges.

Hunger pains racked his gut as he stood, threatening to make him squat back down to the floor, but Richie fought through them. The doorway invited him, so he entered with a penlight in hand and put his foot down on the first step.

A subtle scratching sound tickled his ears, making him stop dead in his tracks. Richie clicked off the light immediately and listened. More scratching. He grinned before turning back to the door.

"Rats," Richie announced without shouting.

Buddy ran to the doorway, placing both palms on the frame to stop himself from colliding with Richie's unmoving form. They looked at each other and grinned. It may not be much, but it would be meat.

"I'll get the sling," Buddy whispered, "Should we close the door?"

"I think it's fine. They weren't trying to come this way."

"Good enough for me."

"Yeah," Richie said, "I'll check things out in here for now. Going down."

Richie turned back toward the dark stairwell, clicking the light back into life as he reached the landing, and began to walk the perimeter of the room. There was a smell that he hadn't had in his nose for a while. It was tangy and almost like the urine one expels after drinking soda or beer all day. None of them had drank anything but water for so long that their own piss didn't have an odor

---

anymore. Richie was looking for the source of this when his light happened on an animal that didn't resemble a rat, at all.

"Fuck me," Richie breathed before squatting to his haunches, "Haven't seen one of you in a while."

Buddy was walking down the steps now, his footsteps flooding the basement store room with a scraping sound. Richie looked over his shoulder and in Buddy's direction.

"No rats," Richie told him, still pointing his light at the furry resident of the place.

"Is that a fucking cat?" Buddy blurted out, his astonishment made obvious by his tone.

"I think so. To skinny to be anything else."

"How in the hell is that possible? How's he alive down here?"

"He must be pretty fucking smart," Richie admitted, "Probably has a way in and out that we don't see."

"Are we going to eat it?"

"I don't know, man. Seems like we shouldn't."

"Yeah," Buddy agreed, "But I'm hungry enough."

"Bet he ate all the rats," Richie said sourly.

Buddy patted Richie on one shoulder and grinned at the green eyes reflecting what little light existed in the basement. Richie looked up at him and his own frown disappeared. If given the chance, Richie would've said exactly what Buddy stated next.

"Elvis would've loved it."

Neither man bothered the feline that traipsed around the basement area as they searched it. The expedition, though void of rats, did prove a fruitful one. A few gallons of fresh water were stored on a low shelf near what was likely the station manager's old desk. In the desk itself were their real prizes, one they hadn't been lucky enough to find in any other place. An unopened bag of extraordinarily stale Doritos, the nacho cheese variety, was stowed away in the top right-hand drawer along with three packs of ramen noodles. Richie nearly jumped for joy at such a find.

Later, as they continued on their journey, they passed the bag of flavored tortilla chips around. They each had a few of the chips and smiled as all but Richie licked powdered cheese off of their fingertips. Richie let the cat taste the remnants of his share.

They hadn't beckoned the animal, or tried in any way to take it with them. Buddy thought the thing had surely gone feral after a year or more of living on its own devices, but the cat seemed as needy of their company as they were of it. Richie suggested they call it Elvis, but Buddy balked at the notion. Instead, on Amanda's suggestion, they named it King.

***

The follower was frustrated with their progress. They'd slowed down quite a bit after leaving the gas station and only eighteen miles had been traveled by the time the group stopped at another one to sleep for the day. They'd probably found food, which was counterproductive to what he was planning. They needed to stay hungry, at least a little, to keep up the desperate pace.

He dug his den for the day, one shovel full at a time, hoping that he would manage to get deep enough to be comfortable in the cool soil. It wasn't easy to excavate a perfect tunnel within a couple of hours, but he would manage as he usually did. The follower had found that three feet worth of depth was too little a few weeks back, no matter how much cooler it was this far north, and had spent the day in near agony. Five feet seemed to work fine. He could pull enough dirt over himself to shield from the sun's rays and insulate from the heat for the most part.

Long miles back, he'd had to start digging much earlier in the night and dig much deeper holes. Trial and error had lost many miles for him, had left him far behind the group of travelers. He'd survived all of it, though, and would continue to live through the days. He would follow them until it was time to make himself known. They needed to move faster.

The bandage around his calf badly needed a change. He'd known this through most of the night, but was determined to wait until the next round of darkness. He felt that the leg could wait a while longer without risking an infection, but no longer than one more day. It was always a shame to put a clean white bandage around his wound just before immersing himself in the dirt for such a long period. If the nastiness of the soil wasn't bad enough, the sweating would make it uncomfortable.

He was a contact lens wearer in his old life, the one before all of this, and would sometimes wear a pair of the disposable lenses for months at a time. He compared the bandages to the contacts. New ones always felt awkward and ineffective until they'd worn in for a while. He'd had eye infections due to the long time wear, also a comparison to the dressed wound, but not unless he had worn the things for so long that they were close to falling out anyway. He felt that the two things were incredibly similar.

More digging. The pile of dirt grew tall and fat as he frantically scooped earth from his hole. He would be done and ready to sleep very soon. He would eat when he woke, as long as the bandage hadn't gotten too filthy in his sleep. He might have to attend to that immediately upon waking.

Chapter 3

Whitehorse, YT
July 14, 2021
1:19 AM 78*F

For what felt like the millionth time, Richie stood at the beginning of a new highway. He looked from left to right, from northbound shoulder to southbound shoulder, and saw no discernable difference between this road and every other road they'd been traveling. The pavement was uneven in places. The lines had grown faint, barely visible against the gray backdrop of the asphalt. The dust across the thing was the same dust they'd been walking on for more than a year as far as he could tell.

"Why are we stopping?" Amanda asked him.

"This is the Alaska Highway," he rasped in return.

She said nothing, just stood with him to look at what was ahead. Buddy had been listening when Richie named the road and wondered if they should be celebrating or something.

Abby paid no attention. She took advantage of the break by sitting in the middle of the road and calling to King, the striped orange tabby immediately came to her for a well-deserved petting. The little girl wasn't smiling, Richie noticed upon looking back, but she looked content in a way that was almost heartrending. King had followed them of his own free will, but he was theirs now.

"Fucking cat," Buddy grunted, "I can't believe we have a cat during the apocalypse."

"It's like we're a gay couple with a little girl and her cat," Richie chided.

"There are more people here. We don't have to be the gay couple with the cat."

"Don't get defensive, Buddy. With our limited population you've become quite the catch," Amanda said with an impish grin.

"That's true. But I wouldn't date a guy with one eye," Buddy returned.

"Maybe you liked me before the eye thing," Richie added, "You wouldn't leave because I was injured. Maybe our love is too strong for a trivial thing like that to separate us."

"And it got way creepier than I thought it could," Amanda said before turning back to the others.

Dylan had walked up to where they stood, passing Amanda on her way to join Abby. His gaze was on the road, seeing the next leg of their journey with eyes that weren't quite squinted.

Richie took a moment before speaking again, to look at the man. He was thin, like the rest of them, but more than ten years older than Richie and Buddy. He was closer to Amanda's age and that was made more obvious by his graying hair than it was by a wrinkled face. He had laugh lines and crow's feet, but the true wrinkles of age seemed more Richie's uniform than Dylan's.

"Ready to walk up the Alaska Highway, Dylan?" Richie asked him without much hope for a response. The man was quiet and communicated more with grunts and body language than words.

"I never planned to go this far north," Dylan began, "But I owe you people something that I couldn't pay back if I didn't come with you. The little girl, too.

"I lived in DeBolt for most of my life and had a family there before all of this. I wanted to die there, just like they did. Was going to if Abby hadn't been brought into that place."

"You were just going to let them eat you?" Buddy asked.

"Wouldn't have mattered to me. They kill you before they really get started. They just take little pieces from you while you're alive. That group was like that, anyway."

Both of the younger men were mystified by the way their fellow traveler was talking. He was calm, so calm that he could've been talking about a handful of pebbles rather than the loss of his own life. His face was without expression as he spoke, so neither Buddy nor Richie could see whether the idea caused him any real pain.

"Either way, boys. I thank you for what you did for Abby and me. I won't forget it and I won't leave you until I've done something to return the favor."

With that, Dylan shrugged his shoulders to distribute his pack along his back bone, and began walking forward.

"That was different," Buddy whistled.

"Yeah," Richie agreed as they watched the man's back, "That one's a real card."

***

The day kept them inside, as it always did, but allowed them time to rest, think, and talk about the last leg of their trip. Abby, who seemed able to sleep on command and stay that way until rough waking was endured, slept through most of the day. Buddy was deeply jealous of this ability and had made it known that Abby would have to teach him her ways before she was able to part company with him. The girl mainly giggled at him when he ranted about it.

"How do we look on supplies?" Richie asked.

"We have one pack of ramen noodles left, some Dorito crumbs, one full meal pouch, one half meal pouch," Amanda paused, "We found one bag of dried beans when we got here tonight. We have plenty of medical supplies and a shit load of antibiotics and Vicodin."

"Good to know," Buddy remarked, "How long will the beans last."

"If we're careful, we can get a week out of them. The noodles and meal pouches will feed us today, so we won't have to break into the beans."

"We need to get more calories going than that," Richie said, "Let's finish off the chips."

Amanda nodded her agreement and went about the preparation of their day's meal. Richie was staring at his guide book, studying it as if the thing might change on him at any minute. Buddy watched, itching to talk about the highway, but knowing that Richie would let him in on the particulars when he was ready. His stomach rumbled angrily. They needed to find more food.

Richie was holding the pocket watch in one loose fist as he perused the book in his other hand. When he needed to turn a page, he let the watch fall against his collar with an audible slap. He would grab the thing as soon as he was able again. The talisman had been his savior on many nights' walks, helping him to hold on to their reality, and he was melancholic to be without it in any way. Richie seldom opened the thing for any purpose other than checking the time, but there were still moments when the picture of Amanda and the small endorsement below it were needed.

The night is real, he thought.

So is the day, he reflected with a shiver.

"If I'm right," Richie told Buddy, "We could be across the border and into Alaska in two weeks."

"Two weeks?"

"Let's say three just for shits and giggles. I don't want to be crucified for estimates later on."

"We've been walking for more than a year, Richie. If you miss something by a week nobody's going to put you up on a cross."

"Either way," Richie went on, "That means we need to find an extra week's worth of food just to make it there. After that..."

"We'll figure it out," Buddy reassured him.

"We need to figure it out soon. We've been lucky the whole way. We're heading toward starvation right now, Buddy. You know that, don't you?"

His friend nodded without looking away.

"The other thing we've gotten lucky as shit on is shelter. Hopefully, and I really mean hopefully, we'll be able to find service stations every twenty miles."

"There's always the walk-in freezer method," Buddy allowed.

"Maybe."

"Any thoughts on how hot it gets during the day up here?"

"Not a clue," Richie said, "But I have an idea on how we can figure it out."

"It doesn't involve me losing an eye because I've been fucking with you, does it?"

"Not yet."

"Then what?"

They were eye-to-eye, so Richie could count on Buddy's attention when he nodded toward the cat. The animal was cleaning itself, as it seemed to for the better part of most days, and paid no attention to them. Buddy looked in the direction of Richie's gesture. His shoulders slumped instantly, his gaze falling to the floor. When he turned back to Richie his face showed defeat.

"That sucks," Buddy whispered.

"It does."

"What about Abby?"

"Bet she wants to live, too."

216

"It's pretty fucked up, Richie. We're just going to throw him outside right before sunrise?"

Richie flinched as if Buddy had struck him. The look on his face was one of shocked horror.

"Hell no. What kind of a person do you think I am?"

"Then what?" Buddy asked.

"The back office, upstairs. It doesn't have any windows."

Buddy nodded. Most of the stations they'd squatted in had an identical room. It was close to the center of the building, its walls windowless protection. Richie had obviously been wondering if they could be above ground and out of the sun without risk. It made sense, but who would want to try it without knowing. They would lock the cat inside when they went downstairs for the day and release him upon their own exit. It was risky for King, but would give them knowledge that they didn't yet possess.

"Alright," Buddy relented, "But you have to talk to the kid."

"I figured."

Chapter 4

<u>**Ibex Valley, YT**</u>
<u>**July 15, 2021**</u>
<u>**3:58 AM 81*F**</u>

Abby sat on her sleeping bag, King cradled in her lap, when Richie sat down across from her. She looked up with wide eyes, knowing what he was going to say. They'd all talked about what would happen as they walked, but she wasn't pleased with the idea.

King was the only cat she'd seen in a year. He was just like Mrs. Hoffman's cat. Abby and her parents had lived next door to the Mrs. Hoffman and she always jumped at the chance to hold and pet the feline. She had always wanted a kitten of her own, but her parents wouldn't hear of it.

Now, in this terrible version of the world, Abby had a cat that would sit with her all night if she wanted. It wasn't fair that King might not be alive in the morning, but Abby wouldn't cry or whine about it. She just wanted a few more minutes with her furry friend.

"It's time, Abby," Richie said, "We have to take King upstairs."

"I know. Can I take him?"

"Sure."

"Can we give him a little food? He'd feel better being alone if he had a treat."

"Abby, we don't ha-," Amanda began, but Richie cut her off.

"We can give him a few scraps and some water. How's that?"

Abby nodded, tears welling up against her eyelids. *Don't you cry!* the girl scolded herself as she stood awkwardly with King in her arms. She walked toward the stairwell, a little girl of only ten that didn't deserve the pain she

218

was feeling. Richie felt for her, but knew that there was no other way to discern if they'd be able to survive beyond the next town. There was no way for him to numb her grief.

Her small footsteps diminished as she climbed the steps. Buddy had been scrounging in his pack for something during the exchange and came up with it just as Richie was bending to their supplies. He held the packet, shining plastic in the lantern light, up to Richie.

"Don't be pissed. I was saving it back for Alaska or if we got hungry enough," Buddy said softly.

The packet of tuna continued to reflect the light against the dimness of the basement. Richie looked at the thing for a long time before taking it from his friend. He nodded, his jaws clenching at the thought of ripping the pack open and devouring the contents, and followed Abby. It would be good for the cat to have something like this. It might even be King's last meal. Why shouldn't it be a special one?

He found the child in the office, sitting on the floor with the cat. She was stroking him and murmuring something that Richie couldn't hear. His eye was watering, making the scene look like an impressionistic painting in some long ago museum. Instantly, he wondered if all of the paintings had been destroyed, but dismissed it just as quickly. He had more prominent things to think about.

Without a word, Richie sat down beside Abby and scratched King's head for a moment. She wasn't the only one who'd enjoyed having the furry thing around.

He sniffed hard, clearing his nose, and blinked his eye a few times before tearing the top off of the package of tuna. His mouth began to water even more than his eye. Again, Richie was tempted to scoop the contents out and cram them into his mouth. Abby watched as Richie emptied the package onto the floor just in front of them. King jumped to the pile and began to devour the stuff ravenously. He would completely finish it in seconds.

Richie stood, holding his hand out to Abby. She stood with him, her small hand linking with his, and they left the office. Richie closed the door as quietly as he could, hoping not to interrupt the animal in its feasting. As they walked down to the others, their own door closed and locked, Richie heard the mewling of the cat, but chose to ignore it. Abby's tears were flowing now, but no one would be able to give her comfort.

***

Ibex Valley, YT
July 15, 2021
7:45 AM 104*F

King was alone again. He didn't have the mental capacity to understand that if he survived the day his people would return. He only knew that he was trapped in another place, like he had been for so long before his people had let him out. King wasn't confused. King wasn't scared. King was lonely.

He'd lived a wonderful life with his first person, a young woman who'd been kind enough to give him a home and feed him every day. She even liked to take him with her to work, as had been the case on the last day he'd seen her. She had brought him to work at the truck place and let him go downstairs.

King liked it downstairs. There were high boxes to climb and plenty of places to hide. He could even hunt there if he wanted to, which he normally didn't. Why would he hunt for food if the person gave him food every day? Eventually, though, when his person hadn't returned, King began stalking the rats and mice for food with great success.

220

It was a long time between being locked in the basement and being let out by his new people, but King didn't know *how* long. Time was different for him than for the people. He knew days by the sun. He knew nights by the moon. In the basement, much like now, there had been no sun or moon. It had just been one very long night as far as King the cat, who had once been Buddy (Wouldn't Richie have had a great time with that old name?), was concerned.

The temperature of the room raised a bit, making King uncomfortable, but no worse than the long ago basement had made him. He searched the floor for more of the fish that he'd been given and cleaned his fur. From time to time he would let out a resounding "MEOW!" to see if anyone would come to let him out. He drank from the water they'd left for him. He sat in a world of dim images. He didn't find a way out of the room.

***

Ibex Valley, YT
July 15, 2021
8:06 PM 84*F

"Can we check now?" Abby asked Richie for the third time in as many minutes.

Richie looked up at her from his maps and considered. He didn't want to know if the cat had died, would be forever saddened if it had.

His bad eye was aching a bit, the flesh around it tender for some reason that he couldn't even think about at the moment. He looked to Buddy, hoping that his friend would volunteer for the task. Then to Amanda. Then to Dylan. No help from anyone.

"Okay," he sighed, slowly rising to a crouch.

221

When Richie stood, closing his functioning eye for a moment, he thought of a dead ball of fur laying in the middle of a concrete floor. He thought of a small girl crying uncontrollably. Richie was not looking forward to climbing the steps, opening the doors, or finding King dead. If the cat hadn't survived, it was a good possibility that they would all be joining him in the afterlife in the very near future. It would also mean Abby having her heart broken.

Moments later they stood outside of the door that had held their new friend captive for the daytime hours. Richie was holding his breath without meaning to. Abby was impatient, but keeping herself at bay.

They heard nothing in the room. No sounds of movement could be discerned through the border between them and the mystery that was King the cat. Richie turned the knob. As the door swung open, he realized that he'd also closed his eye against the sight that awaited them. Richie opened his eye to see King lying in the center of the room, tucked into an unmoving ball.

"King," Abby beckoned, "Here kitty."

Nothing. Richie saw no rise or fall of the shoulders to indicate breath. He wanted to cry for the girl, to kneel down and hold her in his arms. He looked down to her, noticed the steady drip of tears from her eyes. Richie shook his head, clinched his own eye shut against tears that wanted to come. It was worse than he'd thought it would be, finding King this way, and he wanted to take their test back, to let the animal live. Abby would be devastated.

"King?" Abby said again, taking a step toward the small furry body.

When the animal's head popped up, its feline eyes opening to reflect the dim illumination of their penlight, Richie nearly jumped out of his skin. When King stood, stretched, and walked over to Abby for the petting that he very much deserved, Richie wanted to jump for joy. He smiled, as did the girl, when King the cat jumped into her arms.

"Well, I'll be damned," Richie exhaled, "We're alive."

***

The follower watched as they exited the truck stop. Their pace was stronger, but he could see the weakness in their movements. It wouldn't be much longer, now.

As he followed them, not actually seeing the group anymore, he thought of how it would be soon. He would reveal himself in a few days, just as they were approaching their goal. Part of him was hesitant, wondered if he could just keep watching, just stay out of sight. The other part of him, the more cynical part, knew that their business would have to be finished soon. His leg wasn't going to hold up for much longer. The follower would have to do something about the wound that surpassed just wrapping the thing in clean bandages. He could smell it.

The load he was carrying, the physical one, was taking its toll on him. The packages would have to be delivered if he wanted them to keep going. He thought that it might be best to leave his gifts for his fellow travelers while they hid for the next day. He would decide when they stopped.

They *were* fellow travelers. They'd all been walking the same lanes for quite some time and he would be sorry to see them gone from his routine. The craziness of it all wasn't lost on him. He knew that this obsession wasn't something that he could continue living through for all of the time to come, but it was good enough to keep him going for now. He had a goal, after all.

He'd noticed more pain when he awoke. The twinges of agony that stayed with him, the ones caused by the ever-open wound on his calf, had spread to his thigh. He didn't have to be a doctor to know that he was losing the leg. He might even have to cut it off if he wanted to continue living. Luckily, that

223

wasn't what he'd kept in mind for all of these miles. Everything would be over soon.

Maybe they could make it a few more days without sustenance. He would watch. He would know.

Chapter 5

Canyon, YT
July 20, 2021
12:02 AM 78*F

The night was cool, almost refreshing, as they moved along the faded white line of the shoulder. The road had become gravely and loose, but the roadside was made of dirt and was easy to walk on.

Richie was lagging behind, letting everyone else make way for him as he pondered the final depletion of their food. They were empty of any type of ration at this point, and had been for the last two days. Water would have to be enough until they stopped again. He wondered how long they could make it without eating, but dismissed the thought quickly. There was no reason for his deliberations on the subject. Nothing could be done.

King followed them, his tail out and curled toward the sky, with a spry step. Abby would look down every once in a while and smile at her claimed pet. Richie could not help but do the same, though the smile on his face wasn't nearly as angelic due to his scars.

Scars. That was something to think about. Scars upon flesh. Scars upon the mind. He decided to stick with hunger as his topic of speculation. After all, there were worse things than a hollow belly.

"I'm thinking that you need a nickname, Richie," Buddy called back to him.

"Let me guess. One-eye?"

"You never get tired of that, do you?" Dylan remarked, eliciting laughter from everyone.

The laughter was forced, but all of them needed to force an emotion. Buddy, who was grasping at straws to keep himself occupied, felt that chiding Richie would be the best way around their current mood. He decided that something else was in order.

"Dylan, my old friend, tell me a story."

"What might you like to hear, Buddy?" Dylan asked amiably, "Fairy tale?"

"I would like to hear the story of Dylan," Buddy answered.

Amanda smiled at the notion. Dylan had been a bit of a mystery, only interjecting small facts about his life from time to time. It would be nice to hear something new.

"None of the sad shit, mind you. You're screwed the same as the rest of us and we already know that. Tell us the good stuff from before the great tan we almost got."

"Okay," Dylan said thoughtfully, "Give me a minute to gather my thoughts."

Dylan looked up to the night sky, one that was oddly more beautiful in the world they now lived in. There was so little light left on in the night that it couldn't affect the amount of stars within view. The sky seemed an ocean of heavenly illumination now, starlight shining upon them from forever. If given the time to truly stargaze, a man could look beyond the furthest depths of imagination and see more yet to come. Richie joined Dylan in his glance at the worlds that weren't theirs, and found himself longing for a somewhere that he could never reach.

"I was a kid in DeBolt. I already told you that. What I didn't tell you about is the way I grew up there," Dylan began, breathing deeply of the clean air, "My father was a bison rancher. He was also one of the most aggravating men I've ever known and loved nothing more than to work his hands until they were callused and chafed. Liked it when my own mitts were in the same condition."

"Didn't I say 'no sad shit'?" Buddy interrupted.

Dylan raised his eyebrows and smiled. For the first time, Richie had registered the man's accent as he spoke. He sounded like most Canadians that Richie had ever met, but Dylan sounded almost French when he really got to talking. Richie waited through the pause.

"Ain't sad, my friend, just facts. You ever known a farmer that don't work too hard? I never met one."

"Go on," Buddy allowed with an embellished wave of his hand.

"Anyway, since I'm not getting interrupted, I was saying that my old man liked to work. He liked to mend the fence and then fix the stall doors where we kept the horses," Dylan said, nodding when Abby's eyes got wide, "We sure did have them horses. They were ornery as the bison, but never really mean for no reason. We used to corral the bison with 'em. I was good on a horse, too, but might just be because they were sweet as candy when you were riding them. Only time I ever seen one of those mounts kick was when daddy put a saddle on too loose. Makes 'em uncomfortable.

"So we would be riding around, looking for stray bulls or something, and daddy would point at some tree or plant and tell me that I shouldn't ever eat it 'cause it would give me the runs. I'd just laugh 'cause he knew I wasn't gonna eat a tree or plant when we had all that food at the house. He'd laugh right along with me like we had our own little joke. I guess we did, 'cause he never said anything like that to any of the hands we'd hire during the branding.

"I didn't stay in the ranching business, if you hadn't guessed. When I was old enough to go get a job, I went to work at the general store for a while. Once I saved enough money, I moved out of the home place and got into a place of my own. Still didn't leave DeBolt. Grew up there, so probably I grew roots to the place. After a while I went to work in the oil fields when a job came open and worked there up until the sun went bad.

"Had me a wife who was from the same place and lived there all her life, just like me, and before long we had a little boy who liked horses."

The man smiled again, this time with more pain than happiness, but he went on with an upbeat tone that Richie and Buddy both admired. At the mention of a son, Amanda's face fell a bit as Abby's raised. The two had different views of the thing, one seeing it from childhood as the other saw it from adulthood. Amanda was already on the verge of crying as she thought about the man's loss. Abby was fascinated with a story involving a child. When she interrupted Dylan, it was with the next logical piece of the tale.

"You took him to your daddy's farm!"

"You got it, little bean. I took him riding from the time he was old enough to catch a stirrup. He liked it better than anything at all. My little James would ride as fast as I'd let him, but I always made him slow down when we passed certain plants and trees. Why you think I did that?

"Because if he ate 'em, he'd get the runs?" Abby giggled.

"That's right, bean. He giggled just like you do, with his *whole* belly."

Dylan went quiet, still smiling the smile of a man who couldn't bear to let a memory go bad. Buddy thanked him with a pat on the back. Richie watched Amanda smile through salty tears.

***

It was an anxiety filled night for the follower. The reason for his anxiety was the fact that he wasn't following anymore.

The stranger had started moving before the group came out of their hole and had been nearly running for half the night to stay ahead of them. It was time for his gift, but he wouldn't be giving it to them in a face to face manner. He had to plant the packages at their next stop. They were hungry enough now.

He arranged the things as if they'd been on the shelves waiting for Richie, Buddy, and the rest. He had even gone as far as sprinkling road dust on the packs to make sure they *looked* left behind. Again, the situation was nerve racking. What if they were suspicious? Would they eat what was inside? Would they be able to tell where they'd come from?

So many questions ran through his mind that he'd actually stood in the service station for much longer than was planned. If he'd stayed in there for even an hour longer, he wouldn't have had time to dig out his shelter for the night. Just before leaving the place, the stranger had felt weakness for the first time in months, and actually grabbed one of the packages for himself. He was tired from the pace of his night of travel and would need the thing to recuperate. It wouldn't matter.

Once his shelter was ready, the follower sat waiting for them, watching the road intently for the movement of the group. He'd been behind them for so long that being in front of them actually felt surreal. He couldn't truly rest until they appeared a few miles away from him on the road.

He wrapped an extra layer of bandage around his gnarled calf before turning to look at them again. He badly wanted to watch as they found the presents he'd left for them, but didn't have the energy to stay awake. He slipped into his hole, spread a weathered tarp over the lower half of his body, and began to pull the earth over him.

Chapter 6

"How sweet it is," Buddy sang out as he walked the center aisle of the truck stop, his fingertips grazing the shelf full of dehydrated meals, "To be loved by you!"

"The fuck are you going on about?" Richie asked as he walked up.

"Do you not see the love that our lord has bestowed upon us?" Buddy asked, pulling his glasses off to wipe his eyes.

Richie looked to the indicated direction and smiled. There would be food for *three weeks* if they stretched what was sitting on the shelves, but everyone would get a full meal today. Both men began piling the packages into their arms and shouting for the others. Everyone was pleased by the sight. All of them carried the load into the storage cellar where they would sleep through the day on full stomachs. High spirits were catching and shared by each of them, including King. The cat was given more scraps on this day than had been available since they'd found him.

Once the group had laid out their bedding, eaten, and sat down to rest, Buddy had a real chance to look at the packages they were eating from. In his ravenous state everything about finding the wealth of sustenance seemed perfectly normal. Now, once he'd had the chance to find reality, there was something off about all of it.

"The dust is a different color," Buddy said to himself.

"What's that?" Amanda asked from the other side of their encampment.

"The dust on the bags doesn't look like the dust on the shelves. It's darker," Buddy explained.

"Like road dust," Richie agreed, looking at his own empty package.

"Yeah. That's it," Buddy nodded.

"Does that matter?" Amanda asked.

Neither man seemed to have an answer. Dylan's light snoring seemed to be the only response in the small space, but that wasn't going to explain anything.

"How does outside dust get inside?" Richie asked finally.

"Maybe it's our dust. Maybe we make a cloud of it when we make camp," Amanda offered.

"Could be," Buddy admitted.

"Yeah, but I don't think that's it. The bags are all sealed, right?"

"Good thought, One Eye," Buddy said, "They are, but there are ways to put shit in food without breaking the seal."

"Do we really think that there is someone running around the end of the world trying to poison people?" Amanda asked.

"We're a band of survivors carrying a cat around with us and not eating it," Buddy said, "Can we really throw stones at weird situations?"

"We'll know soon enough, I guess," Amanda said, tasting some imaginary poison that she was sure hadn't been in the food.

"Nah. Might be poisoned at random."

"Thanks Buddy. That's a big help."

"King tastes everything we eat before we eat it from now on," Richie ordered, "If he's alive after an hour, then we should be fine."

"Good thing we kept that cat."

Amanda looked at the two men with something like exasperation before she could admit to herself that using King as their taster was a solid idea. If something happened to their furry companion, Abby would be inconsolable, but if one of the *people* in their group died...

"Fine," Amanda allowed, "As long as we make it through today."

"If I die before I wake," Richie muttered as he rolled over on his side.

"That's the ticket," Buddy grumbled, "That's the best way to figure out if we've been poisoned."

"Something else about the bags is weird, too," Richie said, his voice muted by the way he was laying.

"What's that?"

"Don't know for sure. I have to think about it."

"Let me know when you get it all figured out, then," Buddy demanded gruffly, "I'll be waiting with baited breath."

***

Burwash Landing, YT
July 25, 2021
1:02 AM 79*F

The cat was happily following his humans, padding along their line from front to back. Richie was watching the animal and being amused by his movements.

All of them were well fed for the moment, but would begin rationing on their next stop. They would have enough food to make it over the border and into the remote state of Alaska. They were just over one-hundred miles away. Richie, who had seen their destination from the opposite point on the north American map, could barely believe that their goal was actually in sight. The ability to place his feet onto the soil of the fabled place was something that he had thought about for so long that he was nearly afraid of it.

The others were talking quietly amongst themselves. Even Abby was joining in on their talk, which was an oddity in itself. She was normally preoccupied with the cat. Richie smiled, again, at the notion of a group of survivors with an actual pet. It was ludicrous but it was their circumstance. When the cat matched Amanda's stride, Richie focused on her.

Amanda's hair was getting longer, Richie noticed, and had started to fluff and curl around her ears. She'd taken to wearing an old baseball cap that she'd found on one of their many stops and it suited her. The team name of the thing had faded away, leaving the traces of a dirty gray outline on a white front. One of Richie's favorite mind games to play was trying to figure out which team the hat had been an advertisement for. He decided not to partake in the game as they walked through this night, but was sure he'd get back to it.

King passed Amanda, walking along side Buddy.

Buddy's glasses were dirty, something his friend would never have put up with in the old world, and Richie almost pointed it out. He decided not to. His companion seemed in a cheerful mood, though his posture was aware and stiff. The man wore the usual pair of cargo shorts and hiking boots, but the weather had actually improved to the point of allowing a shirt. Buddy had picked up a thin cotton tee with a breast pocket. Richie had to hold his breath for a moment when he noticed the dry bandana held in Buddy's shirt pocket. He knew that his friend always held one for their fallen comrade, but usually ignored the fact.

The cat crossed in front of Buddy to keep pace with Dylan.

Though they'd gotten to know Dylan by listening to his stories and watching his actions, the man was still closed off to them. Richie understood the way Dylan felt and didn't press him to open up any more than he already had. Most

233

people would hold others at an arm's length long before all of the horrors they'd been through. The only one of them Dylan seemed to talk with on a truly personal level was Abby. No one would try to say anything against that behavior. To Richie it just made good sense. The girl was the only one who could hurt Dylan with her own death.

Once King had tired of Dylan's pace, the fur ball slowed to walk with Abby.

Richie could only watch the thin girl for a moment. Her face was dirty, making her smile seem much brighter within its frame. It was a heart racking smile that made Richie point his good eye at anything else in the world but her. Her clothes were ragged and ill fitting, as if they hung on the frame of a ghost.

Their pet slowed down once more, coming to Richie.

He looked down, knowing that his looks wouldn't matter to the eyes of an animal as long as the food kept coming its way. He knew that he was barely a shell of the man who had led his friends out of Florida and onto the road more than a year before, but he also knew that he'd survived more than most men could have.

It wasn't a thought filled with pride. In fact, Richie would've gladly traded himself for any of those that had fallen during their journey. Tears wouldn't be shed on this night, not by Richie, but there were plenty of them fallen to the pavement and long dried by the raging sun.

Richie reached down and picked the cat up from the road. A sandpaper tongue touched his chin and he had to smile.

***

"Almost," the follower whispered, startled by his own voice.

He hadn't spoken a word in weeks, silence being an affirmation of his commitment to seeing the journey through. If he verbalized out of turn someone might have heard him. If he talked himself out of the privation to do what he was doing, his own death might quickly follow. He'd made a pledge that he would follow and see all of this through. The follower wasn't a man who broke his promises.

The moon was high and bright, showing him the image of a group of well-fed people walking along the roadside. He smiled to himself. He was the only one of them who knew where the food came from, he was sure of it. If they'd realized the origin of the stuff, they might've rather gone hungry than eat it. Surely he would've seen the dehydrated packs laying on the ground behind them if they'd figured it out. They would've also become more vigilant than they'd been before. The inverse had seemed to happen. They were *less* cautious now.

It surprised the stranger. Honestly, he felt that at least one of the group would've questioned the appearance of such bounty. It was clear that they hadn't.

Only one thing bothered the traveler about the people that walked ahead of him. It wasn't anything that they were doing. It was the fact that he was beginning to feel like one of them. He laughed at their conversations when he could hear them, applauded them for making smart decisions, was saddened by their losses. He was watching them so closely that he almost became a part of their pact. They were all on the same journey, after all. He shook his head as if trying to empty something from his mind by the visceral force of the movement.

Befriending them wasn't part of his plan. He would resist that line of thinking and continue on his original path. It would lead them all to salvation.

***

Amanda was the first to notice the body lying in the road ahead of them. She slowed her steps, holding a hand up to the others and pointing out the new sight. They all braked with her, Richie being the last to see her signal and almost running into Buddy. In seconds weapons were out and pointing at the thing that lay straddled across the faded yellow line. The formation was like reflex to them with Buddy taking the point, Amanda and Dylan flanking him, and Richie turning to guard their rear. Abby stayed in the center of their group with the cat in her arms. She was wide-eyed and frightened by the sudden flurry of her companions' movements.

The body was motionless, its clothing dark and brittle looking as if it had been laying in the sun for quite some time. Richie searched the area behind them and found nothing to be alarmed about. He stepped slowly backward, timing his own stride with the sound of the others' footsteps. Nothing was moving in the area other than them. The coach barrels seemed to float in time with his glance.

Buddy was a few feet from the body, taking his time as he scanned the area. His steps were slow and deliberate, keeping the others in sequence with him. He was nearly sure that the body was simply another fallen person that had been caught in the light, but he wasn't about to approach without caution. It seemed that his friends agreed with him as usual.

He knelt within a foot of the slumped form, blinking a bead of sweat out of his left eye and wishing that he'd taken the time to clean the lenses of his glasses before this. There were smudges around the edges that wouldn't hamper his vision terribly, but could make seeing something off to the side difficult. He would just have to rely on Amanda and Dylan to watch his flanks.

Buddy poked the body with the barrel of his pistol, nudging the entirety of the form slightly, and felt no resistance. If anyone had been in front of him, they'd have seen his brow crinkle in disbelief. The figure should've been tough and unmoving, affected by rigor mortis and the hateful sun. As he started to turn, words of warning on the verge of spilling from his lips, a voice boomed from their right flank. Its words stopped Buddy in mid turn.

"Don't touch him again and don't fucking move!"

All of them turned to see the source, but no one stood within range of sight. The look of confusion on Richie's face was mirrored by the others. None of them moved, not ready to challenge the voice in case they were in more than obvious danger.

"Drop your weapons onto the ground in front of you! Do not test me or you will be shot where you stand and your body left for the sun!"

Richie's mind whirled, as did his eye. The voice was too loud. It had a resonance to it that almost made him think of a child yelling into one tin can that was tied to another. He didn't drop his weapon.

"I repeat! Drop your fucking weapons or we'll open up on you! You will be shot but left alive to wait for sunrise!"

"Megaphone," Richie whispered, finally understanding why the voice sounded as it did.

"What?" Amanda asked.

"Drop your guns," Richie said, finally letting his coach fall to the asphalt, "They've got rifles and scopes on us."

"How in the hell do you know that?" Dylan asked through clenched teeth.

"He's the smart one," a new voice stated, "Drop the guns or they'll put you down."

Richie looked at the bundle that they'd been investigating. The body was up on one elbow now, a dirty face peeking out of the burnt rags it was wearing. The sound of hand guns hitting the ground was the next to be heard.

"Well, fuck me," Buddy said quietly, "What do we do now?"

"We get captured," Richie said. His eye was wide and dreamy.

I hope this is the dream, Richie said to himself just before he saw the two groups of men walking toward them. Their guns, rifles mostly, were pointed at the five of them. Richie reached for the watch, clasping it in his fist like a talisman, and closed his eye hopefully. When he opened the lid, he knew that they were in a bad situation. The men were all much closer, now, and all of them looked fit and strong.

"Any ideas?" Amanda asked the group.

"Pray, I think," Dylan replied mildly, "Because these people look well fed."

Buddy said nothing as the man who'd been playing possum in the road stood, Buddy's discarded pistol in his hand, and threw off the clothes he'd used to cover himself. He pointed the gun at Buddy, the barrel wavering slightly. Buddy smiled at him.

"Cannibals?" Buddy asked the man.

"We like to think of ourselves as survivors, but labels aren't really useful these days, are they?"

"You don't have to do this," Abby said from the coverage of their group, "You can just let us go."

The man smiled as his own companions surrounded all of them. He dropped to one knee, bringing his face level with the girl's, and looked at her with faded hazel eyes for a long moment. His gaze traveled to Amanda. She met the man's look with her own and said nothing.

"If we let you go, honey, then somebody else will just have to go in your place. That's not very Christian of you, now is it?" he asked.

"Let the girl go, then," Buddy said, "You don't need her if you have all of us."

"And if I do that, she'll just die on her own," the man offered, "Wouldn't want her to suffer."

Richie, who had been silent since the men had surrounded them, spoke. His words were sober and annunciated. His manor was calm. What he said didn't fit with the way he said it.

"You can let us be. We'll keep walking and won't try to hurt any of you if you let us go now," Richie said amiably enough, "But if you take us prisoner it won't work out for you. I promise that all of you will die. You'll beg me to kill you fast, but I won't. You'll scream for help but none will come, because the only help for you is one another. I want you to consider that. I want you to think about what kind of pain you can look forward to before you take this path."

Everyone looked at Richie, his own friends included, with surprised countenances. The man on his knee in front of Abby stood, smiling now, and walked to Richie. He tilted his head as if considering what he should do, but he did not look away from Richie's working eye. His smile widened just before Buddy's surrendered pistol flashed out and impacted with Richie's temple. He fell to the ground in a heap.

"Tie them up and let's go."

***

"No!" the follower shouted in a rasping whispery voice, "No! You can't!"

He'd been watching all of them through his binoculars. He'd begun to sweat as the group pulled their weapons, had started to shake involuntarily as they were surrounded, and finally had no other choice than to shout his displeasure to the heavens when they were apprehended. Who were these people to take his group captive? Who were they to hit one of his charges? It was unthinkable.

239

He had suffered in order to make sure they got this far, had traveled so many miles to get the thing he needed from them. These people had just stumbled onto the group and decided to claim them. They hadn't even worked for it.

The follower paced back and forth, looking through the field glasses at the disappearing forms from time to time. Each time they were farther away and he would curse the hijacking bandits for what they were doing. Once he'd calmed down enough to think, they were nearly too far away to be followed. He began to hurry after them, a rifle held in one hand and the binoculars in the other.

They're so fucking close! he thought.

It didn't take him long to catch up to the caravan of travelers. He was alone, after all, and able to move more quickly than a group carrying prisoners. He wondered if there were many more of them, counting eight in the capturing group. He'd have enough ammunition for twenty of them, but no more than that. If there *were* more then he'd have to kill the thieving fuckers by hand.

Richie and the rest weren't *theirs.* They belonged to *him.*

He decided not to wait for them to get to whatever destination they were headed toward. He would have to take the attackers before they could improve their own odds. The follower began to run.

Chapter 7

<u>Burwash Landing, YT</u>
<u>July 25, 2021</u>
<u>2:15 AM 77*F</u>

The world was upside down and obscured by darkened cloth. Turbulence mottled his view with the motion of walking that would normally have been canceled out by his mind. Richie was almost thankful that during his forced slumber he wasn't projected into the dream he'd been trying so hard to avoid in his waking hours. He was being carried.

Voices, murmuring specters in his ears, were evident in his surroundings. The men who were leading them, corralling them really, were talking amongst themselves quietly and excitedly. He didn't take their unintelligible words as a good sign. On the contrary, their speaking was alarming. That meant that they were alive and still able to converse while imprisoning his group.

"Let me down," Richie said weakly.

A sudden stop. He was let easily down to his feet and allowed to hold his friend's shoulders for balance. Finally, when Richie was confident on his feet, he looked up to the face of Buddy, who had been carrying his sleeping body for who knew how long. His friend did not look happy.

"Keep moving," one of the men said, nudging Buddy with the barrel of a rifle.

"Will do," Buddy said, turning toward the direction in which they were being forced, "How's the head Richie?"

"Still there," Richie replied as he began to walk.

"That was some speech back there," Amanda said from Richie's side, "Any ideas on how to make all of that happen?"

"Give me a second to focus my eye. Then we'll decide how to kill all of these assholes."

"You sure are the confident one," Dylan spoke.

"We've managed to keep alive so far," Buddy said, "Richie's usually the guy with the plan."

"Should we be talking like this when they can all hear us?" Amanda asked.

"Doesn't matter. Just be ready."

They all looked to Richie, who was smiling in a disturbing way, Buddy being the only one of the others to grin. Abby hadn't spoken during this exchange, focusing her attention on King as they walked, but Richie could see that she'd heard him. Her thin shoulders bunched as if she was getting ready to run. He put a hand on her shoulder and looked around at the opposing men.

"Last time I'm going to say this," Richie said with a raised voice, "Let us go."

"Want another lump on that fucked up head of yours?" one of the men asked.

"Can't say I didn't warn you," Richie told him, his eye scanning the area off to their right.

"Whatever you're going to do, Richie, you need to do it soon."

Richie grinned at Buddy without actually looking at him. He'd seen what he was looking for as his companion spoke. The moving shape among the dead trees was up ahead of them. It had stopped moving suddenly. The packaging on their dehydrated meals flashed through his thoughts. He'd figured out where he'd seen it before, but hadn't fully understood why they were there until he'd had time to consider the significance. Someone *had* left it for them, but poisoning them wasn't likely to be the motivation behind the gesture.

"As soon as I give the word, tackle the fucker next to you," Richie whispered to Buddy.

Buddy had no idea of what was going on, but he nodded. He knew that he would have to trust his friend. His body coiled in preparation as Richie whispered similar commands to the others.

"Now!" Richie shouted, jumping on the closest man to him.

The others followed suit without question as gunfire erupted around them.

***

The glass on his scope was filthy, but serviceable. He was able to see the men and align the crosshairs with their magnified images easily enough. When the first shot rang out in the distance, a man had already fallen and the follower was taking aim on another.

He had been fast enough to get ahead of the group, which was the best position to be in for something like this, and figured that he had another five shots before he would have to switch clips on the rifle. The second man fell to his shot, blood spurting from his chest just below the collar of a ratty looking polo shirt. He watched the fidgety image in the scope's glass, took a deep breath, and fired on the third man. The bullet glanced off of his shoulder, taking a chunk of meat with it, but did little harm. The follower triggered on him again, this time planting the round in his chest. The target fell hard.

The scope warbled as he searched for his next victim, cursing under his breath at his own impatience. He slowed the barrel of his rifle as he caught another man in his sight. This one was crouched and turning quickly this way and that with a pistol in his hands. The follower squeezed the trigger of his own weapon, catching the man in mid turn. He fell, the pistol firing until his ammunition was emptied. The follower watched him for a moment to make sure he wouldn't be getting up again. He didn't.

His ex-wife had once told him that he wasn't the best with judgment of distance. The follower, a different man in a different life now, silently scolded her for the judgement. He was doing just fine with the rifle, noting the direction of the wind, of which there was none, and allowing for the movements of his targets. He laughed to himself. They weren't even running, the idiots. The ones still standing simply stood there searching for the source of their attack. As the follower took aim on the fourth man, he laughed again, nervously. The man's head snapped back with the impact of the high caliber round.

He felt the dirt kick up at him, looked down to see a burrow a foot or two to his left and got serious again. One of the fellows was shooting at him. He understood the reasoning for the shot and took no offense. The follower merely aimed, obtained his mark, and fired.

***

The struggle between Richie and his own target didn't last long. He'd quickly taken the imprisoner to the ground with a body tackle and begun hammering his fists into the man's head and throat. Once his opponent had gone still, Richie looked around to see that the others had come upon the same luck. Both Dylan and Amanda had jumped on one of the men as Buddy took another down to the ground. Anyone else who might have tried to attack them was dead at the hands of a stranger wielding a rifle.

Stranger? Richie asked himself, I don't think he's that much of a stranger to us.

The rebellion was over in minutes. Five men lay dead as three more lay unconscious. Richie and his friends spent more time relieving the fallen men of their weapons than had been spent dispatching them. Soon their group was outfitted with more ammunition than they'd seen in months.

"These guys?" Dylan asked, waving a hand toward the men snoozing on the ground.

Richie looked at Dylan for a moment as if he was considering something. He motioned toward Abby and waited for the other man to understand. Dylan nodded finally, and coaxed Abby into following him along the road. Amanda said nothing, but followed after the other two, knowing the fate of their would-be captors.

"Let them get ahead a little," Richie told Buddy.

"Should we be worried about this mysterious stranger that just saved our asses?"

"Is he still shooting?"

"No," Buddy answered, "But he could start up at any time, right?"

"I think we're safe."

"Why?"

"We'd already be dead, otherwise."

Buddy watched his friend for a long moment before speaking again.

"Do you know something I don't?"

"Buddy," Richie said with a grin that seemed eerily like the friend Buddy had known in a long ago world, "I have always known something you didn't."

"Fuck you, one-eye," Buddy spat, shaking his head with a smile.

Just then, Richie broke his promise to the men on the ground, killing them quickly with a shot to the head instead of torturing them.

"Yeah. Fuck me," Richie said, holstering the pistol he'd stolen from a dead man.

"Should we have, maybe, asked them some questions? Maybe they could've told us if there are more of them to deal with."

245

"Would it matter?" Richie asked.

"It could."

"There were eight of them. They were carrying a shitload of supplies. There aren't any more in their group."

"But there *could* be, Richie."

"If more come, we'll kill them."

"You have gotten seriously fucking morbid since you lost that eye, man."

"I can see more clearly, now," Richie told him before turning to catch up with the others, "Let's go."

Chapter 8

Beaver Creek, YT
July 29, 2021
4:11 AM 81*F

None of them could sleep once they'd gone to the trouble of setting up camp under the service station. All of them were nervous and excited by the fact that they were so few miles from their destination. Amanda had been the one to dole out the morning meal, smiling as each of them received a full food pack. Everyone was starving and it would be good for them to find sleep with a full stomach.

Buddy and Richie sat on the bottom step of the stairwell that led to the surface, their knees touching in the narrow space, reminding Richie sadly of a long ago night when he'd sat with Elvis in just the same way.

Buddy was continuing to badger Richie about the existence of their strange guardian angel. The man or woman had rescued them from a difficult situation and Buddy had become quite curious about such a person. Richie, however, refused to comment. He had an idea as to the person's identity, but could very easily be dead wrong.

"If it's a friend, we need to talk to him."

"Buddy, we don't even know who it is. Might be a woman just as easily as it might be a man."

"Is it a woman?"

"Probably not."

"So that means that we need to talk to *him*."

"If *he* wants to talk," Richie said tiredly, "Then he'll come to us. If not, we should leave well enough alone."

"We're not done talking about this, eye-patch."

"Says you."

"We're two miles away, Richie," Buddy said softly, "We're almost there."

"Surreal, isn't it?"

The two men who'd traveled so many miles together could only look at each other for that moment. They were both taken aback by the fact that they'd come this far, but also very sad.

"Elvis should be here, man."

Richie looked away from Buddy, suddenly fighting tears, and nodded. Buddy was definitely right on that one. Elvis *should've* been with them, but he wasn't. He'd been stolen from them by circumstance and their own versions of personal failure. Both men believed that they could have done something more to save their friend. To them it wasn't an idea, or guilt. It was a stone cold fact in their minds. Their friend would be with them if either Richie or Buddy had made one move differently.

Men, when faced with the idea that they have succeeded in only part of their own notion of victory, will ultimately defeat themselves with the guilt left over from the things they cannot change.

King the cat came to them, hoping to be stroked or have his ears scratched. Richie leaned down, provided him with a good scratching, and swallowed his tears. His vision was more easily blurred by the damned crying these days and he refused to partake. Buddy chose to mimic his friend, scratching King behind the ears for a moment. His tears flowed freely and openly, the salty streams cutting through his resolve.

"Elvis and Benny," Buddy said in a choked voice, "Alek and the Dundels."

Richie looked up at him with a widening eye and then away again. Buddy didn't notice.

"We're still here, though," Buddy said as he put a hand on Richie's shoulder, "No matter what happened on the way, we're still here."

"And we're with you," Amanda said, kneeling down in front of them, "And I love both of you."

"I love you, too," Richie told her.

"Me too," Buddy said, wiping his eyes with the back of one hand, "I love both of you."

"What about those two?" Richie asked with a grin.

Buddy and Amanda turned toward their two companions, both snoring loudly. They smiled in unison.

"Why not?"

***

Canada- U.S. Border
July 29, 2021
9:53 PM 76*F

The sign was badly faded, but legible from two hundred feet away. The area around it was hilly, but not much different than the entrance of any other state they'd been through. The sun had taken its toll, as it was known to do, on everything.

This sign, though, was different than any the group had passed. This one meant that they'd found the place they'd started out looking for. It meant that no matter how far they had to go to find a place to be, it would be their place. It would be the last place they had to discover.

249

Richie watched the sign as he got closer, wondering if it would blur and disappear leaving him in a dream world from which he'd never escape. The thought made little sense, but it was the one going through his mind either way. Buddy didn't comment on the thing, keeping to himself the feelings that coursed through him the moment it appeared. Amanda smiled a little, thought of Alek and the life that they should've had together, and kept moving. Dylan saw the sign as a way for him to pay back the debt he owed these people, felt that he would be able to find some way to repay them in this new place. Abby, being a child, continued petting the cat she held in her arms.

The goal, one that had been born more than a year before, was in sight. Nothing could ruin this moment for them.

"Stop," a voice croaked from behind them, "That's far enough."

They almost ignored the voice, so close to where they wanted to be, but the sound of a gun being cocked held them, suddenly. Richie, who wasn't surprised at all, turned around first.

"Hello, Mr. Dundel," Richie said before he'd even seen the man fully, "I wondered when you'd be showing up."

"Dundel?" Buddy asked, "Dundel's dead."

"No," the follower said, aiming his pistol at the center of Richie's chest, "I ain't dead."

The man was still tall, but he slumped badly at the shoulders. One of his legs was wrapped in a dirt and blood covered bandage. Eyes that had once regarded them with so much life were buried in scar tissue, almost nonexistent in the space that had once been the man's face. Dundel had been caught out in the daylight and had paid dearly for it. The question that came to Richie and Buddy was an obvious one. *How had he survived?*

"We're here, sir. Why don't you just come with us? You came all this way," Richie offered, keeping his eye on the man whom they'd believed dead so long ago.

"I'm not here to stay with you, son. I'm here to settle this thing."

"What thing?" Buddy asked, "What's there to settle?"

"You killed my girls and left me for dead, boy. You took a ton of my supplies and left as soon as the sun went down and all I had left was two dead little girls."

"That's not what happened," Richie argued, "We didn't kill your girls."

"I know what you did. I saw their bodies. I still feel that damned sun baking me, burning me, and you're the ones who caused it!"

"You don't remember?" Buddy asked him, "You saved our friend."

Dundel shifted the barrel of his gun back and forth, covering both Richie and Buddy. His mind had been made up the moment he'd awakened, covered entirely in dirt outside of his home in Montana with no recollection of how he'd gotten there. The sun had been long set by the time Dundel had begun digging himself out of the dirt he'd been completely covered in. How he'd been buried was still a mystery to him. All he could think was that as a last resort his body had reacted without his mind to control it. He must have scooped the earth out of the hole by hand and fell into it. It was lucky for him, but not for these two.

His girls had been dead lumps on the ground, cooked by the sun. For some reason Dundel couldn't remember how the three of them had been pulled out of the house and into the sun, but the only ones who could've done it were the boys he'd been foolish enough to take in. He'd decided that he would follow and wait, would bide his time until they were on the edge of the place they so wanted to reach. He would take that from them in the same way that they'd taken his girls and his life.

"You wrote us a letter, Mr. Dundel. I still have it. I can show it to you if you'll let me open my pack," Richie told him calmly.

"I didn't write anything for you murderers. You killed my babies and you almost killed me!"

"The sun hurt you, Dundel. It took something from your mind. I know how that is. We can help you if you'll let us."

"You can't help me, son," Dundel said, his voice calming, "Not unless you can bring back the dead."

Richie could say nothing to that. The man's mind was made up. That much was obvious. Richie could only hope that once the man was focused on him, one of the others could do what needed to be done.

"I just wish your other friend was still alive. I'd take this from him, too."

"Don't you talk about him!" Buddy shouted suddenly, "You don't have any right to talk about him!"

Things happened very quickly then. Dundel, set off by Buddy's recrimination, aimed at him and fired without comment. Before the bullet could pierce Buddy's chest, Dylan jumped past him, taking the shot in his own midsection. Richie raised the coach just as Dundel was setting to fire again, and pulled both triggers. Dundel fired at nearly the same moment, before falling to the ground. Richie, who was waiting for the shot to find his own body, never felt it. Somehow, some way, Dylan had kept moving, throwing himself into the second bullet's path. The man fell, blood pouring from two wounds that were surely fatal.

Buddy and Amanda fell to their knees beside Dylan. Richie moved toward Dundel, a sadness in his heart for the man that couldn't be expressed. He knelt by the dead man, their follower for such a long time, and closed the lids of his scarred eyes with the fingers of one hand. The others were calling his name, pulling him away from the fallen.

"He's gone, Richie," Amanda cried, holding Dylan's hand in both of her own.

"He got what he wanted," Richie said, looking to Buddy who nodded his agreement, "Dylan thought he owed us something. He doesn't anymore."

The sound of Abby's cries as she lay across Dylan's chest filled the night with sorrow and regret.

"Should we get her?" Buddy asked without looking at any of them.

"Give her a minute," Richie replied.

They stood, leaving Abby to her grief, and walked to within a few feet of the border between Canada and Alaska. Richie looked into the distance, a tear escaping the cup of his eye, and cleared his throat.

It was a moment of supreme joy and exaltation. It was a moment of great sadness. The emotions all seemed to mix in with one another as they looked down the road at what was to come.

"We need to do right by Dylan," Richie said, "We need to bury him."

"Not here," Buddy said flatly.

Richie nodded his agreement. They would carry him over the border. He would reach Alaska with them as they had all planned.

"Let's go find a spot, then."

The two men stepped over the imaginary line between countries at nearly the same time. They had started for this destination from a long ago place and time. They had once been a group of life-long friends, fighting for their lives and those of each other. The journey had stolen some of those lives from them, but hadn't been able to truly wrench away their spirit.

"This *is* the dream," Richie said to himself, "The night *is* real."

"What?" Buddy asked.

"Nothing. Let's get this done."

Epilogue

When they crossed the border into Alaska, there was little comment. Each of the survivors felt the elation of having accomplished a great feat. Each of them knew that the journey wasn't truly over.

As the group searched for a place, a home to settle into, they found more people to join them. Families and friends, who had all made similar treks, joined them seemingly at random. More hands were found for chores. More eyes were acquired to keep a watch on the night.

Richie, who would never be as whole as he once was, walked with his head down. His emotions were wrought with pitfalls that couldn't be navigated during moments like these. The mixture of pleasure and misery were like a whirlwind in his soul, dragging him between darkness and light.

His scars would remain, both the physical ones on his face and the spiritual ones hidden in his heart. He would always be the leader of his group. He would always *be*.

Buddy seemed only to need an end to the journey. He was a man who had never been truly strong before the world changed, but his strength would inspire people in a way that he'd never dreamed possible. His determination would be the stuff that builds civilizations. Buddy would become another kind of leader, one who creates and helps others to do the same.

Amanda would continue to be their glue, the strong bond that always held the two men together no matter what the problem. More than that, though, she would become the council for so many who banded together in order to make a life in this new and severe world.

I would get to grow up, at least to the ripe old age of twenty-three, and tell of all the things I was witness to. I'll never again see the unmarked grave of the man who sacrificed himself for all of us in some way or another, but I'll always remember him. Dylan did more than save me. In a way, he made me.

I never really knew Elvis, could barely claim to know Richie or Buddy for that matter, but I got to know him through Amanda's stories. She can still be relied on for some fact checking every now and again, though she's getting older and more tired of my prodding by the day.

Along with that, there's an aging tabby that refuses to leave the area in which I'd like to put my feet. The King lives on.

The End

Author's Note:

I hope you've enjoyed this story even half as much as I enjoyed writing it. Please leave a review on Amazon and Like my page of Facebook, if you don't mind. It'll help me to keep the laptop in electricity and such.

Also, if you turn the page just one more time, you'll get a bonus for all of the hard work you put in reading *The Dark Roads*.

So I'm changing some stuff. As you'll likely hear from Elvis if you pick up the next book, I do what I want. You used to see an excerpt from The Story's Writer here and it was really nice, but I do what I want.

This book is the first in a series of three, unless my crazy tells me that I have to write another for the series. These things do happen. If you scroll down a bit, you'll see the first chapter of Walking Back, a novella that might just answer a few of those pesky questions you've got after reading this one.

Wayne Lemmons

April 16, 2016

Other Works by Wayne Lemmons

Walking Back (Book Two of The Dark Roads Series)

The Story's Writer

An Excerpt From: Walking Back

Chapter 1

Valdez, AK
September 2, 2021
12:52 AM 74*

Richie's breath was shallow and labored. He'd been carrying Amanda over one shoulder for almost a mile and the effort was beginning to tax his strength. She was alive, her deep inhalations filling the gaps between his own ragged exhalations, and he took confidence from that. If the sound stopped coming from her partially open lips, Richie might just drop to his knees and give in to the exhaustion that seemed to be wrapping around his body like an overtight ace bandage.

"You're going to be fine," he told the woman, though she was unconscious and was sure to be ignoring his reassurances, "We'll get somewhere soon."

Where you gonna go? the ghost of Elvis whispered into Richie's ear as it had made a habit of doing in recent days.

"Don't know, little brother," Richie replied to his partner in conversation, giving up on waiting for a response from Amanda.

Might be a place up ahead. You can't see it 'cause it's on the wrong side.

"Get bent," he said with a shaky laugh, "Buddy's the one who gives me shit over the eye."

I'm the King. I do what I want, the voice in Richie's mind declared with a guffaw. Richie laughed along with it. The King *did* have a point, didn't he?

It wasn't overly hot, just yet, but Richie was sweating heavily and wishing that he'd managed to grab some water on his way out of the prison they'd escaped. Amanda couldn't be blamed for their lack of hydration, due to the fact that she'd been knocked out just before Richie had finally made a move on their captors.

He shook his head, the rusty laugh coming out again just before his feet caught up in themselves. It was only with incredible luck that he didn't fall to the dusty pavement, spilling Amanda onto the rocky surface to further her injuries. Somehow he caught his balance and kept moving.

What ya' laughin' about Richie?

"Not much. Just thought about the way I managed to get us out of that place. It reminded me of something."

Elvis said nothing in return. His ghostly traveling companion always went quiet when he knew there was a story to be told. Elvis had always been one of the great listeners when a tale was to be spun.

Richie's laugh sounded again as he thought about the half-smile that smoothed his long gone friend's features when they spent time reminiscing. He would grow impatient if Richie didn't spit something out before too long. No one spoke for a long time. Amanda's breath, thankfully, still sounded out in the darkness.

What about it? Elvis asked, finally growing querulous at his silence.

"Okay," Richie said, "Don't get your panties in a wad."

Your panties are in a wad! Elvis shouted, the words littered with giggles.

Richie smiled his odd looking smile. All of his scars made the expression a mostly unpleasant one, but the people closest to him still remembered that he'd once been handsome. Buddy didn't admit to that, refusing to let a man with one eye claim that he had ever been anything else, but he knew it just the same.

So many scars stood out on Richie's skin, a map of torn and burnt experiences that would not easily be read by the common acquaintance, that he'd stopped looking into mirrors out of simple mercy for his remaining eye.

"You are one ugly dude," Buddy had told him on their most recent walk around their new base camp, "But you're still not as bad as some of the mugs we've got around here."

"I don't know what to say to that. Is that... Did you just compliment me?" Richie asked, his brow raised in faux surprise.

"I wouldn't call it a compliment."

"You're hitting on me, aren't you?" he goaded Buddy, "I knew you had feelings for me, but I have to tell you, Buddy, that I don't play for *your* team."

"Well, if I had to pick a guy to get it on with..."

The laughter resonating from the center of Richie's mind stole him back from the memory. Elvis, or Richie's imagined presence of him, still had the loudest laugh on the vestiges of planet Earth. There wasn't much left for people to laugh at these days, but Richie, Buddy, and Elvis had always found some way to catch a grin. Where in the hell *was* Buddy, anyway?

Buddy said to stay but you left camp, Elvis reminded him, Shoulda' listened, Richie. Buddy was right.

"Do you want to hear the story, or not?" Richie asked with a sudden sharpness in his voice.

Silence from his dead friend. He took that as affirmation, and began to talk about something that happened before they'd found themselves hiding from the day like vampires in some cheesy book.

<><><>

Miami, FL

November 3, 2015

2:15 PM 95*

"I'm pretty sure that winter is never coming," Buddy said from the lawn chair to Richie's left.

"It's still hot," Elvis confirmed from the other chair as he fanned himself with a comic book that he'd been paging through, "It's gotta cool off sometime, right?"

Richie said nothing, just kept his head leaned back and his eyes closed. His smirk was the usual cocky one held by most seventeen-year-old boys. If either of his friends were paying attention, they'd have known that he could hear them and was purposely ignoring their complaints. It was true that the warmth was an unseasonably intense wonder this late in the year and that the sun felt more concentrated than it had in the middle of summer, but it was better than being cold.

They were wearing trunks and flip-flops long after the garments should've been shoved into a closet and replaced by jeans and close-toed shoes. That, in itself, was a victory over the less loveable of seasons. Richie had always abhorred being chilly and if his parents would've allowed him to move even further south to stay warm all year, he would've taken them up on it. He would have had to find a way to bring Buddy and Elvis along, probably Benny too, but he was sure that such obstacles could have been surmounted.

"Getting a nice tan, are you, Richie?" Buddy asked with a soft punch to the arm, "The only guy I know who could smile in a frigging oven."

"I *am* looking very olive-skinned, aren't I?" Richie responded without changing his posture.

"You look like one of those old-school Romans. What do you think, Elvis?"

"I think he's gonna turn lobster," Elvis replied with a hard fought smile. He shifted in his seat to grab a soft drink out of the cooler they'd brought outside.

"Not me," Richie proclaimed, "I was born to live in the sun."

"Shit," Buddy said, his tone turning serious.

Richie finally opened his eyes. If Buddy was going to quit the jibing, then there must be something significant on his radar. He saw that Elvis was looking toward the direction in which their friend had thrown the curse word. He grinned as he located the source of Buddy's duress.

"Something to be said for summer sticking around," Richie expressed as he stared at the sight before them.

The girl was much older than them, probably in her early twenties, and wore the same uniform that most of the Miami born Latinas donned when the sun was high in the sky. Tiny jean shorts, low slung on the waist, and a white bikini top were her only coverings. The tan skin was so tan that it made Richie's own pigment look like an albino coat in comparison. Her body was perfect, leading from painted toes to the luxuriant dark hair that swished back and forth as she walked.

The three boys gawked at her mercilessly, Elvis and Richie feeling truly fortunate to be wearing sunglasses, and therefore looking with complete discretion. Buddy, ever the conspicuous one with his clear-lensed, coke-bottle specs, didn't try to hide his admiration. It wouldn't have mattered if he had.

"Alejandra something?" Buddy asked in a low voice.

"Quevas," Richie added for him.

"Yeah," Elvis said, his mouth forming its charmingly dopey smile.

She waved to them, but didn't stop to talk. The girl had lived on the same street as Elvis and his mother for the better part of a decade, and had grown used to the boys' stares as she'd grown into her body. All of them waved, Buddy being the most enthusiastic one of the group. He couldn't hide his interest if he'd tried, so he chose not to try.

"Why don't you go talk to her?" Richie asked his obviously enamored friend.

"Why don't *you*?" Buddy retorted, still holding the grin he'd given to Alejandra.

"I think I will," Richie answered his challenge, standing up from the lawn chair, the sound of wet skin coming away from a sticky surface barely registering.

"Right," Buddy said, "You're going to talk to her?"

Elvis watched in shock as Richie started toward the sight they'd been taking in at a near jog. He was trying to catch up to her, but having a hard time with the exertion in such heat. Buddy shook his head and turned to Elvis.

"You know he's about to get us into some shit, don't you?"

"What do you mean, Buddy?" Elvis asked, confused by the notion.

"She's got a boyfriend."

"So."

Buddy pointed to a Chevy that was parked half a block from where they sat. It was the boyfriend's car and if the guy was in it when Richie caught up to Alejandra, he'd be able to see the funny little white guy hitting on his girl.

Elvis' eyes widened and he nearly jumped out of his chair. Buddy grabbed his forearm, smiling up at him and squinting against the brightness of the day. Elvis was alarmed and badly wanted to warn their friend before he did something stupid.

"We'll go. You know we will, but let's just watch for a minute. This is gonna be good."

<><><>

Alejandra turned to Richie's call with an arched eyebrow. She looked quizzical and beautiful to the younger man and once he caught up to her, his words wouldn't come for a few hesitant seconds. His plan was easy to follow, however, so Richie was able to quickly regain the composure he'd misplaced. Still, it was nerve racking for him to speak with such a lovely woman.

"I'm not trying to hit on you or hold you up. I just want to have a little fun at my friends' expense, if you don't mind," he explained, completing his delivery with a beaming smile that was scant years away from the damage of a furious sun's rays.

She smiled back, was forced into the expression by the quality of Richie's innocent grin. The girl considered him from the depths of her aviator sunglasses for a short time, before nodding. When she spoke to him it was with slightly accented words that sounded, to Richie, like a kind of music. The words themselves weren't necessarily gentle, but the tone was enough to make up for what the verbiage lacked.

"Okay, but don't turn into a little creep about it. My man's not far away, you know?"

Richie looked around, noticing her boyfriend's car for the first time. He couldn't recall the guy's name, but his reputation didn't require one.

He thought quickly, deciding on whether to continue this little joke or run back to the safety of Elvis' front yard. His solution to the problem was uncomplicated and obvious. He'd already started the thing, so finishing it was the best direction in which to proceed. Besides, the looks on his friends' faces would be enough to counter any beating he might receive.

"Nothing creepy, I promise," Richie said with his open palms raised to chest level, "Just normal stuff. We talk for a minute. You laugh like you actually think something I say is worth laughing at. We hug and I walk away smiling. The smile would be faked, but a hug from you might actually paste it to my face for a couple of years."

She laughed, abruptly, and he knew that it was genuine. Richie loved the sound of it even more than he'd loved the accent of her speech.

He couldn't help staring at her from behind the lenses of his cheap sunglasses, the thought of drawing the lines of her face engulfing his mind. She would be beautiful forever, long after the struggles of her life took away the beauty that she currently possessed and replaced it with the lines of age, and Richie could not wait to put ink to paper.

It would be better if he could see her while he drew, but his mind would hold enough of her image to suffice. Alejandra's eyebrows peeked out from behind her own shades as if to ask what was next.

"That's the spirit. Now we hug and I run like hell," Richie said as the driver's side door of her boyfriend's Chevrolet swung open within his field of vision.

"Is that Jaimie getting out of his car?" Alejandra asked with a snicker as she leaned forward to embrace Richie.

"Yes it is. He doesn't look very happy, either."

Richie found himself quietly laughing with her as they hugged for a moment too long. The feeling of her body against his was one that he would always look back on, fondly. It wasn't the seventeen-year-old mentality that made it memorable. Richie just adored beauty in all of its incarnations and Alejandra was a prime example of that splendor. Her laugh was enough to make the entire situation he'd plunged himself into well past worth it. When their hug was over, Jaimie was within ten feet of them and looked ready to fight.

"The fuck are you doing?" the well-muscled man asked as his chest bumped hard against Richie's.

"Nothing, man. Just being friendly," he answered when his reverse stumbling act was over, adding the smile that had saved him from many physical altercations during his short career as a teenager.

The smile said, "Hey, we're all friends here. Let's just get along and enjoy the day without beating anyone up. What do you say?"

Jaimie, who seemed immune to even the most advanced of charming expressions, had chosen not to listen to the message. His fists were balled and ready in front of him as he advanced on Richie's position.

Richie's "Let's Be Friends" smile fell back to his usual grin, the one that helped him to get *into* trouble instead of the other way around. Richie's mouth opened to harass the guy some more, readying itself to give a little bit before the receiving started, but he was interrupted by Buddy's shouting voice.

<><><>

Valdez, AK
September 2, 2021

1:16 AM 74*

Richie coughed in the midst of his laughter. Amanda hadn't moved in quite some time, though he could still hear her breathing. He decided to take a break for a few minutes, as her weight was beginning to wear him down. She wasn't a heavy woman, by any means, but his strength was ebbing. He was becoming more familiar with the lack of food and rest that all of the inhabitants of their once great planet knew so well.

Richie stepped to the side of the road, knelt down as carefully as he could, and set Amanda onto the ground. He knew it couldn't have been very comfortable laying there, but if she didn't like the place she'd been put then she could just wake up and move. That would serve her right.

He sat without anything to lean on and soon gave in to his body's constant screeching for rest. Richie laid back, playing the scene of that day. It was from a time when the world was still alive, and the brief respite from the reality he was facing couldn't be all bad.

He snorted, again, remembering that Alejandra had smiled at him as her man walked toward them with violence on his mind, but didn't try to stop Jaimie from expressing that hostility. Richie, young and cocky in his ways, had shrugged lightheartedly and waited for the bruising that would soon come.

What happened then, Richie? Elvis asked from his grave in DeBolt, Alberta.

"Buddy came running up with you in tow. Don't you remember, little brother?"

Nope. I can't remember a thing about it.

"Buddy bellowed at the guy, calling him all sorts of names and ranking his mother out. It surprised me to death."

Buddy was crazy!

266

"Yeah, but he was fast, too. That guy started chasing him at a dead run, but Buddy stayed ahead without even trying. All you had to do was wait for Jaimie to come by and stick out your foot. He ate enough asphalt to feed him for a month and gave us all time to get out of there."

It was pretty funny. I remember now.

Richie kept beaming for a moment more. It was pleasant to smile, whether to himself or in the company of a dead man. He pushed the thought away, suddenly uneasy, and sat up to check on Amanda.

He didn't know what was wrong with her, or even how she'd been knocked unconscious, but his friend was still alive and that was plenty of reason for him to keep carrying her until they found camp again.

You remember how to get there? Elvis asked him.

"Yeah. I think I do."

He focused his eye on the road ahead of them. He had to check the dust for his footprints to make sure that he was looking in the right direction. There weren't any signs to follow, just yet, so Richie would have to take care to keep his bearings. He used one fingertip to draw an arrow in the dirt, just in case. It would be easy to get lost if he didn't keep his eye on their direction of travel.

Ha! Keeping your eye on it should be easy! Benny shouted from the depths of Richie's mind.

"Oh good. You're here too," Richie said to the new voice, a grimace taking his features.

Only sometimes, Elvis answered for him.

"Man," Richie breathed as his right hand reached for the pocket watch that wasn't around his neck anymore, "This is *not* good."

His fingertips touched skin that hadn't been free of the time piece in a long while. Richie couldn't exactly remember what had happened to his talisman. The only sure thing was that he didn't have it anymore. The ticker would likely silence the voices and keep him anchored in his tangible existence, but the option wasn't a present one. Richie would have to suck things up and soldier through his mind's tricks, or embrace them, until Amanda woke.

In an instant of inspiration, Richie looked at her hair. The tresses were still fairly short, like his own, though none of them had been able to cut their hair recently. It was enough for Richie to know that he was still in the real world, though, not poking around the dream with his dead friends.

He observed the rise and fall of Amanda's chest, seeing that she hadn't joined them in the afterlife. Richie let out a sigh of relief. He was aware that the danger hadn't passed, but was also relieved that it hadn't already taken her away from them.

Where's Buddy?

"At camp, hopefully," Richie answered.

What if he came looking for you?

That was a new thought, one that had occurred in the first week of their being held prisoner, but hadn't come up in the last few days. Buddy wouldn't have stood a chance at finding them at the lair in which they'd been held, but he might now that Richie was on the road again.

He nodded, not seeing his dead friend on the side of the road, but knowing that Elvis was in his mind. It was a good point. They would have to be on the lookout for Buddy and whoever he might've gotten to come with him.

"The night is real," Richie whispered as he sat up, not really needing the words to keep him grounded, but feeling their comfort, anyway.

He struggled to pull Amanda's limp form from the dirt and back onto his shoulders. He tried the fireman's carry, draping her across his upper back to distribute the burden, and found it a bit more comfortable. Richie took a few experimental steps and chose to keep the form for at least a few miles.

"You guys ready?" Richie asked all of his companions.

Too many voices answered.